Colin Youngman

THE

GRAVEYARD

SHIFT

Colin Youngman

The Graveyard Shift

The Works of Colin Youngman:

The Ryan Jarrod Series:

The Graveyard Shift (Book 9)
Bones of Callaley (Book 8)
The Tower (Book 7)
Low Light (Book 6)
Operation Sage (Book 5)
High Level (Book 4)
The Lighthouse Keeper (Book 3)
The Girl On The Quay (Book 2)
The Angel Falls (Book 1)

**

Other Standalone Novels:

The Doom Brae Witch

Alley Rat

DEAD Heat

**

Anthology:
Twists*

**Incorporates the novelettes: DEAD Lines, Brittle Justice, The Refugee and A Fall Before Pride (all available separately), plus a BONUS READ: Vicious Circle.*

Colin Youngman

This is a work of fiction.

All characters and events are products of the author's imagination.

Whilst most locations are real, some liberties have been taken with architectural design, precise geographic features, and timelines.

Seaward Inc.

Copyright 2023 © Colin Youngman

All rights reserved.

No part of this publication, hardback, paperback or e-book, may be reproduced, stored in a retrieval system, or transmitted, in any form or in any means – by written, electronic, mechanical, photocopying, recording or otherwise – without prior written permission of the author.

ISBN: 979-8-86981-443-2

The Graveyard Shift

Colin Youngman

DEDICATION

TO

JAMES

SOPHIE, EMMA,

AND ALL THE TEAM AT 'THE BOUND'

FOR BEING KIND ENOUGH TO TAKE A PUNT ON ME.

'When men carry the same ideals in their hearts, nothing can isolate them - neither prison walls nor the sod of cemeteries.'

Fidel Castro

'I'm not afraid of werewolves or vampires or haunted hotels. I'm afraid of what real human beings do to other real human beings.'

Walter Jon Williams

ONE

He laughed as the door slammed shut in his face, showering him with flakes of dried paint.

'No room at the inn,' the man had told him. Oh, the irony of it: a hostel for the homeless with no beds for those without a home. A sad indictment of modern times.

Billy Coulson shrugged off the rebuttal with the familiarity of one used to exile. He'd been hindered by his appearance all his life. Billy was only in his early thirties so his white hair wasn't a reflection of his age, his pale almost translucent skin not a consequence of illness, nor his pink, bulbous eyes due to alcohol or drugs.

No, Billy Coulson was an albino, and a withdrawn outcast from society as a result. Life on the streets was all he'd known since he'd escaped the abuse heaped upon him by his alcoholic parents in the Tyneside east end suburb of Walker. Tonight, he'd discovered the west end of Newcastle was no more welcoming. In truth, he already knew it.

He'd spent several nights in the doorway of a convenience store on Elswick Road and another outside a Halal restaurant off Rye Hill. On each occasion he'd been robbed of the few pounds he had, or spat upon, or pointed at as an object of ridicule.

His assailants came not from the Muslim or Hindi community which dominated the west end suburbs - indeed, they were respectful and kind towards him. No, his tormentors, both male and female, were always white. Not as white as Billy, of course, but Caucasian, nonetheless.

He'd found some peace last night, secreted amongst undergrowth in the grounds of Hawthorn House, and Billy convinced himself today would be better still. Even a flea-ridden hostel bed was an improvement on no bed at all.

Until the innkeeper turned him away.

When Billy retreated from the door with its flaking paintwork, he turned right onto Westmorland Road and set off downhill towards the city centre where he'd find kindred spirits huddled in soiled sleeping bags or beneath grubby blankets.

The premature darkness overhead bore the heavy burden of a burgeoning storm. Wind screamed from behind the Gurdwara Sri temple and the clouds burst like a water balloon, releasing an autumnal torrent of Biblical proportions.

Billy's holed trainers leaked while arrows of rain rebounded from the pavement, soaking his lower legs. 'Bloody wonderful,' he muttered to himself, hair plastered to his scalp.

A bus bound for Kenton sloshed by, spraying him with water like a man rinsing a spoon.

'Sod it.'

Billy fumbled in his pockets. His fingers brought out a sodden fiver and a handful of loose change. Enough for a pint, or a Costa coffee and cookie, or, better still, a Greggs if he managed to find one open. More importantly, wherever the meagre sum took him, it meant he'd be out of the rain.

He hoisted his battered rucksack higher up his shoulders and scuttled towards the nearest pub - before a thought struck him.

There was another way.

Rain or no rain, he continued onwards, down Waterloo Street, and headed for the city centre.

The Graveyard Shift

The extra five-minute soaking he received would be worth it. This way, he'd be sure to have a roof over his head, a warm bed to sleep in and, with a bit of luck, cooked breakfast to boot.

Billy Coulson knew there'd be a price to pay, and it was a price more costly than money could buy.

**

'You can't go home in this weather, man. Listen to it: it's like somebody's hoying coins at the window.'

DS Hannah Graves stood in suspended animation, coat half on, half off, as she contemplated Ryan Jarrod's words.

'Stay over,' he insisted. 'We're on the same shift tomorrow so we won't disturb each other in the morning.'

Hannah remained still, listening as the downpour lashed against the front door. Gently, she rubbed her belly. The motion soothed both her and the unborn child within.

She sighed and shrugged off her coat.

'Okay,' she agreed, even though she sensed yet another *'discussion'* about future living arrangements aimed her way. Hannah decided to get her equalizer in first. 'But it doesn't change anything.'

'You don't have to remind me all the time,' Ryan snapped.

She lay her hand on his thigh. 'I think I do, Ry. You've got to understand I'm not going to change my mind when baby's here.' She carefully worded her statement. She knew the baby's sex; Ryan didn't, nor did he know she knew.

'I don't think it's right. Our kid needs both of us.'

'And baby *will* have both of us. Just not in the same house.'

'I think you should move in.'

'I know you do. But it ain't happening.'

Ryan rubbed an eyebrow. 'It should happen. I need to bond with my child.'

'You will. Once it's born.'

'No. You're well into your second trimester. At eighteen weeks, baby will begin to recognise my voice. It already knows yours. I want it to know me.'

'You've been googling again, haven't you?'

'Aye, I have.' Ryan was interrupted by the ghostly lament of a wind rattling through the letterbox. 'You don't tell me owt about your pregnancy so I've no other choice but to look stuff up.'

Hannah bit her lip. He was right. She had excluded him. 'It's not you, Ryan. It's me.'

'*It's me*, what?'

She exhaled deeply. 'I love you, but I'm just not ready to make the next step. Not permanently, like. Not move in.'

'So you've said. But you've never told me why.'

'Look, you don't want to leave Whickham, right?' She waited for Ryan to nod his agreement, 'So, why expect me to leave Jesmond?'

'Cos you live in a flat…'

'…Apartment, actually.'

'Either way, there's no garden. No outside space for little 'un to explore.'

'I think you need to do some more googling. Babies don't up and off like gambolling lambs. It'll be ages before ours gets to that stage.' Hannah spoke gently but her humour was misplaced.

'It's not a laughing matter, kiddo.'

Hannah put her hands to her forehead. Massaged her temples with her thumbs. It was several moments before she spoke again.

'Okay. I'll tell you.' She looked at the floor. 'I'm scared, that's why.'

'Scared? What of?'

Hannah crossed her hands in her lap. 'Commitment. Scared everything will go tits up. Scared I'll be left alone. I'd rather start off by mesel'. I know what I'm dealing with, that way.'

The Graveyard Shift

Ryan took her hand. 'You won't be alone, though. You've got me.'

She sniffled. 'Have I, though? I mean, me Mam and Dad split up when I was nee age, then when I thought I'd got some stability back with her and Stephen, she left both of us for some dodgy DJ in Spain. I couldn't stand it if the same happened with you.'

Ryan cupped her chin and tilted her head towards him. He stared into her eyes. 'Hannah, it's not going to happen with me.' He attempted a smile. 'Besides, I don't fancy Greg James - and Sara Cox is too old for me.'

She almost laughed. Fanned her face with both hands and gave one last noisy sniff. 'I know. It's my hormones, I guess,' she lied. 'I don't know what I'm saying or doing sometimes.' She swallowed hard, aware she'd only postponed the subject until another day.

'Anyway,' she smiled. 'I'm here now, and I'm staying here tonight. That's all that matters for now.'

She leant in for a kiss.

'Let's go to bed,' she said.

**

Billy cast his myopic eyes around the interior of The Eagle. Its occupants all appeared to wear the same clothing, almost as if they needed a uniform to gain entry.

This wasn't the place for him. He swiftly closed the door and stepped back onto the street close to Times Square and the Centre for Life.

The second bar a few doors away was too quiet. Four men sat at one table sharing two bottles of wine. At another, a young woman dressed in checked shirt and cheap jeans held hands with a tall girl with long, thick hair in a waterfall braid which cascaded down her back.

Despite his urge to get out of the storm, he resisted the temptation to enter. Billy felt conspicuous even peering through the window, it was so empty.

The nearby blare of techno-pop, like something heard around a Balearic poolside, rippled the puddled streets. Billy followed the noise and rubbed a palm against the establishment's steamed-up window.

He cupped a hand over his eyes, and peered in, past the *JayKay's* logo etched into the glass in a dramatic Aquafina font. The bar was darkened but he saw enough to establish it was busy. Good. He'd easily disappear into the crowd. He hurried inside JayKay's before common sense could grab him by the arms and shake his plan right out of his head.

Billy slipped his backpack off his shoulder, hoped he didn't look too homeless, and picked up an abandoned glass containing the dregs of a pint. He found it hard making much of the gloomy interior. As far as he could tell, few occupants were drinking alone.

He needed to make himself blend in.

A flash of light from a gaming machine set against a wall caught his attention. The stool in front of it stood unoccupied. He made for it, finished his stolen drink, and picked up a fuller glass left invitingly on top of the machine.

He sipped lager from the schooner then, brazenly, downed the remainder in one gulp. *'Nowt beats a free beer'*, he thought.

He shivered. The rain and the cold and the ale cut straight through him. Billy needed a slash.

The sign for the Gents pointed along a small corridor right next to the gaming machine. Very convenient. He'd warm himself up with the hand dryer whilst in there.

There were only two urinals in the washroom, and one was occupied. Billy unzipped himself and felt a warm jet of urine seep from him. The man next to him turned to look at Billy, who forced a smile. It remained in place even when the man's gaze drifted downwards and lingered way more than necessary.

The man shook himself dry and moved to the sink.

'You look cold,' the man said, speaking into the mirror. 'Can I get you a drink? A whisky. Or a brandy, maybe? Something warming?'

'Shit,' Billy swore in his head. This is what he'd come for, to hope someone would offer him space for the night, but now it was here, the thought of what was to come made him shudder.

'Yeah, why not?' he replied.

They stepped out from the muffled quiet of the washroom into the cacophony of the main room. Billy made for the bar. The man took hold of his arm. Leant towards his ear and said, 'Not here. I have somewhere better in mind.'

Billy smiled to himself. *'Yesss! Some warmth for the night.'* With a bit of luck, the bloke might only want a handjob in return. He doubted it, but he lived in hope.

Once outside, the man handed Billy a hipflask. 'Here. This will warm you up.'

Billy sipped from it and screwed his face. Whatever the flask contained, he'd never tasted anything like it before. 'Cheers,' he said, hastily handing back the flask while wiping the taste from his lips with a sleeve.

They engaged in small talk as the man guided Billy uphill, away from the city centre. Billy wasn't really listening. Just muttered a few responses here and there, came clean about living rough, and how hard his life was when the weather was against him.

His companion looked skywards. 'Yes, it's a bugger at times.'

No sooner had he spoken, the rain stopped and a full moon emerged from hiding.

'Where do you live?' Billy asked.
'Out of town,' the man said.
'Not far out of town, though?'
'Far enough.'
'Oh.' Billy stopped in his tracks. 'I didn't realise we had far to walk.'

The man laughed. 'You don't think I'm taking you home, do you?'

Billy furrowed his brow. 'But I thought...'

The man pointed to a brick-built, pebble-dashed building Billy recognised.

'No good,' Billy said. 'I've tried there. It's full. Can't I go home with you? I'll pay... you know, someway or other.'

The man pulled at tangled hair. 'Sorry. You are most certainly not my type. Not in *that* way. I tell you what, though. I know somewhere else close by. They'll take you in.'

'How do you know?'

'They always do. It's their duty.'

'Who's duty?'

The man looked at Billy as if he were from Outer Mongolia. 'The Little Sisters of the Poor, of course.'

'Oh. Okay,' Billy said, cautiously. 'Not what I had in mind.'

The man pulled out a few notes. 'Here, take these for tomorrow. Get yourself some proper grub. Perhaps a Travelodge will have a room for you. But not tonight, yeah? Too late to go hunting one down now. The Little Sister's will be there for you tonight.'

The moon slipped behind an ominous cloud as the man heaved on a metal gate which shrieked in protest from between the lips of a grandiose stone archway.

'Is this it?' Billy asked, 'In here?'

'Nearly. We're taking a shortcut.'

The man's face wore a beatific smile as he dragged the tall gates closed, howling their fury.

The sign on the gateway read: *St. John's Cemetery.*

The Graveyard Shift

TWO

Ryan lay spooned against Hannah, listening to her gentle, contented snore. He had one arm under her body as she lay on her left-hand side, facing away from him. His other arm looped over her and his hands met around her abdomen.

He lay still, patiently waiting to feel movement or a kick from his baby. He knew it was likely to happen any day now. Hannah had mentioned she'd felt the flutter inside her several times already. Ryan was yet to feel his child communicate with him.

He raised his head from the pillow and peered over Hannah's shoulder. The bedside clock read *3:15*. Three hours until the alarm sounded and they set off to start the day with their respective teams.

Ryan kissed the nape of Hannah's neck. The rain no longer rattled the windowpane and the wind, even atop the breezy hill Whickham stood on, had stilled.

Ryan closed his eyes and drifted into a peaceful sleep.

What seemed moments later, the alarm jolted him awake. 'Fuck's sake,' he mumbled. He opened one eye. The clock read 3:52. Ryan rubbed his eyes. Hannah stirred next to him as the obstinate alarm continued.

Ryan sat bolt upright. It wasn't his alarm. It was his mobile.

He reached over Hannah and grabbed the phone. The illuminated display told him Stephen - DCI Stephen Danskin, his senior officer and stepfather to Hannah - was calling.

Ryan swiped to accept just as the call ended.

'Work?' Hannah said sleepily, turning onto her back.

'Yep.'

'Must be important,' she slurred.

Ryan's phone pinged. *'Get your arse in here. Body found in graveyard,'* Danskin's message read.

Ryan sighed. 'I've gotta go.'

His phone pinged again. *'That's an order.'*

He ran his fingers through Hannah's hair. 'Let yersel out. I'll see you at the station later, yeah?'

'Mm-hh.' She turned over and closed her eyes.

Ryan returned Danskin's call, phone cradled under his chin, as he struggled into last night's jeans.

'Jarrod. 'Bout time,' the DCI complained.

'Howay, man. You've just this minute rang.' He pulled the bedroom door closed behind him and crept downstairs. 'What's up?'

Danskin said something which Ryan couldn't make out. The DCI was clearly on the move, using handsfree. 'Say again, sir?'

'Get yersel' to the cemetery in Elswick.'

'Which one?'

'There's more than one?'

'I don't know. Might be.'

'Saint-somebody's, it's called.'

Ryan scooped his car keys from a saucer by the front door. 'I'll find it. What do we know about the body?'

'Young male, according to uniform.'

'We're sure it's murder? Not some druggie overdosed himsel'?'

Ryan heard Danskin spit out a laugh. 'Oh aye. It's murder, all right.'

'Do you mean we already know the cause of death? Aaron Elliot must be chuffed at this early a start.'

'No, Dr. Elliot's not duty pathologist today but I don't think his expertise is particularly needed in this case.'

Ryan started up his Peugeot. 'Why not?'

He almost mounted the kerb when he heard Danskin say, 'Because the poor victim's had a bloody great stake driven through him.'

**

Moonlit trees cast spectral silver shadows over pools of standing water outside the cemetery's gothic entrance. They rippled like curtains in a breeze under the Peugeot's headlights as Ryan approached.

Stephen Danskin's car was already outside, abandoned in the turning circle used by funeral corteges.

Uniformed officers stood on sentry duty at either side of the gateway to Saint John's, checkered tape blocking access and egress. Ryan flicked his lights to full beam. A hundred yards or so inside the graveyard, the glare picked out white-suited forensic officers huddled around a hastily erected tent.

A mobile incident van and a patrol car stood on the pathway leading through the graveyard. The vehicles lights were extinguished in deference to the dead. A figure looked up, hands shielding eyes from the glow of Jarrod's lights, and made towards the Peugeot. The man lifted the tape and ducked beneath it.

'Thanks for coming, Jarrod,' DCI Danskin said.

'Not sure I had much choice, sir.'

'Aye. Sorry about that. I know you weren't on call but O'Hara wasn't picking up his phone. You were the first one I thought of.'

'Thanks. I think. Is Gavin okay?' Ryan enquired after DC Gavin O'Hara.

Danskin shrugged. 'No reason to think he isn't but I don't know. The sod didn't answer, did he?'

Ryan and Danskin moved towards the cemetery gates. The duty PCs held up the tape for them as Ryan nodded an acknowledgement.

'Forensics got here quickly, I see.'

The Graveyard Shift

Danskin walked with hands thrust deep in pockets. 'Aye. It's that young pathologist. He's a bit keen for my liking.'

Ryan rolled his eyes. 'Rufus Cavanagh. For God's sake call him Dr Cavanagh. Last time I dealt with him, he lost his shit when I called him Rufus.'

'I call everyone by their surname, Jarrod,' Danskin reminded him. At home and around Hannah, the DCI deigned to address Ryan by his first name. On duty and to everyone else, it was either Jarrod or Detective Sergeant.

They continued their walk in reverential silence, hemmed in by headstones and memorials. Ryan lost sight of the forensic team as the footpath arced behind a hedgerow towards an older part of the cemetery where the gravestones stood angled like rotten teeth.

Once the incident tent was back in view, a flap opened and the junior pathologist stepped out, a Scene of Crime Officer alongside him. The rest of the forensic team waited on the tarmac footpath.

'Can we go in?' Ryan asked Rufus.

He weighed up the question. Answered with a nod. 'Only when booted up, though.'

Ryan knew the score. Aaron Elliot, lead pathologist to the City and County police, had taught him the drill. He was already pulling on a pair of overshoes.

'There weren't any noticeable footprints near the body,' Dr Cavanagh said. 'I've taken photographs of the murder site for you before anyone trespassed. Just as well I did. Your officers trampled all over the scene.'

Rufus looked skywards. 'Oh, and I wouldn't hold out too much hope of us finding out much, forensically. The storm will have washed away most of it.'

Cavanagh spoke softly and without emotion, as was his norm. Ryan guessed it was a necessary trait of the vocation.

Aaron Elliot used dark humour and acerbic wit to mask the macabre, while Rufus Cavanagh hid behind a façade of indifference.

Ryan took in a lungful of air and stepped inside the tent.

The air was stuffy and humid beneath the plastic, and the ground under his feet churned up like a Passchendaele trench.

He took his first look at the body. 'Hell's teeth!'

'Weird, isn't it?' Danskin said, softly.

William Coulson lay flat on his back. A wooden stave pierced the centre of his torso, driven deep within his chest cavity. Not exactly a stake; something more akin to a giant cricket stump, but both Jarrod and Danskin knew that wasn't the weird bit.

The corpse lay supine, directly on top of a grave. His head almost touched the tombstone, his arms were folded across his chest and his hands clasped together as if in prayer.

'He's been posed,' Danskin commented.

'Looks that way, doesn't it?' Ryan agreed. He stared at the man's face. Even in the darkness of the tent, it shone white as the moon above. Ash white hair, although combed neatly, lay caked with clay-like earth.

The man's sightless eyes, paled in death, gazed upwards. The hint of a smile played on the lips.

'Definitely weird,' Stephen Danskin repeated.

'Has he got make up on?' Ryan wondered aloud. 'He's like, I don't know - a clown, or summat.'

'Oculocutaneous albinism,' Rufus Cavanagh explained from the tent opening. 'He has little or no skin pigmentation and, quite probably, astigmatism or photophobia, or both.' He sneered at their blank faces. 'Poor eyesight.'

'Ah. Right.' Ryan rolled his eyes at Danskin. 'Would I win back some Brownie points if I hazarded to guess he was killed by that pole sticking out of him?'

'None at all,' Rufus Cavanagh replied.

'Seriously?'

'You really should stick to your field of expertise, Detective Sergeant. The absence of significant blood splatter strongly indicates some other cause of death.'

Ryan's mouth lolled open. 'He was already dead?'

'Almost certainly.'

Ryan and Danskin exchanged glances. 'How was he killed?' Danskin asked.

'I won't know until I've conducted a full post-mortem.'

'When's Aar… Dr Elliot back on duty?'

'Are you questioning my judgement, Detective Chief Inspector? I'm perfectly capable, you know.'

'I've nee doubt, but Aaron's our go-to guy.'

'He's back in the country tomorrow, and in the lab the following day.'

Ryan looked at the corpse once more. He hunkered down. 'What's this?'

A thin sliver of blood trailed down the man's neck.

Rufus smiled. 'That's what I intend to find out. It appears to be a puncture wound of some description.'

Danskin thought for a moment. 'If the stake didn't kill him, and there's not enough blood here for his throat to have been slit, was he injected with something? Drugged, like?'

'I'll only be able to tell when we've run toxicology tests. If he was, I doubt the drug was self-administered. I don't know anyone who injects themselves in the throat before hammering a pole through their torso.'

Danskin and Ryan nodded muted agreement.

'Not only that,' Cavanagh continued, 'If drugs are involved, whoever injected it was a novice. Not even a newly diagnosed diabetic would be so ham-fisted as to draw blood.'

Danskin's lips formed a grim line. Ryan mumbled, 'True enough, like.'

Cavanagh turned away from the tent flap. 'Oh, before you ask,' he went on, 'I don't know who the victim is but I believe he was a vagrant of some sort.' Dr. Cavanagh spoke with disdain. 'He's quite grubby. His clothing is stained. He appears malnourished. All things considered, I'd say he's been sleeping rough for a while.'

'How sure are you?' Ryan asked.

'Very. And his rucksack is tucked behind the headstone. You may find some clues to his identity inside.'

'You haven't looked?'

'That's your job, Detectives. Now, I must get on.'

Once they were sure he was out of earshot, Danskin said, 'This gets weirder by the minute.'

Ryan walked behind the headstone. His feet squelched in the mud, pulling at his overshoes until they made a sound like a kid sucking blancmange. 'We'll get forensics to go over the rucksack with a fine-tooth comb.'

'There's no obvious signs of a struggle. No bruising to the face, scrapes on his knuckles,' Danskin observed.

'Apart from the big pole stuck through him, you mean.'

'Aye, but you heard Cavanagh: he was already dead by then. Why didn't he struggle?'

'Perhaps it was self-inflicted, after all. Maybe he did inject himself. Doesn't explain away the impalement, mind.'

'No. It doesn't.' Danskin glanced around the grave site. 'There's no syringes, no tourniquets, no sign of drugs at all.'

'Unless some of that stuff is in his rucksack.' Jarrod looked at the corpse once more. The man was no more than a few years older than Ryan himself. White, dirty hair slicked with rain and mud - and he wore the eerie, smirkish smile on his face. Perhaps it was the effect of death on the facial muscles but, whatever the cause, Ryan found it disconcerting.

'There's no suicide note either, which tends to confirm our suspicions. Unless it's in his bag.'

When Danskin didn't comment, Ryan turned towards the DCI. Stephen Danskin was staring at the headstone, his lips puckered inwards.

'Found something, sir?'

'I don't know. Just a feeling I sometimes get. Can't put me finger on it.' The DCI dragged his eyes from the memorial. 'Anyway, howay oot and have a look around. We might find something of note out there.'

They skirted the grave and ducked out into the damp night.

As they opened the tent flap, a shaft of moonlight fell over the headstone; its inscription worn with age and barely decipherable.

'Thomas Raith
Died 14th February 1808.
Aged 33.
May God protect thy soul.'

THREE

The wall clock ticked over to 8:08 as Danskin and Jarrod stepped from the lift onto the third floor of the Forth Street station.

Most of Danskin's squad were at their desks, but Ryan's eyes rested on a member of DCI Rick Kinnear's team. DS Hannah Graves returned his look with a coy smile.

Ryan thought she looked a million dollars, corkscrew curl teased down her forehead, cheek dimpled in smile. Ryan, on the other hand, looked like a man who'd been up since 3:52.

His eyes scanned his own team. Only Nigel Trebilcock, covering the late shift, and DI Lyall Parker, cruising the Med, were absent. Todd Robson yawned but appeared alert. Lucy Dexter, only recently back on full duties and a shadow of the bubbly young girl she'd been before her encounter with the infamous Benny Yu, beavered away at a keyboard. Ravi Sangar, visible through the tech room windows, was engrossed in his work as usual.

Ryan sought consolation in the fact Gavin O'Hara looked even worse than him.

'Jarrod,' Danskin said over the mumbled *'Morning, sir,'* of his crew, 'Update the guys and make a start on the board.' The team swung their seats towards Ryan. 'Not you, O'Hara.' Danskin clicked his fingers. 'A word. My office. Now.'

Gavin O'Hara shuffled awkwardly into the DCI's room, his gaze nestling somewhere above Danskin's head.

'Nice to see you made it in.'

'Sir?'

'You don't know what's wrong, do you?'

'Not really.'

Danskin stood, hands on hips. 'Where were you last night?'

The Graveyard Shift

'I was in The Traveller's.'

'Until four this morning?'

'No, sir. 'Course not.'

Stephen Danskin's nostrils flared. 'Then why was your phone off?'

'I don't know. Was it? I was pretty pissed, like.'

'You don't need tell me. I can smell it on your breath from here.'

Gavin O'Hara started to say something, then stopped. 'Oh hell. I was on call, wasn't I?'

'You remember!' Danskin raised his hands. 'Praise the Lord.'

O'Hara's eyes fell. 'Sorry, sir.'

'Sit doon, lad.'

Gavin sat. So, too, Danskin.

'Care to explain yourself?'

Gavin ran a hand back and forth across his eyebrows. 'Me and the missus had a falling out.'

'You've been separated for years. Thought you'd be over it by now.' Tact had never been Danskin's strong point.

'We have. I was. Di went back home to Shipley when we split, but her job's been relocated. She's been looking for somewhere else. She asked me if there was owt up here. We got talking and eventually decided to give us another go.'

'When was this?'

O'Hara shrugged. 'Di came back to Burradon about four or five weeks ago. It's not going to work. *'Not compatible'*, she says. *'Night and day,'* we are, seemingly. We had a bit of a barney last night. Well, more than that. I threw the kettle at her. She stormed out to God knows where, I drowned my sorrows in The Traveller's Rest, came home, and fell asleep on the sofa. With my phone off, as you know.'

Danskin sighed, wind taken from his sails. He might lack tact but he had empathy in bucketloads. He'd been there himself, with Hannah's mother. And it took a lot more than one night's drinking for him to get over it. More like ten years drunk.

'Okay. No harm done. I managed to raise Jarrod from the dead so you weren't missed.' He moved around his desk and put a hand on O'Hara's slouched shoulder. 'Do you need a few days away?'

'Nah, sir. Thanks all the same, but I'll be fine. We're already a man light with DI Parker on leave.'

'Sure?'

O'Hara nodded.

'Good man. Howay, then: let's catch the end of Jarrod's briefing.'

**

Ryan fixed a scene of crime photograph of the body on a hastily prepared crime board.

'Funny looking bugger,' was Todd Robson's only comment.

'Different, for sure.' Ryan welcomed Danskin and O'Hara into the group. 'I was just saying we have no ID for the victim, but we do have this photograph.' He pointed at the board. 'We know he's white...'

'Very white,' Todd joked.

'...and appears to have been living on the streets. The contents of his rucksack gave no clues to his identity, sir. Seems it contained a couple of blankets, a change of socks, a shirt, and a thick pullover. All of them well-worn.'

'SOCO confirm that, Jarrod?'

'Aye, sir. Report from forensics was ready and waiting by time we got back here. Obviously, I haven't had time to fully digest it all but that was the gist of it.'

Danskin addressed his team. 'Do you have any questions before we get cracking on the case?'

The Graveyard Shift

Lucy Dexter spoke first, raising her voice above the rumble of a train exiting the adjacent Central Station. 'Do we have any information on the person who found the body? Seems an odd time for a passer-by to wander through a cemetery.' She pronounced the letter 's' as 'sh', a lisp she'd developed since breaking her jaw.

'Good question, Lucy,' Ryan said, keen to boost her confidence, 'Although there's a perfectly logical explanation. The victim was discovered by the cemetery sexton.' He looked towards Todd Robson. 'That's the gadgee in charge of a cemetery for those who don't know. Bloke by the name of Drew Fellowes. He lives in a lodge in the cemetery grounds. Uniform say he's seventy-five and about ready to join the other residents in the graveyard. He's made a statement and uniform will check him out but I doubt he's involved.'

'Have we started door-to-door yet?' Todd asked.

Danskin snorted down a laugh. 'I don't think the neighbours are likely to provide much help. It's a cemetery. The neighbours are all dead people, yeah?'

'Cameras, then?' Todd continued, unabated.

Ryan shook his head. 'We asked. There's none. Too intrusive, apparently.'

Todd exhaled through his nose. 'I know it'll take a while, but what about CCTV around the area? I mean, he's pretty bloody distinctive, isn't he?'

'I'll get onto it,' Ravi Sangar volunteered.

'You give him a hand, Robson. There'll be lots to go through. Start off with the cameras closest to Saint John's and work out from there.'

The sun burst out from behind cloud cover. Low in the sky, its rays reflected off the makeshift crime board. Stephen Danskin closed the window blinds and the contents became visible again.

'Guv,' Gavin O'Hara said, quietly. 'I'm looking at the photograph of the crime scene.' He walked closer to the board. 'Is that a footprint we've got next to the body? Just there.' He put his finger on a smudge in the grass close to the deceased's feet.

Ryan and Danskin squinted at the mark.

'Bloody good spot,' DCI Danskin approved. 'Get the image blown up for us, Sangar. Jarrod, you have a word with Dr. Cavanagh. Ask for all the images he took. He might have caught summat else before uniform churned the place up like the Baseball Ground circa 1972.'

'Speaking of the pathologist, when will we learn cause of death, assuming the stake didn't kill him?' Sangar asked.

Danskin replied before Ryan could. 'Cavanagh's running some tox tests later today. It'll be a couple of days before we get anything back. I'm hoping Aaron Elliot will be available by then. I'm sure Cavanagh's competent enough but he's a bit of a closed book and I reckon we'll learn a lot more from Doc Elliot.'

'Right,' the DCI concluded. 'Sangar and Robson, you get onto the CCTV footage. Dexter, you check over Drew Fellowes statement and see if you can find any holes in it. We need someone to take a look at the fine detail of the forensic report on the haversack and its contents. That's your job, O'Hara. I'll update the Super which means you're in charge oot here for now, Jarrod.'

Stephen Danskin breezed towards Superintendent Maynard's office leaving behind a buzz of static and a hive of activity.

Ryan sensed a long day ahead. He had one priority. A coffee.

A strong one, at that.

**

'I'd be careful, if I were you.'

The Graveyard Shift

'Huh? What?' Ryan jerked himself awake, spilling the cold contents of the coffee mug into his lap.

'Falling asleep at your desk like that. You'll get into trouble with Stephen,' Hannah whispered, a gleam in her eye.

'Look what you've done, man.' He wiped his crotch with his hands. 'I look like I've wet mesel' now.'

'Serves you right.'

'What for?'

'Oh, a few things. Loving me and leaving me like you did this morning, for one.'

'I didn't have a choice, did I?'

'Chill, man. I'm only joking.'

Ryan chilled. 'Aye, I know. Sorry. Been a helluva day and it's not even eleven yet.'

Hannah ran her hands down his back, feeling tension knots near his neck. 'Someone could do with a massage,' she whispered into his ear.

'Now that would get us both into bother,' Ryan laughed.

'Awww. Spoilsport,' Hannah chided. She straightened. 'Anyway, I overheard your briefing. You were pretty impressive.'

'I would hope so, seeing as I'm Acting Detective Inspector.'

She stood back. 'Seriously?'

Ryan responded with Hannah's own words. 'Chill man, I'm only joking.'

'You sod, you,' she chuckled.

He looked at his watch. 'Actually, I suppose I am DI, but only 'til Danskin's back from talking to the Super.'

A look crossed Hannah's face. 'Why don't you ask him?'

'Ask who what?'

'Stephen. Ask Stephen if you can cover Lyall's absence properly.'

'He's only away for three weeks, man. You know the policy.'

Hannah shrugged. 'Suit yourself. Just a thought, that's all. I mean, you are on fast-track and it'd be an opportunity to prove yourself. At least think about it. Now, I must get on with my own booo-ooring work.'

Ryan's eyes followed her back all the way to her desk. He knew she didn't get a kick out of the more mundane work carried out by Kinnear's team, and he appreciated the fact she didn't resent being moved sidewards to Kinnear to accommodate Ryan on Danskin's team.

He also knew she hated the desk duties she'd be on for the next few months. Although there was no detailed policy on when a pregnant officer should be removed from frontline duties, the City and County force took a pragmatic approach: as soon as the pregnancy became visible, it was *'suggested'* the officer *'consider'* stepping back.

Ryan was present when Superintendent Maynard had the conversation with Hannah three weeks ago. Hannah argued that, to a casual observer, she looked to have put on a little weight; that she wasn't obviously pregnant.

Sam Maynard disagreed. Ryan knew Hannah would have raised further objections if DCI Kinnear had been the one giving the advice but, coming from a woman, Hannah reluctantly accepted the decision. She still didn't agree with it, though.

Hannah turned towards him as she took her seat and blew him a kiss. Ryan fought down a blush as he glanced around to check if anyone had seen it. Satisfied they'd got away with it, he strolled to Lucy Dexter's desk.

'Does he seem kosher?' Lucy jumped at Ryan's question. 'Sorry, Luce. I didn't mean to startle you.'

'That'sh okay.' Self-consciously, she tugged a strand of blonde hair over the side of her face where the metal plate had been inserted. 'I don't think the cemetery warden's our man. Drew Fellowes isn't known to us, and his statement adds up.'

Ryan's eyes flitted over her face. Lucy had grown her spiky hair long so it masked her scars, her teeth were pearl-white but false, and the sparkle had gone from her eyes. So, too, the self-assured air of confidence she once exuded.

'What was he doing out in the cemetery grounds?' he mused.

'Walking his dog. It's as old as him and even more incontinent. Fellowes sets his alarm for midnight and three a.m every day. He takes the mutt out, lets it do its business, and goes back inside.'

'Or so he says.'

'I think he's telling the truth. I've tracked down the veterinarian he uses and they've confirmed the dog does have a problem.'

Ryan raised his eyebrows. 'You are on the ball today, Lucy. Well done.'

He squeezed her shoulder. Where once she'd have welcomed his attention, she shied away from his touch.

'Had on,' Ryan thought aloud. 'Does he say in his statement whether he takes the same route with his dog each time?'

Lucy scanned the statement. 'There's no mention of it here.'

'Check it out with him. If he did, and the body wasn't there at midnight, we can narrow down the time of death to a three hour window. It'll save us waiting on the post-mortem.'

Lucy reached for the phone. 'I'm onto it already.'

Ryan wandered to the vending suite. While he waited for a fresh coffee to dispense, he slid a coin into the snack machine and watched a Boost bar tumble into the receptacle like a high diver.

Outside, the sun, freed from its shackles, wallowed in self-glory. A rainbow hue of colours spread across the sky and sprinkled the River Tyne with golden streaks. Ryan found it hard to believe it was only fourteen hours since last night's storm raged, and nine hours since Danskin summoned him to the graveyard.

He wandered to the floor-to-ceiling window and watched lunchtime traffic crawl across the Tyne Bridge like a disoriented worm. The irregular curved roof of The Glasshouse, the new name for The Sage, sparkled in the sunlight as if it were a Christmas bauble.

Christmas.

Ryan felt a flutter in his stomach at the realisation he'd be a father next Christmas. He was brought back to earth by the sound of Todd Robson's voice.

'That's the ugly sod there. It's got to be him!'

Ryan hurried towards the open door of the tech room where Robson and Sangar pored over a bank of monitor screens.

'We've found him,' Todd exclaimed quietly.

Ryan looked at the grainy image. Had it been anyone else, he'd be unable to tell with certainty but, with the distinctive rucksack on his back and the stand-out white hair, Ryan knew Todd Robson was right.

'Where's this?' Ryan asked.

Ravi checked the co-ordinates on the bottom of the screen. 'Clifton Road, near the Primary School.'

'I'm not familiar with it.'

'We're one street north of Elswick Road,' Ravi explained. 'Not half a mile from the cemetery.'

'Bingo,' Ryan said. 'Now all we need do is track him.'

'Where to?'

'All the way to his grave, that's where.'

FOUR

Stephen Danskin emerged from his half-hour update meeting with Sam Maynard three hours later.

She'd roped him into a video conference with the Police and Crime Commissioner where they discussed budgets, targets, recruitment levels, and other *'Non-coppering bollocks,'* as Danskin described it.

Danskin rested against the glass wall of the Super's office, observing proceedings. Ryan roamed between the team, checking progress and providing direction. Trebilcock had arrived and was working on tasks already delegated to him by Ryan.

A smile spread across Danskin's face as he watched his protege at work.

'Impressive as ever, I see,' Maynard said as if reading his mind.

'Aye. He's a good 'un. He'll go far, if he doesn't get distracted.'

'The baby, you mean?'

Stephen nodded. 'Hannah reckons he's a bit too keen.'

'Is it possible to be too keen? Many a woman would be delighted to have a partner as enthusiastic as DS Jarrod.'

Danskin spoke softly. 'Well, it's up to them. I'm not interfering unless it affects his work.'

'And you think it might?'

'Time will tell. For now, though, he's doing aal reet.' He levered himself from the office wall and walked towards the hive of activity.

Ryan saw him coming. 'Can I have a word, sir?'

'About the case?'

'Well, indirectly, I suppose.'

'Gan on. Make it quick - and direct. I need to catch up on developments.'

Ryan took a deep breath. 'You know you mentioned me covering Lyall's duties?'

'Uh-huh.'

'Will it be official, like? You know, temporary promotion?'

'For a couple of weeks? I divvent think so.'

'Just ... Hannah and me have been talking. It'd look good on my CV. I mean, I'm on the fast-track scheme. That means they'd expect me to reach DI within three years...'

'...in the Met. Not here.'

'Perhaps, but it's been well over three years and I'm no further forward.'

Danskin's breath came out like a whistle. 'Do you want to move away?'

'What? With the baby on its way? No chance.'

'Then, forget about DI. There's only two posts here and they're filled by Parker and Brownlee, from Kinnear's team. You'll have a long wait.'

'But, sir...'

Danskin held a hand in front of him like Gandalf casting the Balrog back to the shadow.

'Listen, Jarrod. I've just been lectured about budgets and such shite as if I was on a GCSE Economics course. Three hours I've listened to the Commissioner's crap when all I wanted was to get on with some proper coppering. I don't need hear your crap, an' all. Understand? Right, what's the latest?'

Knowing when he was beaten, Ryan told the DCI about the victim's last known location.

Danskin turned towards Todd Robson. 'Robson - any more footage of our victim?'

'Nah, but we're still looking, Rav and me.'

'Any theories why he might have been around the spot the cameras picked him up?'

'Possibly,' Todd replied. 'There's a hostel for the homeless not a kick in the arse away. He might have been staying there.'

'You haven't checked?'

'Trying to find more images of him. See which way he was heading, like.'

'Makes sense,' Danskin concurred. 'Okay. Jarrod, get uniform to check out this hostel place. See if our bloke is known to them.'

'Sir,' Ryan said, picking up his desk phone.

'Oh, and congratulations, Robson,' the DCI said.

Todd looked puzzled. 'Congratulations for what?'

'The birth of your second brain cell. I think the hostel's a good shout of yours.'

'Cheers, guv. I think.'

Ryan set down the phone again. 'The wheels are in motion, sir. Uniform will report back soon as.'

Danskin moved to the sparse crime board. It bore little more than a map of the city, a map of the cemetery with an 'X' marking the spot where the body was discovered, a timeframe *'Midnight-3am'* and a few photographs of the crime scene which Rufus Cavanagh had e-mailed in response to Ryan's request.

'Any more on the footprint? Danskin asked, pointing at an enlarged image of the ground near the grave.

'Not had time to follow it up, sir. It's on the list, though.'

Danskin pursed his lips. 'Forensics come back with anything on the rucksack?'

'DC O'Hara confirmed they found no clues to the victim's identity inside it, as we suspected. Gav says he's still awaiting a detailed report.'

The DCI nodded. 'Aye. Still early days.' His eyes fixed on the corpse lying atop the grave of the young man called Thomas Raith. 'Any news on a listing for the post-mortem?'

'Nothing confirmed, sir,' Ryan said. 'With a bit of luck, it'll get scheduled for tomorrow.'

'Good. We need someone there, I think.'

Jarrod's stomach churned. Post-mortems weren't his - or any other officers - bag. He changed the subject. 'We mightn't have a motive, suspect, or cause of death but we do have an approximate time without having to wait for Cavanagh or Aaron to do the PM.'

'We do?'

'Aye. The sexton bloke, this Drew Fellowes, walked his dog at midnight and again at three. Lucy's checked and it turns out he took the same route both times. No corpse at midnight, body at three.'

'Brilliant! And when was our bloke caught on camera?'

Ryan checked his notes. 'Ravi says the image we've got was taken at nine fifty-five.'

Danskin traced a finger across the map. 'So, where did you go for two or more hours? And why come back to the same place to be killed?' He stopped talking to himself and addressed Ryan. 'We need more images of the sod. And we need them quick.'

Ryan stifled a yawn. 'Todd and Ravi have been at it non-stop. Do we need another set of eyes on it?'

Danskin looked around his team. 'Everyone's pretty bogged down. I'll ask if Rick Kinnear can spare someone.'

'I'm happy to help.'

The Graveyard Shift

DCI Danskin looked towards Ryan and spoke softly. 'I know you are, son, but you're shagged out, man. Get yersel' yem to bed for a while. You're done for the day.'

'Sir, you've been on the case longer than me...'

'Aye, and I get well paid for it.'

'So would I if you let me be DI for a bit.'

He saw Danskin's look. Held his hands up in surrender. 'Okay, okay. I get it. I'll keep it zipped.'

'I'll hold you to that, Jarrod.'

As Ryan turned to leave, he added, 'You'll get there soon enough, lad. Trust me. You're a good 'un. You know I rate you.'

Ryan gave the guv'nor a sheepish smile. 'Thank you, sir. See you tomorrow.'

'Aye, you will. And get here sharp again. Early shift for you if I'm letting you go now.'

'No such thing as a free lunch,' Ryan muttered.

**

Kenzie sensed his approach.

The young German Shepherd, growing as fast as Jack's beanstalk, perched on the back of the sofa, ears pricked, tongue lolling, tail wagging. His breath condensed on the window of Norman Jarrod's living room as Ryan made his way up his father's garden path.

The dog disappeared from view before Ryan heard its paws scratch against the door as he pushed it open.

'Just me,' Ryan called.

'Aye. Kenzie telt is,' Norman chuckled.

'How's he been?'

'Canny, man. Ran himself ragged on The Glebe but behaved himself.'

Ryan crouched down so the dog licked his face. 'You always do behave, don't you?'

'Most the time. Except when he scoffs me sausages.'
'Again? You shouldn't leave them out.'
'I'm still getting used to him being here.'

Ryan straightened. 'I think having him is doing you good, an' all. Gives you an interest apart from the telly and the Toon.' He pointed at his father's stomach. 'Exercise paying off. You're waistline's shrinking.'

'That's got nowt to do with exercise and everything to do with the mutt eating me scran.'

'Hadaway, man. You love having him.'

'I plead the fifth amendment.'

Ryan sat down opposite his father. 'It makes sense, though; you having Kenzie. I'm at work aal hours and it's not fair on the dog. It was different with old Spud. Little dog like that could cope on his own for a few hours. This lad, though, needs more attention. Don't you?' he said, ruffling the dog's neck 'Yes you do. Yes you do!'

Kenzie gave a yelp of delight.

'Aye, it's company for us,' Norman conceded. 'You're not around much, your Gran's in a world of her own in the home, and wor James is still infatuated with that lass of his.'

Ryan shook his head. 'Aye, I never thought me brother would be matched up with somebody like that but they get on well enough. I can't figure her out, still.'

Norman stood. 'I was going to make a brew. Fancy one?'

Ryan checked his watch. 'Gan on, then.'

He played tuggy with Kenzie and a heavily knotted rope while Norman busied in the kitchen.

'You're finished early,' Norman shouted from the kitchen.

'I've been on the job since the middle of the night, though.'

Norman returned carrying two overfilled cups. 'Busy day?' He slurped noisily.

'Most are.'

Norman knew better than ask about the job so he settled on taking over tug-o'-war duties from Ryan.

Eventually, Ryan broke the silence. 'I've been at a cemetery.'

'Ah, that's nice. Good lad. I've been meaning to gan mesel'.'

Ryan frowned. 'Oh. No, not THE cemetery. Not Rhianne's. Another cemetery.'

'I thought you meant you'd visited your sister. Ah well, whatever turns you on, I suppose,' Norman said, tapping Kenzie on the forehead with the rope he'd wrestled from the dog's jaws.

'Just a bit of an odd case, that's all.'

Norman sat back. 'Not like you to talk about work. Something up?'

'Murder case. Pretty nasty. And very weird.'

'Want to tell me more?'

Ryan shook his head. 'Not a great deal to tell yet. It's early days. Anyway, it hasn't hit the news so I can't talk about it even if I wanted to.'

Norman looked at his son. 'Howay, man. After what we've been through with your job, you can trust me.'

Ryan sighed. His father was right. Ryan had exposed his family to too many horrors over the last couple of years. Which was exactly why he wasn't about to open up about the case.

'Nah, I should be getting off. Didn't get much kip last night and I'm on earlies tomorrow.'

'Owt yer like, son. But I'm here, yeah?'

'I know you are, Dad. Cheers.'

He gave Kenzie one last pat and headed for the door. As he did so, his phone vibrated in his pocket.

Once outside, he checked his messages.

'Humph. First you bail out on me in the middle of the night, then quit work without so much as a tara.' The winking emoji told Ryan that Hannah was joking.

'*Can't let you have too much of a good thing lol,*' Ryan responded.

Moments later, his phone vibrated again. '*That's a shame. I was going to suggest I stayed again tonight.*'

Ryan sighed. '*Would love you to but I really need get some sleep.*' He hesitated. Deleted half the message until it read '*Would love you to*' and added a tiger emoji and *xx*.

'So much for a good night's kip', he mused as he put the Peugeot into gear and pulled out of Newfield Walk onto Larkspur Road.

FIVE

Streetlights confirmed the city centre was awake, but the roads hadn't yet regained consciousness.

The only traffic on the usually crammed city streets were delivery vehicles. The occasional shift worker shambled by, a taxi or two ferried dirty stop-outs back to their homes, and pigeons peered out from nesting spots on the Central Station portico.

And Ryan Jarrod rubbed at his eyes as he stepped through the doors of the City and County HQ on Forth Street at four-twenty AM.

In the elevator, he rotated his neck until it cracked, and stretched his arms high above his head before the doors slid open on the third floor. Ryan yawned as he left the lit hallway behind and entered the darkness of the open-plan CID room.

Sensors triggered the lighting as he made straight for the vending suite. He pressed a series of buttons and waited for black coffee to fill the Styrofoam cup.

He slurped from it and collapsed into his chair, sloshing liquid over his hands. He didn't care. At least it woke him up; enough to think about last night.

For the first time, he'd felt uncomfortable making love with Hannah. Nothing about her, of course, more the unnerving thought that their unborn child may have an awareness of what Mum and Dad were up to.

It clearly hadn't bothered Hannah. Ryan did the usual man-thing and immediately put it down to her hormones but, whatever the cause, Hannah Graves was more liberated than he'd ever known her. 'Shagged out' had never seemed a more appropriate description, he thought.

He rubbed a hand against the underside of his desk to dry it, then licked the residual coffee stains from the back of his hand. He turned it over. Looked at his palm. The scars from the fire several years ago were almost invisible, but they'd remain in his head for life.

Ryan stretched again and yawned noisily. He shook his head to clear his mind and wandered to the crime board. His movement caused the office lighting to flick on and off like the set of a cheesy game show.

One look at the photographs on the board reminded him that this was no game.

He massaged his eyebrows as his gaze roamed the board. One thing leapt out at him. An addition to the board. A name.

'William Coulson.'

'Aye, things have moved on a bit,' a voice next to him said.

More coffee spilled from Ryan's cup as he jumped at the sound. 'Bloody hell. Where the hell did you come from?'

Ravi Sangar smiled. 'The bog. Thought I'd have a wash and brush up before I got back to it.'

'You been here all night, mate?'

'Yup. No point going home when I hardly ever sleep.'

Ryan looked at Sangar. He appeared bright-eyed and bushy tailed. 'I don't know how you do it, Rav. I'm knackered, still.' Ryan almost smiled at the memory.

'I had a couple of hours kip at me desk. That's more than enough for me.'

Ryan shook his head in wonderment. 'I see we've a name for him, then.'

'Yep. Turns out Todd's hunch was right. He was a regular at the hostel but it was full up last night. The owner - is that what he is: 'owner?' - anyway, the gadgee in charge knows Coulson of old. Doesn't know owt about him, but at least he knew his name.'

'Did I miss anything else?'

'Not yesterday, no. Danskin told us to call it a night there and then.'

'Good. At least we've got a name and an approximate time of death. We're starting to get somewhere. I'll get someone to run a full check on this Coulson bloke once the cavalry arrive.'

Ravi had a smile on his face. 'What?' Ryan asked.

'I said that was all that happened *yesterday*.'

They both looked towards the door at the arrival of Rick Kinnear's early starter, saluting them from across the floor.

Ryan turned back to Sangar. 'Meaning?'

'Meaning I found out something *today*.' He turned his wrist. 'About half-an-hour ago.'

Ryan tugged at an earlobe. 'And now you're going to make me ask what you found, aren't you?'

Sangar chuckled. 'It'd be nee fun if I told you straight away.'

Ryan tutted. 'Howay, man. What is it?'

'Walk this way,' Sangar sang in his best Steve Tyler voice as he led the way to the tech room.

**

Matty Neill clung to the kitchen bench as if his life depended on it. He looked up at the clock on the wall, blinked twice as he tried to focus on it, then took another slug from the bottle of brandy next to him.

He'd established that it was something-past-four, and probably something-past-four in the morning, which was good enough for him.

His head swam. He rested it on the cool tiles of the kitchen wall. The bass beat from the speakers in the room above sent shockwaves running through him.

If he hadn't consumed half a bottle of Bacardi, two ciders, and become good acquaintances with Remy Martin, Matty might have felt sorry for the neighbours. As it happened, he never gave them a thought. Not that there were many, anyway.

The thud of the speakers coursed through him like a heartbeat, drowning out the shouts and exaggerated laughter of his fellow partygoers. He needed some air.

As he turned, his trailing arm caught a stack of empty beer cans which clinked to the laminate floorboards like scattered ninepins. The couple entwined on the floor paused what they were doing, laughed, and re-engaged as if nothing had happened.

Yes, the party had reached *that* stage; where folk had either paired up or were desperate for someone to pair up with.

'*The scene*' had never been Matty's scene. Now, though, even the house parties he attended weren't for him. He felt older than his thirty-seven years. Older and lonely, but not too old to long for companionship. Even in his stupor, he realised he wouldn't find what he wanted here.

He stepped over the couple and swayed into a corridor.

Matty screwed up his eyes. The light was too bright. At the end of the passageway, the glass panel of the back door beckoned him towards a welcoming darkness beyond.

He lurched along the corridor like a man on a rolling boat. He fumbled with the door handle. Pushed at it twice before finally realised he should be pulling. Two young men - boys, almost - watched him with a sneer of disgust.

The door yielded and Matty tumbled out into a pitch-black back garden.

'*Who lives in a house like this?*' Matty thought. He didn't know where he was, or how he'd got there. He swallowed down a

The Graveyard Shift

sense of self-pity - or was it self-disgust? - and swayed into the darkness.

He staggered into a dense privet. Felt its bony branches prick him. He stretched out his arms. Matty's fingers touched the rough and pitted surface of a waist-high stone wall.

He bent over it and vomited thickly, spitting out mustard-flavoured bile and the bitter sting of spirits.

'I think you've had too much,' a voice said from behind him. A hand was around his waist, steadying him.

Matty kept his head down, hiding the tears of self-disdain from the man's view.

'Are you okay?' The voice was calm, benign, and soothing.

Matty said nothing at first, waiting while his stomach settled and his wits returned.

'I'm fine,' he said, eventually. Matty straightened and looked at his saviour. Taller than Matty, he had Elvis-black hair in an outdated curtain cut. The man flicked back the hair from his eyes. Ran a hand through it, then lay a fingertip on Matty's cheek.

'Hey,' the man said, 'You been crying?'

'No,' Matty lied. 'It's just being sick, you know? Always brings tears to my eyes.'

'Okay.'

Matty appreciated the non-judgemental tone in the man's voice. He also appreciated the man's touch. He wasn't especially attracted to him, but the warmth in the touch meant something to Matty.

The man smiled at him. Matty smiled back.

'You have had too much, though.' the man repeated.

'I always do,' Matty said, still smiling.

'Here on your own?' his new companion asked.

Matty felt something stir inside him. 'Aye. I'm all dressed up with nowhere to go.'

The man looked deep into Matty's eyes. 'We could go somewhere.'

Matty sensed a movement further back in the garden. '*No. Not now. Please don't let us be interrupted.*' He stared beyond the man, towards the house and the raucous noise coming from within.

Nothing moved. No-one spoke. He'd been mistaken.

Matty relaxed. 'Somewhere special?' Matty teased.

'Oh yes. Somewhere very special.'

The man reached out and took hold of Matty's fingers. He led him through a gate in the garden wall, beyond a row of trees, and into an open space beyond. A field, Matty assumed.

Out in the open, away from the sweaty, crowded house, the air felt chilled. Matty shivered.

'Cold? Don't worry.' The man looked skywards. Silver tints gave the first hint of the approaching dawn. 'It'll soon warm up. It'll be light soon. We should hurry.'

Matty felt a tingle of excitement at the thought of impending sex. They stepped through a hedgerow - and Matty stopped in his tracks.

'What the...?'

The silvery tint revealed just enough for Matty to pick out a row of stones protruding from tufted and neglected grass.

'Is this...?'

'Never done it in a graveyard before?' the man asked. 'Exciting, isn't it?'

'Well...no. I mean, I don't know.' But Matty did know. The man was right - it WAS exciting.

'Here,' the man said. 'This will help make it even more special.'

'I don't do drugs,' Matty countered, stepping away.

'Relax. It's not drugs. Look.' The man held up a hip flask. Matty saw him tip some of its contents into an odd-shaped cup.

The Graveyard Shift

Matty took the cup from the man as if commanded by an unseen force. He heard the contents fizz and, with it, the realisation they were wrapped in absolute silence, further from the house and its overbearing guests than he'd imagined.

There was just him, his companion, and the dead.

'Go on,' the man encouraged. 'Drink it. It'll help you relax.' He hunkered down in the grass. 'Here, join me.'

Matty accepted the man's invitation. He took a sip from the cup and screwed his eyes tight. 'Yukk. What is it?'

The man chuckled. 'It's an acquired taste, but you get used to it.'

Matty heard a tinkle as the lip of the hipflask met his cup. 'Have another.'

He took a sip from the cup. The man had been right. Second time around wasn't so bad.

Matty felt himself tip forward. Dewy grass scratched at his face.

'Whoa. I think that was the straw that broke the camel's back,' Matty giggled.

The man dropped to his knees alongside Matty. He leant towards him. Matty groaned as the man nuzzled his neck, tongue licking at his throat. The man's fingers stroked the side of Matty's face. Matty moaned softly and reached for his own belt, struggling with it against the pressure.

A shadow fell over the two men, as if someone was watching. Matty's eyes opened wide, searching the black void.

There was no-one. Just him and his lover.

'Your name,' Matty murmured. 'What's your name? I want to whisper it in your ear.'

'My name? You mean you don't know?' The man's voice came out muffled against the side of Matty's throat.

'Tell me,' Matty said.

He felt the man's lips pucker the flesh of his throat. Then came a sharp, piercing sensation.

'Owww!' Matty groaned, half in agony half ecstasy.

His eyes snapped open.

And he saw the stars blink out, one-by-one.

SIX

DCI Danskin's team assembled in front of the crime board assigned to William Coulson. Ryan had briefed Danskin on Ravi's latest sighting of Coulson and he'd pleaded for Danskin's permission to lead the briefing.

Danskin consented, aware it added to Jarrod's growing stature.

'Okay, guys: well done on yesterday. We have a name for our victim,' Ryan tapped the board's heading, 'And an approximate window of opportunity where the killing occurred.' He indicated the *'midnight-3am'* legend. 'We still don't have a cause of death. Any news when Cavanagh's likely to do the post-mortem?'

'Not yet,' Gavin O'Hara replied, 'But I've asked we be notified as soon as they know the timeslot he's been given.'

'Good.'

'And, even better, Elliot's secretary reckons the main man himself is coming in to do it. Seems Dr Cavanagh expressly asked him to after you and the guv'nor spoke with him.'

Ryan beamed. 'I'm beginning to warm to Rufus Cavanagh, you know. That's great news. I'll attend the post-mortem. Gav - fancy doing it with me?'

O'Hara paled. It didn't escape Danskin's attention.

'I'm afraid I've loaded O'Hara with a mountain of urgent paperwork.' He looked Gavin in the eyes. 'He's got enough going on for now, with one thing or another,' Danskin excused, mindful not to reveal anything of O'Hara's domestic concerns.

'Thank you,' Gavin mouthed silently.

'Trebilcock, you can accompany Jarrod,' the DCI ordered.

The Cornishman looked as if he'd been asked to consume his own excrement.

'Right,' Ryan continued, 'What do we know about our guy?'

'He's not active on any social media platform,' Ravi Sangar informed the team, 'And there's no mobile phone records. There again, I wouldn't expect anything else, Coulson being homeless an' all.'

Ravi received universal nods of agreement.

'And I presume we'd have heard by now if he was on wor books?'

'There's no trace of him on the database,' Lucy Dexter contributed. 'I find that strange. A lot of homeless guys are known to us in one way or another.'

Ryan puffed out his cheeks. 'Okay, Lucy. Keep at it.'

'I will. I wonder... d'you think we should run checks on hospitals and such like? He might have medical records somewhere.'

'Good point, Luce. Not sure whether it'll help us in any way but worth a go. I reckon with his albinism he'll have a medical history or treatment record somewhere.' He took a slug of water from a bottle. 'You chase it up, Lucy.'

'What I'd like to know,' Todd mused, 'Is where did he go after we got him on camera?'

Ryan chuckled to himself. This was going well. 'Et voila,' he said as he pinned a blurred image Ravi Sangar had retrieved from the streetcam to the board.

'This is our man fifteen minutes after he was caught on camera at Clifton Street. Ravi tracked it down in the wee small hours.'

The team took a moment or two to digest the image and the timings.

'Where's this taken, Jarrod?' Stephen Danskin interjected.

'Outside a hookah bar on Rye Hill. That's hookah with an 'a' and an 'h' for your benefit, Todd.' The squad laughed. 'A

The Graveyard Shift

shisha lounge, if you prefer it. Now, I know the picture's crap. Remember, it's pissing down, murky, and generally Godawful but, fortunately, our guy is quite distinctive.'

'Aye, that's him, like,' Todd agreed. 'I spent hours looking through the footage for him. His mug's engrained in me memory. I'd recognise him a mile off.'

'Which leads me nicely to Todd's question: where did the bugger go after this?'

Ryan looked at his team for inspiration and got none. What he did get was the sight of Hannah Graves, newly arrived for DCI Kinnear's late shift, watching his address from afar with pride.

Danskin brought him out of his trance. 'Was that a rhetorical question, Jarrod?'

'What? Err, no. Right, we know Coulson tried to gain access to the hostel up the West End. We know he was denied entry and was spotted a few hundred yards away from both the hostel and St. John's Cemetery. Next, we pick him up here.' Ryan annotated the map with two red crosses, connecting them with a hastily scrawled arrow.

'Looks like he's headed towards the city centre,' Gavin O'Hara suggested.

'Haymarket area, I'd guess,' Lucy said. 'We get a lot of homeless hanging out around there.'

Her comment was met with a murmur of agreement.

'Possibly,' Ryan considered, 'But remember the weather conditions. This is a man who we know tried to find a bed in a hostel even before the weather broke. My guess is, he'd be looking for cover somewhere, out of the storm. Somewhere,' he said, tracing a finger along the trajectory of Coulson's route, 'Like here.'

The direction of travel took his finger to the railway arches running beneath the Central Station.

To a man, the squad looked out the windows of the Forth Street police HQ. Barely a drop-kick away from the City and County force's offices lay Orchard Street - and the tunnels which undercut the railway lines.

The thought of Billy Coulson spending his final moments within spitting distance of where they stood, staring at photographs of his mutilated corpse, brought Danskin's team to a sober silence, broken by Ryan.

'We've plenty CCTV coverage around the area of the Central Station. Ravi, I suggest we narrow your search down to this area initially. It's a much smaller haystack to search for our needle, and you should start trawling through footage ten minutes after his sighting in Rye Hill.'

Hannah Graves still stood just inside the doorway. A convoy of patrol cars left the compound below the office windows, blues and twos sounding. She shut the window so she could better eavesdrop on Ryan's briefing. She basked in his reflected glory, proud to see the bashful youth, five years her junior, blossom into the leader of men he had become; yet still retain a childlike vulnerability beneath his veneered exterior.

The more she saw, the more she knew her decision to bring their child up apart from Ryan was the right one. Although there was more than a grain of truth in the story she'd told Ryan about her insecurities caused by her upbringing, the real reason was his career. It was blossoming and neither she nor their child should get in its way.

Sleepless nights with the baby, hurrying to finish a shift to get back to them, and the possibility he'd shy away from difficult situations because of fears for their child, were all factors which would prevent Ryan from reaching Detective Inspector.

Hannah, with regret, knew she'd use her full maternity leave caring for their child at her Jesmond apartment. Alone.

The Graveyard Shift

After that, she'd reconsider - but she knew 'now' was not the moment for Jarrod to take his eye off the ball.

'It's what's best for Ryan,' she convinced herself.

With the street noise extinguished, Hannah heard Ryan's melodious voice address the squad again. She also heard DCI Kinnear's pointed 'Harrumph' as he looked at her and tapped his wristwatch.

'Ah well,' she thought as she stroked her stomach, *'Back to paperwork boredom for us, little one.'*

**

DCI Danskin observed the impact Ryan's update had on his troops. He'd allocated tasks to them all, and they were eager to get on with the job.

Except one.

Todd Robson's chair creaked as he sat back in it, feet on his desk. He gnawed on his pen like a rabbit with a carrot. His demeanour didn't escape Danskin's attention.

'Before you all start beavering away,' Danskin interrupted, 'Is everyone comfortable with what's been discussed?'

'Yes, sir,' the majority replied.

'What about you, Robson? You look a bit unsure.'

Todd swung his feet off the desk's surface. Thought for a moment. 'Aye, to be honest, I am. I don't think we'll find Coulson anywhere near the arches.'

Nigel Trebilcock rolled his eyes. Gavin O'Hara tutted.

'Now, now. Let's here Robson out,' Danskin stressed.

'Aall I'm thinking, like, is what I would do on a night like that. I mean, it's pissing more than me after a sesh at the rugby club.'

Trebilcock spoke up. 'Which is why he'd have taken shelter, so he would.'

'Okay, clever shite - tell me this: if he walked all the way from Elswick to the city to find cover beneath the station, why the hell would he then gan back up hill to where he started out from? His body wasn't a kick in the arse from where we first picked him up. Nah, I'm not buying it. I think we're barking up the wrong tree.'

Danskin's crew remained silent. They knew Robson's observation was relevant.

The DCI himself spoke first. 'Dexter, I want you to put out an APB. We're looking for a man called Todd Robson, 'cos this bloke here's an imposter. He's made more observations in forty-eight hours than the real Robson has in fifteen years.'

When the chuckles died down, Danskin asked Robson for his theory.

'If it was me, and I was caught out in a storm, I'd dive in the first boozer I came across. Ride the worst of it out there.'

After a group intake of breath, heads nodded.

'Good thinking, Todd,' Ryan praised, 'But do you know how many boozers there are within half a mile of the hookah joint where we last spotted Coulson?'

'No, but I'm happy to visit all of them, just in the interests of research, you understand. No, seriously, he wouldn't go to any of the upmarket bars, would he? Nee cash, for starters. He might try the Beehive or Old George, I suppose, but that's the best he'd go for, I reckon.'

'Ravi, concentrate the CCTV search on the Bigg Market, will you?' Ryan suggested.

'Can we just think this through a minute,' Lucy Dexter lisped. 'If he did shelter in a pub, it still doesn't explain why he later went back to a place which he knew didn't have a room for him.'

'Shit. You're right, Lucy,' Ryan cursed.

Todd stood up. Moved towards the map on the board. 'Unless he was meeting someone. Somebody who already had a room in the hostel. A room he could share.'

'Gavin - get onto the hostel supervisor. I want the names of everyone who had a room there that night.'

The Graveyard Shift

O'Hara reached for his telephone, while Ravi Sangar joined Todd by the board.

'There's another possibility,' he said. 'If we follow Coulson's route towards the city centre, instead of carrying on down Fenkle Street way towards the station, he might have turned off here,' Ravi's finger jabbed at the map then trailed at right angles. 'Down towards Grainger Town way.'

'What's down there for him?' Gavin O'Hara dismissed. 'We could go on like this forever, man. Let's focus on the station and the Bigg Market, I say.'

'Had on,' Danskin mused. 'Let's not see what we expect to see here but, if he did meet someone; let's say, a stranger, there's no better place than Grainger Town.'

'Why's that?'

Danskin and Ryan looked at one another. They spoke together; one questioningly, the other with more authority.

'The pink triangle.'

SEVEN

Gavin O'Hara set the phone down. 'I've got the names for you from the hostel.' He ripped a sheet of paper from a notepad and handed it to Ryan.

Jarrod studied the seventeen names scrawled on the note. None of them leapt out at him. 'Well done, Gav. Run checks on them. See what you can find, then we'll send uniform up to speak to them.'

He turned towards Lucy Dexter. 'Have you come up with anything on the medical records for Coulson?'

She looked up at him, squinting as a ray of sunshine speared her in the eye. 'Still working on it. Nowt so far.'

'Okay. Keep at it.'

Ryan turned back to his keyboard.

'Follow me, Jarrod.' Stephen Danskin's voice.

'Hell's teeth. What have I done now?' Ryan wondered. When he looked up, Danskin was holding open Superintendent Maynard's office door for him.

'I don't understand, sir.'

Danskin inclined his head towards the interior. 'You will.'

Sam Maynard looked up from her paperwork and met them with a stare of eyes the colour of Polar ice.

'Stephen? Ryan? What can I do for you?'

'Sorry to intrude, ma'am. I'm after your opinion, if you don't mind.'

'Of course not,' she said setting down a pen.

Danskin considered his words. 'I've been observing DS Jarrod during this investigation, ma'am.'

Maynard's eyes flitted over Ryan. 'And?'

The Graveyard Shift

'Well, ma'am, he's shown real leadership qualities. I think it's time.'

Ryan's brow furrowed. Sam Maynard was no more clear. 'Time for what?'

It was Danskin's turn to look towards Ryan. 'His Inspector exam, ma'am.'

Ryan's mouth fell open. Maynard smiled, but there was something else in her face. Doubt?

'Stephen, we have no positions free...'

'Hear me out, ma'am,' Danskin continued. 'I'm aware of that. I'm also aware the timing is not great, given DS Graves condition.'

'She's pregnant, Stephen. She doesn't have a condition.'

'Aye, but you know what I mean. Anyhoo, if Jarrod takes his exam, he's at least on the list...'

'...assuming he's successful.'

'He will be. I've every confidence in him.'

Sam Maynard stared at them. 'So have I.'

'Then you agree, ma'am?'

The Super sighed. 'Sit down, gentlemen.'

They sat, gazing over the Tyne.

'I'll put Sergeant Jarrod's name down.'

'Wow! Great. Thanks, ma'am,' Ryan beamed.

'Just a second. Wait - I haven't finished. I'll put him down in three months' time.'

'Three months? Why three months?' Danskin asked, puzzled.

Maynard tilted her head back. Sighed. 'Because that's when his progression bar ends.'

'My what?'

'Ryan, I didn't think you'd need to know but, after your Operation Sage *activities*', she chose the word carefully, 'You were precluded from consideration for promotion. It expires in three months, and I'll be delighted to throw all my weight behind you at that time.'

Ryan and Danskin gawped like landed trout. 'I don't understand. I thought I was cleared.'

'Of disciplinary proceedings, yes. But you must admit your conduct was, shall we say, unorthodox. Now, I know you acted with the best of intentions - you always do - and I managed to persuade the PCA to take no additional action.' She saw the look of horror on Ryan's face. 'There's no mark on your record, no reference to it anywhere on file, and in twelve short weeks I will gladly endorse your well-deserved application. Now, if there's nothing else…?'

It wasn't a question.

Outside, Danskin swore. Ryan swore worse.

'Can there be any more surprises today?' Jarrod wondered out loud.

'Ryan!,' he heard Trebilcock's west country accent, 'Where 'ave you bin'? Oi been lookin' for ya.'

'You've found me, now. What is it?'

'Coulson's post-mortem. They're doing it as we speak.'

**

Heavy traffic meant the two-mile uphill drive through the city took over ten minutes. Nurses picketing outside the hospital entrance and student demonstrations at the adjacent University slowed the journey even more.

Ryan almost dragged Nigel Trebilcock through the bowels of the Royal Victoria Infirmary until they arrived outside the morgue.

They arrived too late.

Rufus Cavanagh was scrubbing down work surfaces and the familiar figure of Aaron Elliot rinsed off a bone saw before holding the implement up to the light where it glinted like a mirror.

The Graveyard Shift

Dr Elliot peeled off his surgical gloves and sanitised his hands. When he saw Ryan outside, he beamed a smile and Ryan lipread his silent 'Come in.'

'Sorry you missed the show, Sherlock.'

'Good to see you, too, Aaron,' Ryan smirked. 'Seriously, though, I asked to be notified well before you began the PM.' He stared at Rufus Cavanagh.

'Ah, that was my fault,' Elliot explained. 'Dr Cavanagh did tell me but I was so keen to get started it slipped my mind. Apologies.' He smiled at the Detectives.

Ryan and Trebilcock narrowed their eyes as harsh lighting reflecting from white and chrome surfaces gave off a celestial glow.

The thing on the table was anything but heavenly.

Billy Coulson lay under the spotlight, the Y-shaped incision on his body hastily stitched in a ragged fashion. Ryan guessed the dead weren't fussed about scars, but it seemed anomalous to sew the incision yet leave a raw, jagged hole where the stake had pierced him.

Ryan moved closer to the table. Trebilcock moved further away. Ryan gave him a concerned look but Trebilcock nodded that he was okay.

Ryan noticed Coulson's chest was slightly concave, a result of his innards being removed and inspected before the medics had hastily returned them to the cavity.

'So, how did he die?'

Rufus Cavanagh answered. 'We don't know, unfortunately.'

'You *still* don't know - how come?'

'Initial toxicology reports show nothing. A trace of alcohol but nothing of significance. No signs of any drugs, prescription or otherwise.'

Ryan drew in breath and wished he hadn't. The overpowering stench of chemicals, antiseptic, and death filled his lungs. He cleared his throat.

'We're sure he was dead before the stake was driven through him?'

'Absolutely,' Aaron Elliot asserted. 'Almost no blood loss as a result of the impalement shows the man was already deceased. He had no underlying medical issues as far as we can tell. Perhaps a little malnourished, some evidence the man was a smoker at some point but, otherwise, Mr Coulson appears a healthy specimen. Apart from being dead, of course.'

Ryan smiled. He was well used to Elliot's macabre humour. 'You have nothing to give us at all, then.'

'Oh, that's not what I said,' Elliot smiled. 'We know Coulson had sexual relations shortly before he died.'

'Does that mean you've got DNA?'

'Indeed it does. But, sadly, it's Mr Coulson's own.'

'Are you sure? There definitely isn't any belonging to the woman?'

'We're running tests but I'm confident we won't find female DNA,' Rufus Cavanagh said.

'You're not certain, though.'

Elliot spoke. 'I can't speak for Dr Cavanagh but I'm certain, yes.'

'How come?'

'Because Mr Coulson was penetrated by a male, and traces of a lubricant indicate the use of a condom.'

Ryan's eyebrows shot skywards.

'Like I say, we're awaiting more detailed lab results but…'

'No, no. I don't doubt it.' Ryan glanced at Trebilcock. 'Todd was right. He said as much, didn't he?'

Trebilcock nodded.

'The sex was consensual?' Ryan asked.

'In my opinion,' Rufus interjected, 'I'd say so.'

'Aaron?'

Elliot hesitated. 'If I were to testify in court, I couldn't give a definitive answer.'

Ryan exhaled. 'Okay. So, really, we have zilch suspects and no cause of death, am I right?'

'I'm afraid so. It's as though Mr Coulson's heart simply stopped beating,' he clicked his fingers, 'Like that. Dr Cavanagh and I found no evidence of myocardial infarction nor any catastrophic haemodynamic deterioration.'

Ryan rolled his eyes. 'I'll take your word for it.' He moved around the cadaver. 'What about the puncture wound to the neck?'

Aaron Elliot smacked his lips together. 'That, my friend, is another mystery but, whatever caused it, I promise it didn't contribute to our friend's death.'

Ryan opened his mouth but before he could speak Aaron Elliot continued.

'Oh, and for what it's worth, there's actually another puncture wound.'

'What? Where?'

'Just here. See, it's barely visible. I may have missed it had Dr Cavanagh not been assisting me.'

'Well done, Dr Cavanagh,' Ryan felt compelled to say. 'It's a good spot. Does it help us, though?'

'Not in the slightest, I'm afraid,' Rufus apologised.

Ryan sighed. 'Okay. Anything else you can tell us?'

'The man was in his mid-thirties, I'd say. As you know, he had a condition commonly referred to as albinism but that in no way accounted for his death. Oh, I'd put time of death at around…'

'…Midnight and three o'clock,' Ryan answered.

Aaron clapped, the noise echoing like a hollow thunderclap in the laboratory chamber. 'Well played, that man,' he said.

'Actually, I'd narrow it down to between one and three but, for an amateur, I'm impressed.' Elliot said without any air of condescension.

Ryan ran a hand over his mouth, then tugged at his ear. 'I suppose if that's all you've got for us, we'd better get back. Keep me updated though, docs, yeah?'

'Of course,' Cavanagh said.

'With pleasure,' Elliot added.

'Can oi arsk a question?' Nigel Trebilcock spoke for the first time.

'You may,' Elliot told him.

'The second puncture wound - how close is it to the first?'

Elliot's eyebrows pulled inwards. He picked up a pair of surgical callipers and lay them against Coulson's throat. '4.4 centimetres,' he concluded.

Trebilcock pulled at his bottom lip. He slipped his fingertips into his mouth and brought them out, fingers apart. He brought them up to his eyeline.

'It wouldn't be a bite, I'm thinking, would it?'

Aaron Elliot responded. 'I'm not at all sure how to answer given the double negatives in your question but, no: they aren't teeth marks.'

Ryan gave Nigel Trebilcock a look of disdain. 'Okay, thanks again for your time, gentlemen.'

They turned to leave when Ryan remembered something.

'Dr Cavanagh, thanks for the crime scene photographs. They're already proving useful to wor enquiry. One thing, though: I know you said forensics trampled over the scene after you took the images but there's one with a very clear impression of a footprint. That's going to prove invaluable, I believe. I know we've had our differences but you should know how much we - I - appreciate it.'

Rufus smiled. 'And I appreciate your appreciation, DS Jarrod.'

Trebilcock pushed open the door.

The Graveyard Shift

'They're a size nine,' Cavanagh said. 'A pair of Clark's Cottrell Edge.'

'How...?'

'Because I'm afraid it's my footprint. Unfortunately, it was the only place I could stand to get the right angle for the shot of the neck wound. I'm sorry if it's been a distraction.'

'Ah bollocks,' Ryan cursed.

**

Ironically, just when Ryan could do with some thinking time, the return journey to Forth Street took a matter of minutes. He and Trebilcock arrived to find the third-floor office a hive of frenetic endeavour with its air drenched in the musky scent of pheromones.

Ryan wanted to update Danskin on the post-mortem but he was swept along on a tsunami of activity. 'What the hell have we missed?' he asked Gavin O'Hara.

'Loads, man. We've got more info on Coulson.' He hurried towards his desk, shouting, 'Lucy will update you,' over his shoulder.

Ryan spun his head in his attempts to locate Lucy Dexter. He found her by the crime board, which now read '*Ronald William Coulson.*'

'That's why we had nowt on him, Ry. He's known as Billy but he was named after his father, Ronald.'

'Great work, Lucy. How did you find him?'

'He had some appointments as a kid at the eye infirmary. Hasn't been back for years but, from his records, it's him, aal reet. He went for a few checks with him being an albino but then went off grid.'

'Do we know why the appointments stopped?'

Lucy paused. 'Yeah. He was taken into foster care. His parents were total shithouses and abused him. He spent most of his childhood between social services and foster parents, then at the age of fourteen he just disappeared. I presume that's when he started living on the streets. He was known to Social Services as Ronald Coulson. Probably dropped his father's name later 'cos of the way he treated him.'

'What else do we know about him?'

'Born on Valentine's Day 1990, which makes him thirty-three.'

'Ties in with Doc Elliot's approximation, doesn't it, Nige?'

Trebilcock didn't answer. He'd wandered off somewhere.

'Owt else?'

'No.'

Ryan surveyed the floorplate. 'That doesn't explain all the activity. Something else is up, isn't it?'

'Yes,' Lucy agreed. 'Ravi's just spotted him on CCTV. Looks like Todd was right - Coulson was seen at the toon end of Scotswood Road. Coulson went into The Eagle.'

'The gay bar?'

'That's the one.'

'Well, get someone down there. Now!'

'The DCI says it's not worth it 'cos Billy Coulson didn't stay. He came straight back out again. The DCI's in with the Super asking permission to flood the area with uniform, but The Eagle is one place we know he wasn't at, at least for any length of time.'

Ryan shook his head. 'We should be down there.'

'With what? We haven't the resources.'

Lucy Dexter was right and Ryan should have known. He took a gulp of air, dispensed a coffee from the vending suite, and returned to the crime board.

Trebilcock was next to it, staring at the crime scene images.

'What do you make of it all, Nige?' Ryan asked.

Trebilcock didn't answer.

'Something troubling you?' Jarrod persisted.

'You's can call me a superstitious oik, but this ain't right, so it's not.'

The Graveyard Shift

Ryan removed the photograph of the footprint from the board. It was no longer relevant, seeing as it belonged to Dr Cavanagh. 'Gan on, then - what are you thinking?'

'Well, where I comes from, folk believe in fairies and pixies and all sorts of imps and spirits.'

Ryan sighed. 'Yep, you're right. You're a superstitious oik.'

Trebilcock looked at Ryan, coldly. 'But it's not right, all this.'

'All what, man?'

'The bite marks on Coulson's neck...'

'...You heard the doc. They weren't bite marks. Puncture wounds, they were.'

'And when did Lucy say Coulson were born?'

'February fourteenth, 1990.'

Trebilcock shook his head. 'This ain't right. Oi'm not liking it.'

'For fuck's sake, man: what?'

Ryan stopped mid-sentence. Trebilcock was pointing a finger at the photograph of William Coulson spreadeagled in front of the gravestone.

'Jesus,' Ryan said.

'Exactly.'

The gravestone still read:

'*Thomas Raith*
Died 14th February 1808.
Aged 33.
May God protect thy soul.'

'Co-incidence, surely,' Ryan protested, 'That Coulson's birthday's the same date this Raith guy died.'

'He was the same age as well, Ryan.'

'Co-incidences happen,' Ryan said, with less conviction.

'And Coulson had a stake through his heart.'

Ryan tisked. 'That's a bit of an exaggeration, mind. He had a bit of wood in his chest.'

Trebilcock shook his head. 'Do you know who Thomas Raith is?'

Jarrod sighed. 'I've a feeling you're going to tell me.'

'Thomas Raith is a character in *The Dresden Files*.'

'So?'

Trebilcock looked at Ryan. His pallor was deathly white.

'Ryan, Thomas Raith was a vampire.'

EIGHT

'Hadaway, man,' Ryan laughed contemptuously. 'You can't seriously expect me to go to Danskin with your cock-and-bull theory.'

Trebilcock shrugged. 'Just sayin' what my fellow Cornish folk might be thinking, that's all.'

Ryan shook his head. 'You're an even weirder lot than I thought, doon there. Must be all that cider. Or dancing naked around big stones in the ground. It can't be good for you.'

'Okay. Forget it. Let's move on. You think I be bamfoozled, I can tell, so don't tell Danskin aught. I still say it's all peculiar, mind.'

Ryan shook his head. Trebilcock had lost it. And yet...

'No, don't even think it,' Ryan told himself.

He didn't have time to think it. Todd Robson gave a triumphant bellow across the floorplate. 'We've got a possible witness. Bloke who runs a bar on the corner of Marlborough Crescent. Uniform say he's pretty sure Coulson was in his bar that night,' he shouted, telephone handset still in his grasp.

'Get in! Let's get up there and have a word. Howay, Todd - you're coming with me. Nigel, update the DCI, yeah? Mind, nee mention of...' Ryan didn't need finish the sentence.

Trebilcock was already miming a zipper-pull across his lips.

**

Given the proximity of the bar to the station and the potential for traffic delays, coupled with the bonkers one-way system, Ryan and Todd decided it was quicker reaching JayKay's on foot. It wasn't far - but it was uphill. They hadn't reached the top of Forth Banks before Ryan found himself lagging behind Robson.

'Had on a minute, Todd. I'm struggling here.' He stood bent double, hands resting on his knees.

'Soft shite,' Robson joked. 'I thought you used to be a gymnast an' all.'

'*Used* to be a gymnast. Past tense. Been a canny few years now,' Ryan gasped.

'You need to work oot more, young lad like you. I'll put a word in at the rugby club, if you like.'

'How man, what do you expect? I've had nee kip for days. Hardly eaten a proper meal. I've been living on coffee.'

'Sounds like your being ower defensive to me, like,' Todd said, giving Ryan a half-wink.

Ryan's phone pinged, saving him from coming up with a suitable retort. 'That's Lucy. She's e-mailed us details of the witness. She's attached uniform's preliminary report, an' all. The witness seems kosher enough, they reckon.'

'What's his name?'

'John Kaye.'

'Like the bloke on Breakfast News?'

'I've nee idea. I always seem to be at work when that's on, these days.' Ryan straightened. 'Right. Not far now. Let's get it over with.'

They cut by the Centre for Life and walked up to John Kaye's bar. It was nothing from the outside - small, panelled windows with a door which opened directly onto the street. A good lick of paint wouldn't go amiss so, all-in-all, a pretty mundane establishment.

Ryan pulled open the door and peered inside. The bar was past its best, but he could tell it had once been pleasant enough. Besides, most city centre pubs look tawdry during daylight hours - especially when they're as quiet as this one.

Ryan and Todd looked around.

A couple of women in their thirties sat at one table, glasses of Coke in front of them. A youth - probably a student - sat with legs crossed at the thigh. He hammered away at a laptop. A couple of older guys propped up one end of the bar. One wore a trilby with a coloured feather protruding from its band; the other smoothed beer foam from a moustache, above which a thread-veined nose glowed red.

They glanced up but quickly lost interest and resumed their conversation.

The only other occupant stood pump-side of the bar. Smartly dressed and wearing John Lennon glasses, the man had stylish dark hair. He gave Ryan and Todd a shy smile.

'Mr Kaye?' Ryan subtly flashed his warrant card. 'I'm Ryan Jarrod. This is my colleague, Todd Robson.' He didn't announce their status. No point driving away what little custom Kaye had.

John Kaye glanced around the premises. 'Shall we go through the back?'

'Aye, that sounds like a plan.'

Kaye held up a Del-Boy type hatch for them to pass through, and shouted through an open side-door, 'Charles - can you cover for a few minutes? Deed as a dodo but you never know - we might get a busload of tourists at any moment.' He gave an exaggerated eyeroll. Ryan laughed. He was warming to the man.

Todd appeared more comfortable in the back room, not so concerned about being spotted in a gay bar. 'I hear you were working on the night Billy Coulson was killed.'

'Yeah, that's right.'

'Were you busy that night?'

'Oh aye. Rammed, we were. Usually are at night, not that you'd think it at the moment, mind.'

Ryan thought for a while. 'How are you so sure it was Coulson, if you were that busy?'

'Plenty of reasons. My clientele are regulars. Lovely boys and girls. Polite, friendly - almost always in couples. We don't get many single guys in. It's not that sort of place, if you know what I mean.'

Todd grimaced. He did know what he meant.

'Any other reason he stood out?'

'He was scruffy. Extremely scruffy. Plus, he was quite distinctive with his white hair, an' all. I was a bit wary of him.'

'Did he give you cause to be wary?'

'Oh no, nothing like that. It's just…well, we don't like trouble here and you never know what a stranger's motives are. I kept an eye on him just in case he was looking for bother.'

'Was he alone?'

John Kaye pointed his head towards the bar. 'Sat by himself next to the bandit, most the time.'

'You said, *'Most of the time?'*

John Kaye paused. 'You must remember it was busy. I couldn't spend all my time watching him.'

'I sense a *'but'* coming,' Ryan encouraged.

'He was with another guy for a while. I'm not sure how long they were together.'

'There's another *'but'*, isn't there?'

Although no-one could hear the conversation, John Kaye lowered his voice. 'I saw them come out the toilets together, and then they left.'

Todd pulled a face, imagining all sorts of things about *'the toilet together'* bit. Fortunately, Ryan was more discrete.

'Could you describe him; this other man?'

John Kaye pouted. 'Tall. I'd say, around your height, Mr Jarrod. Well-built. Not in a bodybuilder way, just well-put together. Again, rather like yourself,' Kaye said with a twinkle in his eye. 'He had dark hair, as I recall, but the lighting isn't great in here.'

'Clothes?' Todd asked.

'Oh yes, he had clothes on,' the proprietor smiled.

Todd sighed. 'Can you describe what he was wearing?'

John Kaye pondered the question before replying. 'Not really. He had dark clothing on, either navy or black, but that's all I remember. Sorry.'

'No, no,' Ryan reassured, 'This is all very helpful. I wonder, do you think you could help a sketch artist pull together a photo fit for us?'

The man bristled. Took off his glasses and wiped them on his T-shirt. 'Oh. Well... I don't know. I could try.'

'It would help us a lot, I think.'

'Okay. I'll give it a go.'

'Great. Someone will be in touch. Thank you, Mr Kaye. That's been really useful,' Ryan said.

'Or, if it's easier,' John Kaye suggested, 'You could always just look at our CCTV.'

**

Kaye led them to a pokey back room besieged by an army of stainless-steel beer kegs.

He loaded a VCR - *'Bloody hell, who still has these?,'* Todd remarked - into a grubby recorder plugged into a tiny TV set.

'It's all yours,' Kaye said.

'Okay. Give us a clue, then,' Ryan pleaded.

John rolled his eyes, pressed a few buttons, fast-forwarded through a sequence of blurred black and white images displayed with all the clarity of an original Felix the Cat cartoon, paused the screen, and declared, 'That's him.'

Ryan and Todd bent towards the screen. 'Where?'

Kaye lay a finger on the screen. 'There.'

The man sat shrouded in shadow, almost directly beneath the camera. 'But you can't make out his face,' Ryan complained.

John Kaye tossed back his fringe and held his hands aloft. 'I don't tell my customers where to sit.'

Ryan exhaled through his nose and peered at the image. 'Is he wearing a beanie hat?'

'No, that's his hair, silly boy.'

'Do you have a shot of him entering?'

'Possibly, but you'll have to rewind the footage. I've no idea when he arrived.'

'What about Mr. Coulson?'

'That's easier. I remember when he came in.'

Kaye pressed the remote control again. Time flew by. Customers popped in and out of focus, yet their suspect remained stationary in the corner of the screen.

'There he is,' Kaye exclaimed.

A bedraggled man with a rucksack looked around sheepishly. His white hair glowed like a fuzzy halo on the grainy footage. They watched him pick up a glass and drain it. Coulson made his way to the corner of the screen, almost disappearing from view.

'What's he doing?'

'Playing the bandit. Or, at least, pretending he is.'

'How long did he sit there?'

Kaye shrugged. 'Can't be sure. Not long.'

While they watched, the top of their suspect's head moved closer to the camera before disappearing from shot.

'Where's our bloke gone?' Todd mused.

'To the washroom. It's just along the corridor.'

'No cameras there?' Ryan asked, hopefully.

John Kaye gave a shocked look. 'Of course not! Why would we want to? Besides, it would be a gross invasion of privacy.'

'Aye, that's a point,' Ryan conceded.

Coulson swung around on his stool, slipped from it, and followed the suspect out of view.

'Is this where he gans to the bog?' Todd asked.

'Seems to be.'

Ryan and Todd held their breath, waiting for them to re-emerge. When they did, they were disappointed. Whilst Coulson was easily identified, his companion kept his head down and face away from the camera.

'Bugger and hell,' Ryan cursed as the door closed on their last sighting of victim and suspect.

'Mr Kaye, I presume you've no objection to us taking the surveillance footage with us?'

'Please - be my guest, Detective Sergeant' he said, ejecting the cassette and passing it to Ryan.

'Do you think Ravi will be able to do owt with it?' Todd asked.

'Can't do any harm, that's for sure.'

Ryan turned the cassette over and over in his hands. 'Given what we've seen or, more to the point, haven't seen, I'm sure you'll understand I'd still like you to work with our sketch artist.'

Kaye groaned. 'I suppose. Is tomorrow okay? I've a lot of business to attend to today, not to mention a bar to run.'

Ryan considered for a moment. 'Aye. Tomorrow will be fine. I'll make sure you're expected.'

They shook hands. 'Thanks again for your time,' Ryan held up the cassette, 'And this.'

'My pleasure,' Kaye simpered.

Ryan and Todd slipped through to the bar, passed the female couple, and the student, and the two chaps standing at the bar.

Once they were outside, John Kaye puffed out his cheeks, winked at Charles - the relief bartender - with a tight smile, and spoke to his customers.

'Now, can I get any of you good folk another drink?'

**

Back in the tech room on Forth Street, Ravi Sangar's lips curled in distaste at the object in his right hand.

'You look as if you've been given a dog turd for Christmas,' Todd laughed.

'If I'm honest, I think I'd prefer it to this.' He turned the cassette around. 'I'm a bloody digital forensic specialist, man. This is more suited to a historical archivist.'

'You can't do anything to enhance it?' Ryan asked.

'I'll have a go but I think one of the blokes off Repair Shop would be a better choice.'

Ryan squeezed Ravi's shoulder. 'Just give it your best shot, yeah?'

'Owt you say.' Sangar's voice displayed little enthusiasm for the task.

Outside, in the sunlit room previously known as the bullpen until Sam Maynard demanded the squad ditch the Americanism and refer to it as 'the floorplate', Ryan brought Stephen Danskin up to speed.

'We're getting there,' the DCI said. 'The squad's done well. YOU'VE done well, Jarrod, lad. Would you like the honour of updating the Super?'

'Aye, I will - but she's not going to change her mind about the three-months thing, is she?'

'To be fair, that's not her call. She did her best to keep you out of the clarts. In fact, you could've been up to your neck in it without her backing.'

'I suppose,' Ryan moaned. 'Aye, I'll do it.'

'Good. Once you've done that, get yersel' yem. You still look knackered. I need my top man at the height of his game.'

'Thanks, sir.'

Ryan stretched as he made his way towards the Super's office, then rubbed his face to bring some colour to his cheeks.

'You okay, Ry?'

He turned to see Hannah Graves watching him with concern.

'Just washed out, that's all. I need some kip. The DCI's letting me off early.'

Hannah fumbled in a pocket. Held up a set of keys.

'Why not go to mine? You can rest up there and, when I get back, I'll rustle up some scran for us. Then,' she stroked his cheek, 'Who knows what might happen?'

'*Nah, not today, love. I need to get me heed down,*' Ryan said - and was astonished when the words 'Sounds just perfect,' came from his mouth, instead.

He took the keys to Hannah's Jesmond flat wondering what the hell he'd just done.

NINE

Deep down, he'd known yesterday he'd regret it.

Ryan woke no more refreshed than when he went to bed. Hannah's idea of *'rustling up some scran'* involved a large Hot'n'Spicy from Domino's with a side of pepperoni dough balls.

After a mercifully brief bout of bedroom gymnastics, he'd spent the next two hours with indigestion severe enough to floor a Vietnamese potbelly pig. Worse, Hannah passed the entire night snoring like said hog.

'At least,' Ryan thought, *'I didn't get a four o'clock wake up call.'*

He illuminated his smartwatch and groaned. Three thirty-four: still time for the call to arms.

Next thing he knew, Hannah was hitting him with a pillow. 'Wake up, sleepy head. It's after seven.'

'Sleepy head? I wish,' Ryan muttered as he slid out of bed.

They showered together, towelled each other down, before Ryan dressed in yesterday's clothes while he watched Hannah massage a Holland & Barrett lotion over her - their - bump.

Hannah drove to the station in her Renault, Ryan his Peugeot, and they rode the lift to the third floor in a silence punctuated by the protests of Ryan's stomach.

'Ah well, here's to another day of paperwork,' Hannah sighed as they exited the elevator.

'I'd swap you any day of the week, the way I'm feeling

today.'

She squeezed his buttock. 'What's the matter? Can't keep up with me?' Hannah teased.

'If I'm honest, no; not at the minute I can't.'

'Just think yourself lucky I don't bite,' she winked.

They pushed open the office door and Ryan's eyes immediately settled on the puncture marks in Billy Coulson's neck.

**

John Kaye was another who'd spent a sleepless night.

He unravelled himself from Charles' arms and lay on his back, staring at the ceiling. They were well-used to the late nights that came with running a city centre bar and, over the years, the couple had become accustomed to switching off for sleep.

But not last night.

John knew he had an appointment at Forth Street and the thought disturbed him. In his mind, he'd gone over and over the face he was to construct. He consoled himself with the thought photofits always looked more like a Doctor Who villain than a human being.

John kissed the somnolent Charles on the forehead and slipped from beneath the sheets.

**

Detective Constable Gavin O'Hara didn't have a clue where he was.

Then, the world swam into focus and he recognised his own living room. With an effort, he turned his head away from the arm of the sofa. He rubbed his cheek which bore an imprint of the open weave burlap fabric.

For a moment, he wondered why he was on the sofa and not in bed next to Diana. He swung his legs to the floor and knocked over an empty spirit bottle.

That's when he remembered why.

'Shit. What a mess,' he said out loud, ruffling the knots in his hair. 'What a fucking mess!' The bottle rolled under the TV unit, sent there by O'Hara's vicious kick.

His phone pinged.

'God. Don't let it be Danskin.'

It wasn't.

The notification consisted of four images. He scrolled past the first one, spread finger and thumb apart on the screen to better-see the second before dismissing that, too.

He rubbed his eyes and stared at the third. His finger hovered over the image for a second or two before he closed it.

O'Hara coughed up phlegm and gagged as he swallowed it back down.

The fourth image caught his attention. He enlarged it. Smiled briefly. Before he could think, *'What the hell am I doing?'*, he tapped on it and began a finger dance over his phone's touchpad.

O'Hara snapped shut his phone cover as soon as he sent the message.

In the bathroom, he found a deodorant spray and almost bled dry its contents over his crumpled attire.

He made for the front door.

'I'll be shot with shit if I'm late again,' he said to himself.

O'Hara had done a lot of talking to himself, lately.

The Graveyard Shift

**

Davey Hall manoeuvred the tractor-mounted tree trimmer along Gateshead's Saltwell Road. Despite leaving the council depot at an ungodly hour to avoid disrupting the morning commute, a trail of vehicles soon built up behind him like Formula One cars waiting for the safety car to pit.

Davey was grateful for the ear defenders strapped to his head. Not to mask the thunderous rumble of his wheels, nor to drown out the angry horns of queuing traffic, but to avoid listening to the constant yakking of his companion in the cab.

Health and Safety decreed tree trimming a two-man job and, this morning, Davey was paired with an annoying apprentice: Rogan 'Josh' Cantwell.

Josh was a rarity - an apprentice who was keen to learn the ropes and before they'd even climbed into the cab, Rogan had asked, 'How does this thing work, Davey?'

'Doubt you'd understand, son.'

'Try me.'

Davey sighed. 'Reet. The cutter is three-point link mounted and it's driven by the PTO. The PTO rotates at 540 rpm...'

'What's a PTO?'

'Power Take-off unit. It drives the pump which operates the cutter motor.' He saw Josh's glazed expression. 'See, I telt you it wouldn't make sense.'

With that, Davey pulled the ear protectors over his bobble hat, where they remained in situ throughout the journey as the tractor rumbled onwards.

The Gaudi-like gothic turrets of Saltwell Towers appeared to shimmer in the distance through a film of mist before

Davey turned into a lane which led to a patch of allotments. Before the tractor reached the gardens, it veered through a narrow entrance inaccessible to the general public.

From there, Davey Hall drove Josh down a sloping tarmac path into the oldest part of the cemetery.

**

Ryan made straight for the tech room where, he was sure, Ravi Sangar would have spent the night reviewing the CCTV footage from JayKay's.

He was wrong. The room remained empty and unlit. Ryan opened his mouth to ask Todd if he'd seen Sangar, when the man himself stepped into the open-plan floorplate with a breezy, 'Morning all.'

'Blimey. The Prince of Darkness has actually been to bed.'

'I do, sometimes.'

'Right - let's get cracking on the tape.'

Sangar chuckled. 'No point. I've done all I can with it. It's not much clearer. Come on, I'll show you.'

Ryan followed Ravi into the technology lab where Sangar quickly loaded the tape. He'd pre-set the timer and ran the tape forward to the required juncture. He'd lightened and de-pixelated a triangular funnel of the recording, spreading from the front entrance out to either side of the oak bar top. The rest of the establishment remained dark and fuzzy.

'I can't do owt with the rest of it but we can see the entry point.' Ravi flicked a couple of buttons. 'This is where our PoI enters. See, he keeps his head down all the way from here to here.' Ravi used a digital pen to draw an arrow on the screen like Jamie Carragher analysing a VAR error.

Their suspect, a man around six feet tall dressed in dark

The Graveyard Shift

clothing skirted the edge of the bar, stepping in and out of the highlighted portion of the screen.

'He never once raises his head,' Ryan commented, 'Which means he's familiar with the layout and camera coverage. This isn't the first time he's been here.'

The man disappeared into the blurred portion of screen, where he remained. Only the top of his head was visible.

'Does he never move?'

'Nope. Not until he goes to the loo but, again, there's no coverage of that area.'

'What about ordering a drink?'

Ravi drew another line on the screen. 'This dark shadow here, that's the edge of the bar. He's close enough to order a beer from where he's sitting. Look.'

Sure enough, a hand appeared from behind the bar and set a full glass on the surface of the bar. The suspect's hand placed a note on the counter and took the pint.

Ryan puffed out air. 'And that's it, is it?'

'Aye, 'fraid so. Unless you want to see Coulson's movements.'

'No. Todd and me have already seen it. We watched them with Kaye, so we know the CCTV didn't capture the suspect's face on the way out, either. Bugger,' he swore.

'Couldn't have put it better myself.'

'Hang on - it was a busy night. Surely there wasn't just Kaye behind the bar?'

Ravi shrugged. 'No, but all we see are pairs of hands. The camera doesn't cover behind the bar, either.'

'The system's about as much use as Teflon Sellotape. Good

job Kaye's coming in to do a photofit.'

'Well,' Ravi considered, 'Why don't you ask him who else was working? They might have a better description for us.'

Ryan lowered his head and massaged his forehead. 'The bloody obvious questions are the ones you never think to ask.'

'Is that another of Danskin's sayings?'

'No. It's the first of Jarrod's sayings,' Ryan replied.

**

Davey Hall explained how to calibrate the cutting arm and inched the tractor along the treeline at the rear of Saltwell Cemetery.

Davey used one of the hydraulic levers to manoeuvre the cutting arm and a second to alter the blade angle. 'Ready or not, here I come,' he said through the cab window.

The flail heads moved at such speed they appeared not to move at all.

Young Josh pulled his ear defenders down for the first time. The high-pitched buzz rattled his teeth before the sound of splintering wood drowned out even that.

Twigs and leaves and debris peppered the tractor cab windows like a hailstorm.

'Where does all the shit go?' Josh yelled.

'What did you say?' Davey shouted back.

'I said, *'Where does all the crap go?'* You know, the cuttings and stuff?'

'Ah, well. That's why we've got to get the calibration right. If we do, it all drops into the masher. Get it wrong and we're shafted. We'll have to pick it all up by hand.'

Davey switched off the engine and moved the levers to the off position. 'Your turn,' he said, standing on the tractor wheel and jumping to the ground. 'Shift ower.'

His apprentice shuffled across to the driver seat. In the mirror, a row of neatly shorn trees stood at odds with the long grass.

'Don't know why we need bother,' Josh commented. 'Neebody's been arsed to cut the grass.'

'Different department,' explained Davey. 'Besides, look at the graves, man. They're so owld you can't even see the inscriptions. Nobody's visited here for donkey's years.'

'So why do we do it?'

'Cos of that lot.' He waved an arm in the direction of a row of houses now visible through the trimmed-back trees. 'That's Whitworth Close. People who live there have a right to light. Let the trees grow ower high and the cooncil could get sued. None of the buggers are arsed about a bit of lang grass, though.'

Josh nodded. It made sense.

He turned on the ignition, pulled at the flail head lever, and drove too fast for Davey's comfort.

'Whoa. Had on, man. Slow doon.'

'Sorry.'

Josh slowed the tractor and dragged the cutting blade along the line of ragged trees. He glanced in the mirror.

'Aw shit.'

'What's up now?'

'I didn't think you'd cancelled the calibration. We've got half a forest to pick up.'

Davey swung a look behind him. 'What a bell-end. You've barely gone thirty yards and there's tons of the stuff to pick up. Bollocks, man - I was hoping we'd be in The Ninepins for brunch. Nee chance of that now.'

They climbed out the cab.

'You start that end, I'll start this,' Davey Hall ordered.

They scooped up armfuls of leaves and twigs scattered far and wide, some covering the headstones and graves.

Josh picked up a couple of thick branches and tossed them into the masher. Davey whistled while he worked. 'There's a brush in the cab. Once we've picked up the big stuff, we'll sweep the rest of the crap into the trees or long grass. It'll be fine.' He sniffed the air. 'I smell bacon after all,' he laughed.

'Ow, this is bloody hard work, this,' Josh complained. 'Me arms are scratched to ribbons and me feet are soaked.'

'Tough titties, young 'un. That'll larn you.' Davey grunted as he pulled at a branch buried deep in the detritus and hoisted it into the masher.

'Can we not just start brushing it now?' Josh asked.

'Let's get rid of these big 'uns first,' Davey said, heaving at another branch protruding from behind a headstone shaped like angel wings.

'Owt you say. You're the boss.'

Davey grunted again. 'Bloody hell, this one's wedged in aal reet.'

Josh Cantwell swept brambles from his clothes. 'I'll get the brush out ready,' he promised.

Josh mounted the cab and jumped back out, broom in hand.

'Did you hear me? I've got the brush. Should I mek a start? Davey - should I make a start?'

'Rogan.' The voice was quiet, almost whispered.

'*Rogan?* Bloody hell. I divvent think you've ever called me

The Graveyard Shift

that before.'

Davey was staring at an upright branch stood proud above a headstone green with moss.

'Rogan, get ower here. Quick.'

The voice remained hushed.

Josh hurried across, pulling thorns from his trousers. He stopped, eyes wide, mouth open.

'Fuck me,' he whispered.

The workers were staring down at a naked corpse, hands folded across his chest.

The man was pinned to the ground by a five-foot branch driven clean through his body.

TEN

Stephen Danskin rolled a mint imperial around his mouth until it rattled against his teeth as he drip-fed coins into the vending machine. While the Styrofoam cup filled with Americano, he sensed a presence alongside him.

Gavin O'Hara collected an energy drink from the dispenser and pulled at the tab. Like many ex-drinkers, Danskin remained hypersensitive to the smell of alcohol and his nose picked up the stale aroma swaddling his DC.

'I hope you haven't been drinking already, O'Hara,' Danskin said through clenched teeth.

'At this time? I don't think so,' O'Hara answered, but the slight flush in his cheeks gave away his lie.

'I don't believe you.'

'Honestly, sir. I haven't.'

'How many did you have last night, then?'

O'Hara's sigh masked the sound of his phone pinging with a message. He ignored it. 'A few,' he said.

'A few too many,' Danskin asserted. 'You stink like the Tyne Brewery. You'd better not be drunk, still.'

O'Hara slurped down his drink. 'I'm fine.' His phone chimed again.

DCI Danskin looked down towards the man's pocket. 'Trouble with the missus again?' he asked, more sympathetically.

O'Hara shook his head. 'It's not her.'

'Then who?'

'Nah, man. I meant it's not her messaging. I've heard nowt from her since...well, since the other night.'

The Graveyard Shift

Danskin looked around him. A couple of Rick Kinnear's squad queued behind them at a respectful distance.

'We need to talk about this, O'Hara. My office. Now.'

Once inside, Stephen Danskin ordered Gavin to shut the door and gestured for him to take a seat. O'Hara did so with the attitude of a naughty schoolboy.

'Look, I know this must be hard for you. Heaven knows, I've been there,' Danskin's eyes briefly glazed over as he thought of the acrimonious split with Hannah Graves' mother, 'And, from experience, I can tell you drink isn't the answer. It's the highway to hell.'

'Can't be any worse than being sober.'

Danskin breathed in through his mouth before smacking his lips closed as he almost tasted the vinegar-like odour of O'Hara's stale drink. 'Trust me, it's a lot worse.' He popped another mint in his mouth to deflect the memories and offered the packet to Gavin.

O'Hara's phone chirruped again, a wolf-whistle sound. He fumbled in his pocket to silence it.

'Check your phone, for Christ's sake. It might be Diana.'

'It isn't.'

'You haven't even looked at the bloody thing.'

'It's not Di.'

'If you're so sure, switch the damn thing off. It's getting on my tits. In fact, so are you. You need something to focus on…'

The office door flung open.

'Sorry to interrupt, sir,' Ryan said breathlessly, 'But it looks like our killer's struck again. A couple of council groundsmen have stumbled across a body; posed and impaled.'

'Shitting hell,' Danskin swore. He pushed back his chair. 'Howay, O'Hara: you're with us. It looks like we've found something for you to focus on.'

Gavin O'Hara looked as if he'd rather be focusing on the bottom of a brandy bowl.

**

Danskin rolled the unmarked car to a halt outside the main entrance to Saltwell Cemetery. The uniformed officers prepared to move the cordon so he could steer the car along the narrow cemetery road.

Danskin declined the offer. He explained to Ryan and Gavin that he wanted to survey the surroundings as they progressed towards the scene on foot. 'It'll help us make a comparison with the Coulson case,' he explained.

It was with a sense of déjà vu Ryan walked through the cemetery's open gates alongside DCI Danskin. They walked down a slight incline for almost half a mile in palpable silence, Gavin O'Hara trailing behind his senior officers.

'It's a helluva long way to drag a body,' Ryan mused as the slope began to level out with the crime scene still not in sight.

'Depends how they entered,' Danskin observed. 'Might not have come this way.'

'Fair comment, sir,' Ryan conceded. 'How much further?'

Danskin shielded his eyes against a silver-grey sky mottled with dark clouds. 'Up there.'

He pointed to a spot where dappled blue light intermittently lit up a row of trees and hedges.

'Aye, I see it,' Ryan said. 'I thought St Johns was a canny size but this place is huge.'

Danskin began an uphill march towards the hidden patrol cars, passing wooden bench seats planted alongside the footpath at irregular intervals where the aged could rest and ponder how long it would be before they moved in permanently.

Ryan took time out to scrutinise the brass plaques which adorned the seats, looking at the names etched upon them. Satisfied none of them were dedicated to a Romanian Count, he asked over his shoulder, 'You alreet, Gav?'

The Graveyard Shift

'I suppose. My guts are playing up a bit.'

Gavin jumped as a grey squirrel dashed by clutching its forage before it scaled a tree and scuttled along a branch where it disappeared amongst foliage beginning to rust and wither.

As they approached the source of the shimmering blue light of the squad cars, a cold wind blew across the open land. Ryan turned up his collar against it. The clouds thickened, casting ominous flickering shadows across ebony and ivory headstones.

Danskin stopped and crouched down alongside a wastebin. 'Interesting,' he mumbled.

'Have you found something, sir?'

'Whippets, Jarrod. More than half a dozen of them.'

Ryan knew Danskin wasn't talking about dogs. A scattering of small, metallic cylinders lay beneath the raised bin.

'Nitrous oxide,' Ryan affirmed.

'Could be kids messing about with laughing gas but it's worth getting forensics down here.'

'And telling Aaron Elliot, too.'

'Aye. Summat for him to assess.' Danskin made a note of the location and set off once more.

At the crest of the rise, the footpath cut through hedgerows and into a section of the graveyard unlike the other. Here, the headstones were mottled with age, half-hidden by long grass, with epitaphs eroded by weather and moss.

Before them, illuminated by the lights of two patrol cars and a forensic van, a tent had been erected. It stooped over the crime scene like the Grim Reaper's cloak.

Stephen Danskin showed his ID to the officers standing guard. He deliberately paused a moment to talk with them, hoping the delay would give the morose and silent O'Hara time to gather himself.

'Have we started door-to-door yet?' the DCI asked.

'Yes, sir. We're starting to get a few reports coming back already,' the SOCO confirmed.

A thought hit Danskin. 'O'Hara, escort forensics to where the nitrous oxide whippets are. I want them dusted and checked for anything which might give us a lead to their users.'

Gavin breathed a sigh of relief. He had no wish to step inside the tent of horrors.

'You, Jarrod, follow up any promising reports from the door knocks,' Danskin suggested. 'I'll call the station to find out what the team has been up to and update the Super while we wait for Elliot to inspect the body.'

He checked his watch.

'We'll meet back here in half an hour.'

**

A quick scan of the incoming reports from the door-to-door offered one promising lead. A neighbour reported there'd been a party at a house across the back from where she lived.

Ryan checked the address and made his way to a bungalow on Whitworth Close. He heard classical music coming from inside. At first, he assumed it was a radio playing loudly before he realised there was only one instrument.

Ryan rang the doorbell and waited. He rang again. Still the music played. He was about to try again when the music stopped.

A tiny, bird-like woman opened the door. She held a flute in her left hand. 'I'm sorry,' the woman trilled, 'I wanted to finish the sonata. Bach, you know. Johann Sebastian, of course; not Christian – his brother was a terrible fellow.'

The woman studied Ryan. 'Can I help you?' she asked.

Ryan produced his warrant card.

'Oh. Police again. How exciting. Come in, come in.' She used her flute to wave him inside like ground crew marshalling an arriving aircraft.

The Graveyard Shift

Ryan declined the offer of tea and took a mink-coloured armchair next to an overgrown houseplant. 'I'm Detective Sergeant Ryan Jarrod, City and County CID. Could I have your name, please?'

'Mrs Bradshaw. Kate Bradshaw. Was it drugs?'

'Was *what* drugs, Mrs Bradshaw?'

'The party. Yet *another* party. They happen all the time, you know.'

'What makes you think there were drugs involved?'

Mrs Bradshaw gave a high-pitched laugh and rolled her eyes. 'The things that go on over there, you wouldn't believe. Mr Hawkins had nice tenants at one time, but with the cost of housing and all no-one has occupied it for weeks. Ever since then, it's been a free for all. Folk coming and going all the time.'

Ryan held up a hand. 'Sorry, I don't understand. The house isn't occupied, you say. So how come there's so many parties?'

'Because Mr Hawkins lives abroad, somewhere. He doesn't know what goes on, and probably doesn't care. He's got enough money not to care, he has.'

'Mrs Bradshaw, that doesn't explain how the house hosts parties.'

She laughed again. 'You can see it from my bedroom. The back door's unlocked. Folk come and go as they please. The street it's on is just an access road to the cemetery. Mr Hawkins bought the land and built on it. Just the one house. No neighbours as such, apart from the dead and me.'

'Would you mind if I went into your bedroom, to see what you can see?'

Kate Bradshaw giggled. 'It's been a long time since someone asked me that. Yes, of course you can. It's through there,' she pointed her flute at a cream door. 'I'm making a tea. Are you sure you won't join me?'

Ryan relented on the basis it would give him an opportunity to survey the party house.

While Mrs Bradshaw tra-la'd a piece of music and tinkered with teacups, Ryan looked over the house out back from her bedroom window.

It was large, at least four bedrooms, he guessed, with curtains closed and blinds drawn. The garden was small and overgrown, but Ryan could see enough to notice the other garden – the one facing Saltwell Cemetery – was significantly larger. The house door was closed but there was no way of knowing if it was locked or unlocked. He made a note to check it out and report to forensics.

Kate Bradshaw returned with a tray holding two floral China cups and a matching teapot; the flute, for once, missing from the woman's hands.

'Thank you,' Ryan smiled. 'So, you were telling me about the parties.'

Kate Bradshaw grimaced. 'Yes. Awful things. Awful people making an awful noise.'

'What sort of noises?'

'Well, I suppose they think it's music but to me it's all noise. Then there's the shouting and shrieking and who-knows-what else.'

'And you think there's drugs involvement?'

Mrs Bradshaw nodded, then looked down. 'And sex,' she said sheepishly.

Ryan cocked his head to one side, encouraging the woman to continue.

'I went in the garden after one of the parties. Terrible mess all over. And I saw lots of...' she struggled to say the word and settled for, 'French letters.'

Ryan looked at the house again. 'And there was a party recently?'

The Graveyard Shift

'Yes, I told your officers when it was.'

Still looking at the house, Ryan asked, 'You don't think the house was one of ill-repute?' adopting Mrs Bradshaw's antiquated turns of phrase.

'No. Not in that sense.'

He looked at her. 'What other sense is there?'

'Look,' she bristled, 'I've nothing against them, you understand.'

'Nothing against who?'

'You can tell them a mile off.'

'Who, Mrs Bradshaw?'

'*Them*. I'm not prejudiced but, well, you know...'

Ryan gave her a look which told her he didn't know.

She crossed her arms in front of her chest, Mrs Brown-style.

'Homosexuals,' she mouthed.

ELEVEN

Ryan made his way back into the graveyard where O'Hara had joined Danskin outside the forensic tent.

'Good timing, Jarrod. I've just had word that Dr Elliot says we're free to step inside. Did we learn anything from the door-to-door?'

'No direct witness reports but certainly corroborating information of what goes on in the house ower there.' Ryan dipped a head in the direction of party central.

'Okay: you can fill me in later. Let's get this over with.' Danskin moved towards the tent before stopping. He spoke to Gavin. 'Tell you what, you stay with the SOCO and pick out any trends or commonalities from the rest of the door-knocking statements as they come in, then report to me.'

Gavin once more felt his eyes sliding shut with the relief of avoiding whatever lay within the tent.

'You're with me, Jarrod,' Danskin said as he disappeared through the tent-flap.

**

This one stunk to high heaven.

'Bloody hell.' Danskin spluttered and held a sleeve against his nose.

'Hell, indeed,' Aaron Elliot said from his crouched position next to the corpse. 'This one has been here a few days, I'm afraid.'

Ryan took an initial look inside the makeshift tent. At first, the naked corpse didn't seem real. The body appeared snow-white. Translucent, even; like an alabaster statue of a nude David.

Until he stepped closer.

The Graveyard Shift

From alongside the corpse, he could see the flesh was more grey than white. The victim's lips were bluish purple and patches of green decay formed below the man's bloated abdomen.

The smell was overpowering, but it wasn't the stench which did for Ryan. Nor was it the branch spearing the man's chest.

It was the sight of a centipede squirming from the man's nostril and the heaving mass of maggots pulsing within the chest cavity which forced Ryan out of the tent and into the bushes where he vomited thickly.

He came back with profuse apologies and drool hanging from his mouth.

'I'm disappointed in you, Sherlock,' Aaron Elliot said with a half-smile. 'You've seen worse than this.'

'Aye, but it's just the whole set-up, man. It's creepy; like being in my own horror movie.'

Elliot glanced up from the body. 'Try walking in my shoes. This is my whole working life you see before you.'

'That's as maybe, but you enjoy it 'cos you're creepy, yersel'.'

The pathologist laughed. 'That's more like it, old boy.'

The tent flap rustled as Dr Rufus Cavanagh ducked in. 'Sorry I'm late back from my break, Dr Elliot. I've been talking to the detective's colleague – Detective Constable O'Hara, I believe - outside. He tells me there's a possible drugs connection.'

Danskin greeted the newcomer with, 'Bloody hell. Buy one pathologist, get one free today, is it?'

Elliot laughed, even if Cavanagh didn't. 'I thought it'd be useful to have Dr Cavanagh here. I wasn't at the scene of the other killing so I felt it would be a good idea to compare notes with someone who was.'

Danskin gave a thumbs-up. 'More the merrier. I take it there's no doubt it's the same killer?'

Rufus Cavanagh answered. 'Almost certainly. You can see we have two puncture wounds here and here,' he pointed at the victim's throat, 'And the impalement would certainly indicate someone of a similar mind, shall we say.'

'We've kept details of the previous murder as low-key as possible so it's highly unlikely anybody would know about the killer's methods. We're not looking at a copycat,' Danskin concurred.

'There is one difference, though,' Ryan pointed out. 'One wore clothes, this one didn't.'

'I'd say he wore clothes but they've been removed,' Cavanagh corrected.

'Yeah, but we know there were sexual overtones to the previous killing. I'd suggest the fact this bugger is naked points us roughly in the same direction, wouldn't you agree?'

'Let's not assume anything, Jarrod, and leave the doctors to do their job.'

'Thank you,' Cavanagh said. 'There is another thing the victims have in common, however.'

'Yes?' Danskin prompted.

'They were both dead before they were impaled. Hopefully, we'll find out what did kill him when we are back at the lab.'

'We found some nitrous oxide cannisters down the hill. That's the drug connection O'Hara mentioned to Dr. Cavanagh. Will you be able to check if that was the cause, this far after the event?' Danskin asked Elliot.

The pathologist nodded. 'Certainly. N_2O remains in cell tissue for up to a month after death. A few days is nothing.'

'A month? So, if this guy tests positive, does that mean there's still time to test Coulson's tissue for it?'

Elliot offered Danskin a sad smile. 'We already have. It's as I said: there was no sign of any chemical substances in the previous victim's system.'

The Graveyard Shift

'Shit.'

After a brief silence, Ryan asked if there were any hints of the latest victim's identity.

'None. We may extract some clues from medical records once we have a look inside our friend here, and there might be some identification in his clothing but, of course, he hasn't any clothes – and finding them is your department, not mine,' Aaron Elliot pointed out.

Danskin ran a hand over his shaven head. 'I think I'm about done here. I can't think straight for the smell. Howay, Jarrod; let's head off.'

Ryan opened the tent flap - and walked straight into Gavin O'Hara making his entrance.

'Come up with anything?' the DCI asked.

'Nowt substantial yet but it's still early doors. There's another neighbour who's mentioned the party the other night but, other than that, the only other thing that's cropped up is a bloke complaining his neighbour keeps him awake at night playing a flute, and another old codger who thinks a wife a few doors down is a witch.'

Ryan pulled at an earlobe. The mention of witches and the supernatural reminded him of something. He walked up to the headstone and scrutinised it in detail. It was impossible to read the inscription, so weather-beaten was it.

'You onto something, Jarrod?'

Ryan hesitated. 'Nah. Just something Nigel Trebilcock said.' He rubbed his palms together. 'I don't suppose we know whose grave this is, do we?'

'What's that got to do with the price of fish?'

Ryan shrugged. 'Nowt, really.'

Gavin O'Hara knew what Ryan meant. Trebilcock had mentioned his *Thomas Raith* theory to him, too. 'Let's see if I can read it,' Gavin suggested.

He pinched his nose as he closed in on the headstone and the corpse.

'Matthew Neill,' he said in a whisper. 'My God. It's Matthew Neill!'

'The name on the headstone? It means something to you?'

O'Hara continued to stare downwards.

'O'Hara? Gavin: does the tombstone mean something?'

Gavin shook his head. His voice came out flat and distracted. 'Not the grave. The...' he couldn't say the word. Instead, he pointed to the remains. 'That's Matty Neill.'

'Is he known to us?'

The silence seemed to go on forever.

'I don't know about you, sir, but he's known to me.'

'How?'

'I went to school with him. We were best mates.'

**

Whilst Stephen Danskin wrapped things up with Aaron and Rufus, Ryan went in search of O'Hara who had left the forensic tent in a daze.

Danskin told Ryan to tread carefully, that O'Hara had stuff going on, and not to ask too many questions. 'Just be there for him, yeah?' he'd said.

'I will. Gav was my mentor, remember. I owe him one,' Ryan reassured the DCI.

Ryan found Gavin on a park bench, staring into space. Jarrod wandered over, hands thrust deep in his pockets, and sat next to him.

'I haven't seen him in years,' Gavin said without looking Ryan's way. 'Yet, I recognised him straight away. You never forget some people, do you?' O'Hara didn't wait for an answer. He bent forward, head between his knees, and covered his face with his hands. 'God, I can't believe it.'

Ryan remained silent, allowing Gav to get it out his system.

'We hit it off straight away, Matty and me. As soon as we met the first day at George Stephenson High School, we had a bond. All the others were typical Killingworth lads, into football and all that. Me and Matty were quieter. We liked art and reading. I think the other lads thought we were a bit odd in that respect.'

Gavin sat up straight and raised his face to the passing clouds. 'I can't get my head around it,' he whimpered.

'You need to go home, Gav. Danskin will understand.'

'No. I'll be better here. Just give us a few minutes.'

They sat in silence, a cold wind lapping around them. Ryan thought Gavin looked almost as grey as Matty Neill, but he kept his counsel.

'I wish I'd kept in touch with him,' Gavin berated.

'We all lose touch with folk over time,' Ryan replied, thinking of Barry Docherty and other friends he'd drifted away from over the years in the job.

'I guess. He went to art college, you know. London. Down Greenwich way, somewhere.'

'Is that how you lost touch?'

Gavin shook his head, vigorously. 'No. That was all my fault. We saw each other a couple of times after that, but he'd changed. Perhaps we both had. Matty had got into fashion. Not wearing it: designing it, yeah? He mixed in arty-farty circles and soon fell into their arty-farty ways.'

'What ways?'

'Gay ways. Looking back, I think I probably always knew he was but it never became an issue. We were mates, and you never really think about your mates as anything but mates, do you?'

Ryan saw Danskin emerge from the forensics tent and look around. He spotted them and began walking towards them.

'So,' Ryan said, 'Why and when DID you start thinking of Matty differently?'

O'Hara swallowed down a bitter laugh. 'I started seeing Diana, that's why. She didn't want me mixing with others, especially someone like Matty. She didn't approve of his lifestyle.'

'And you went along with her?'

Gavin nodded.

'Doesn't sound like the Gavin O'Hara I know.'

Gavin used the back of his hand to wipe away a tear. 'No-one really knows Gavin O'Hara, Ry. No-one. Not even Gavin O'Hara.'

'Are you ready to go, Jarrod?' Danskin asked.

'Give us a minute, sir.' Ryan put an arm around O'Hara's shoulder. 'Don't overthink things, mate. Are you sure you're okay?'

'I'm sure.'

Gavin quickly stood and just as quickly swayed. He sat back down.

'Right,' Danskin said, 'I've seen enough. I'll head back to the station and update the Super and the rest of the team. Jarrod, you make sure O'Hara here gets back home safe and sound. Get one of the uniform lads to drop you off.'

'But, sir...'

'No buts, O'Hara. It's an order. Get home. Get some rest. If you're up to it tomorrow, you can come in then. But not before, okay?'

'Sir,' Gavin relented.

'I'll see you back at the station when you've got him settled in,' Danskin told Ryan. 'We've work to do.'

TWELVE

Outside Gavin's terraced house on Burradon's Station Road, Ryan ordered the driver of the patrol car to wait for him as if he were a cabbie with the meter running.

He took Gavin's keys from him and opened the front door. If the house had been unprepossessing from the outside, sandwiched as it was between a convenience store and the junction leading to Camperdown industrial estate, the interior was even less salubrious.

'Bloody hell, have you been ransacked?' Ryan said, only half-jokingly.

'No. At least, if I have had burglars, they've tidied the place up a bit. I thought it was more of a mess than this.'

A litany of takeaway cartons, beer cans, and crumpled tissues covered the carpet. A pile of unwashed clothing lay against one wall. The TV had been left playing.

The air reeked of body odour, curry, alcohol fumes, and sour milk.

'You're not okay, are you?' Ryan asked with concern. 'By the looks of it, you haven't been for a while.'

Gavin's chin began to quiver. Only the wolf-whistle of his phone prevented his entire face from crumpling in on itself. He checked the screen and quickly put it back in his pocket.

'You know you can talk to me, don't you?' Ryan said. *'Christ, I'm a bloody Agony Aunt now,'* he thought.

'I can't talk to anyone, that's the trouble. I've always kept myself to myself, and that's the way I'll always be.'

Ryan considered his next words carefully. 'But you've told the DCI.'

'He told you? You know about it?'

Ryan shook his head. 'No. Danskin wouldn't do that. All he said was, you weren't yourself.' Ryan looked around the room. 'And I think he's right.'

The phone pinged once more, masked by Gavin's sharp intake of breath. 'Sit doon,' O'Hara said.

Ryan moved a snot-stained cushion and sat.

'You know I was married, yeah?'

'I thought you were separated.'

'Oh, I am. At least twice.'

Ryan's brow wrinkled in puzzlement.

'Diana and me separated years ago. She went back to live in Yorkshire but she came back a while ago.'

'That's great.' Ryan saw his old mentor's face. 'Isn't it?'

Gavin shook his head. 'Worse thing that could have happened. Got me hopes up and it's all gone tits up again.' The phone wolf-whistled again. 'Bloody thing!' Gavin swore.

'I'm sorry to hear that. But you've obviously still got plenty of mates who care about you.' Ryan nodded towards the phone lying on the sofa where O'Hara had discarded it. Just then, the screen lit up and the phone pinged once more.

Gavin laughed loudly. 'Friends? I don't think so.'

'Hadaway, man – your phone's never stopped.'

Gavin adopted the head-between-the-knees pose again. 'You really want to know?'

Jarrod stayed silent. If O'Hara wanted to offload, he would. He didn't need Ryan's consent.

'Okay, I'll tell you. It's not friends. It's a dating app. I'm such a loser I've joined a dating agency for a bit of company. There, are you satisfied?'

Ryan didn't know what to say.

'Me and Di – we had a lovely bungalow up the road on Cheviot Grange once upon a time. We drove passed it on the way in. Now, thanks to her, I'm living in this shithole.' He

The Graveyard Shift

sniffed. 'And I'm reduced to tashing around chasing strangers.'

'There's nowt wrong with that, Gav. Just…just tidy the place up a bit. Make it more like a home. You'll feel better, I'm sure.'

'That's fine for you to say, with a gorgeous girlfriend and a kid on the way.'

Ryan lay a hand on Gavin's knee. 'There's more to life than that, man. Besides, I never had you down as a lady's man. I remember when you were on a stakeout at the Masonic Lodge in Whitley. You and what's-her-name from Kinnear's team. Todd took the piss out of you summat rotten because he thought you were embarrassed to be with her.'

Gavin laughed at the memory. 'Aye, but that was before Di came back. And went again. I guess it made me realise what I've been missing.' He looked around. 'Actually, though; you're right. I do need to clear this place up.'

A phone chimed. Ryan's, this time.

'I need to go. The Super wants a word with me and Danskin. You sure you'll be alright?'

Gavin thought for a moment. 'Aye, I reckon I will. Do us a favour before you go, though. Pour some of the booze down the sink, please.'

Ryan smiled. 'That's ma boy.'

'Oh. You don't have a packet of mint imperials on you an' all, by any chance?'

This time, they both laughed.

Ryan left Gavin O'Hara's terraced house and sucked in cold, fresh air with the relief of a man set free from prison.

**

The moment Ryan stepped back on the floorplate, he felt at home. Not just for the welcoming dimpled smile Hannah gave him from her desk next to Rick Kinnear, equally for the sense of normality the office gave him.

No overwrought colleagues to support, no cold autumnal winds, no morose pathologists, and no rotting corpses with stakes driven through them. Just the everyday busy-ness of detectives doing their utmost to track down a killer.

Ryan returned Hannah's smile and received a mouthed '*In the office*' and a finger pointing towards Sam Maynard's room in response.

He knocked, waited for the invitation to enter, and took a seat next to Danskin across from Maynard.

The Super's welcome of, 'Thanks for joining us, Acting Detective Inspector,' was as uplifting as it was surprising. 'How's DC O'Hara bearing up?'

Ryan told as much – and as little – as he thought Gavin would want.

'Will he be back tomorrow, do you think?' Maynard asked.

'My guess is he will, yes, ma'am.'

'Good. We need all hands on deck for this one from what Stephen tells me.'

'I presume you haven't called me in to share the results of the post-mortem, have you? It won't be done already, surely?'

'Of course not. They'll barely have got the bugger back to the lab yet. Mind, Elliot did promise us he'd give it priority.'

'That's good, sir, assuming it'll reveal something, of course.'

Danskin gestured for Sam Maynard to continue. 'I understand you commissioned a sketch artist to work with the owner of JayKay's, yes?'

'Oh aye. When he gets here, I want to ask him a few questions. He said he was working alone the night of Coulson's killing but the CCTV shows he wasn't. I want to know why he was lying to us.'

'I'm afraid you missed him. Mr Kaye has long since been-and-gone.'

'Bollocks. I'll head off and have a word with him now.'

The Graveyard Shift

'Not yet, Ryan,' Maynard continued. 'The portrait he's come up with is quite revealing in its detail. I think it'll be very helpful in identifying our suspect.'

Ryan beamed. 'Great. We need a break on this one. When will we get sight of it?'

'That's why I asked you to wait here a moment. We already have it.' Sam Maynard typed on her keyboard before swivelling the monitor so Ryan could see the screen. 'I wanted you to see it before we print a copy for the crime board.'

Ryan sat back in his chair. 'You're kidding me.'

Danskin and Maynard looked at one another. 'No. Are we missing something here?'

'Has Todd seen this yet?'

'No. Why?'

'Excuse me, ma'am,' Ryan said, scooting his chair backwards. He opened the office door. 'Todd! Get in here, please.'

Todd Robson ducked under the door. 'You rang?' he said, imitating Lurch's bass voice.

'John Kaye's been in. He's come up with a picture of our suspect.'

'Let's see, man,' Todd said.

Ryan pointed at the screen.

Todd's reaction mimicked Ryan's. 'You're pulling me nob, right?'

'That's what I said, more-or-less.'

'Why the hell would he do that?' Todd exclaimed.

Sam Maynard sighed. 'Gentlemen, will someone kindly tell me what's going on?'

Ryan allowed Todd the honour.

'Well, if the guy in the sketch had a haircut and you hooked a pair of specs roond his lugs, John Kaye has just given us a portrait of himself.'

**

It had been another long day and Ryan was running on fumes as he and Todd Robson approached the entrance to JayKay's.

They could tell the bar was already busy by the noise coming from inside as they neared. Despite the late rush-hour traffic, the sounds were clearly audible from the street.

Todd pushed open the door and stepped inside. When busy, it appeared an entirely different establishment to the one he'd visited previously. No-one looked twice as he and Ryan made their way to the bar. Most of the occupants were same-sex couples, meaning another pair didn't look out of place.

'I can't see Kaye, can you?' Todd asked.

'Nah. He must be out the back.'

'Or not working today. Not everybody works every hour God sends, I suppose.'

'Don't they? Lucky beggars,' Ryan remarked.

They hung around as if waiting to be served until a man with surfer's blond hair approached.

'What's your tipple?' he asked.

'Actually, we're not here for a drink.' Ryan surreptitiously produced his warrant card. 'I'm looking for John Kaye.'

'Can I ask why?'

'You can ask, aye,' Todd said without answering the man's question. 'Who are you?'

'Charles. Charles Proudlock. I'm John's partner.'

'Business, or...' Todd's question was halted by Ryan's dig in the ribs.

'Is Mr Kaye in?' Ryan asked.

'I'll get him.' Charles disappeared.

Ryan leant towards Todd. 'He was on duty the night Billy Coulson was killed.'

'How the hell do you know that?'

'I recognised his hands.'

'...the fuck?'

The Graveyard Shift

'Aye. Well, not so much the hands, more the rings. Didn't you notice Proudlock had a load of gold bullion on his hands? One of the blokes behind the bar the night Kaye said he was working alone wore them. I remember from the video.'

'Jeez, get a life, man, Ryan,' Todd wheezed.

'This way, gents,' Charles said before Ryan could respond to Robson.

In the office, Ryan noticed John Kaye's jaw was clenched tight. The man was worried.

'What can I do for you?' Kaye said with a failed attempt at a smile.

'The night of the murder, you didn't mention anyone else was working behind the bar with you. Why was that?'

Kaye stiffened. 'Is it important?'

'Aye, it could be,' Todd retorted. 'They might have been able to tell us more aboot what happened that night.'

'What else could they see that wasn't on the CCTV? I mean, you have looked at it, haven't you?'

Ryan clicked his tongue against the roof of his mouth. 'Of course. How else would we know that Mr Proudlock was working that night?'

'He was?'

'Yes, he was. You might think your video didn't show him, but it does show his hands. Very expensive jewellery he wears.'

'And distinctive,' Todd added.

'Alright. Yes, Charles was working. I didn't want him involved. He worries, you know.'

'Someone else was working that night, an'all.'

John Kaye's eyes flitted from Ryan to Todd and back again. 'You're very observant,' he remarked. 'Yes, there was a third person. It was Sherry.'

'Sherry who?'

'Sherry Proudlock. Charles's daughter.'

Todd's mouth opened. 'I thought he was gay.'

John Kaye shook his head and smiled sadly at Todd's ignorance. 'Gay, bi, hetero - we're all the same, you know. Yes, Sherry is Charles's daughter. She helps us out now-and-again. But it's cash in hand. She doesn't get taxed and we don't get lumbered with National Insurance. That's why I didn't mention her.'

Todd looked at Ryan. The glance they exchanged recognised there was more than a grain of truth in what Kaye had said.

'Is that all?' John said, standing as if to signal the conversation was at an end.

'Not quite.' Ryan produced the sketch from an inside pocket. 'Why did you tell our artist to draw a picture of you?'

John Kaye tilted his head for a better look.

'That's not me. That's the guy in the corner. The one who left with that poor man.'

Todd took a step towards John Kaye, who cowered away. 'That's you,' he said, pointing to the John Kaye in the sketch.

'It's not. It's nothing like me. Look at the hair. It's different.'

'Aye, and you've got specs on,' Todd reached out a hand and removed the man's glasses from his face. 'Now, look in the mirror and tell me that's not you.'

'I can't,' Kaye said.

'And why not? Is it because it *IS* you?'

John Kaye smirked at Todd.

'No, I can't look in the mirror and say it's me because I can't see a bloody thing without my glasses on.'

THIRTEEN

On the way back to Forth Street, Ryan and Todd agreed Kaye's behaviour was odd, the fact he'd described himself to the sketch artist, weird; and the whole JayKay set up strange.

However, Kaye had told them nothing which warranted further investigation. For now, at least, they agreed he'd remain on their radar as a Person of Interest but nothing more.

Todd offered to brief Danskin - and Ryan wasn't inclined to turn him down. He needed sleep and needed it badly. He drove straight home without calling into *di Biasio* chippy at the top of Lobley Hill despite his hunger.

Once inside his house on The Drive, famished but, more than anything, tired as an old shoe, Ryan dragged himself upstairs. He hauled a change of clothes out a wardrobe, thought *'Bugger it,'* and lay flat out on his bed instead.

He woke with a start, still fully clothed but chilled to the bone.

Something had woken him.

There it was again. A creak. Someone climbing the stairs? Ryan held his breath, straining to hear.

A final squeak, followed by a thud of what sounded like wood on wood.

Ryan trailed an arm over the edge of the bed. Reached for the golf club he kept beneath it. As his fingers brushed against the club, a half-light angled across the bedroom.

Something had triggered the external security light.

Ryan turned his head towards the window. Through the curtains, he watched a silhouette skim by so swiftly he didn't comprehend what it was.

The image returned. Magnified by the exterior light, a leathery-winged creature beat against the window before disappearing.

The light flicked off.

Ryan felt himself swallowed by the night.

He breathed out. Turned his head away from the window.

Even in the darkness, he sensed a shadow fall over him.

The security light flickered to life again.

A grinning John Kaye leered over him, naked and proud. He clutched a sharpened wooden stake in his hand.

Kaye's mouth opened in a smile, revealing dagger-sharp incisors.

Ryan screamed.

He sat bolt upright, bathed in a cold sweat.

He flicked on the bedside lamp.

Ryan was alone and, this time, REALLY awake – not as he'd imagined in his nightmare.

'Fuck,' he whispered, fighting to bring his pulse rate under control.

**

'Alreet, son?' Norman Jarrod greeted his eldest son.

Ryan didn't answer. Instead, he indulged in some rough and tumble with an excitable Kenzie.

'I've just popped some toast in. Do you fancy a couple of slices?'

Ryan thought of the long day ahead. 'Gan on, then. You've twisted my arm.'

Burnt bread leapt from the toaster like meerkat lookouts. 'Do you want first dabs?'

Ryan looked at the sacrificial offering. 'You have those ones, ta all the same. I'll do my own,' he insisted.

He returned from the kitchen a few minutes later to find Norman Jarrod brushing crumbs off his sweater with one hand and scratching his crotch with the other.

'So, Norman said, 'What are you after?'

'Nowt. Just thought I'd call in while I had the chance. Pretty much tied up on a case at the moment.'

'The cemetery thing?'

Ryan had forgotten he'd mentioned it to Norman after the first killing. 'Aye. It's a new hobby of mine. I call it grave spotting.'

'Good name for a movie. They should cast Ewen McGregor and Robert Carlyle.'

'I think summat like that's already been done,' Ryan said, wiping crumbs from his bottom lip.

'Likely to run for a while, this case?'

Ryan shivered. 'Hope not. It's creeping me out a bit.'

'I'm sure you'll get to the bottom of it soon enough.'

Norman flicked on the TV. Images of air strikes on Gaza on one channel, drone attacks in Ukraine on another. 'What happened to stories about dogs on surfboards?' he mused.

'That's life, Dad.'

Ryan was too young to understand why his father almost choked on his last mouthful of toast.

Norman silenced the TV and set down his plate for Kenzie to lick. 'You haven't seen your gran for a while, kidda.'

'Have you seen your mother lately?'

'Fair comment. We should make the effort, you know. While she still knows who we are.'

Ryan felt a pang of guilt. 'I know, Dad.' He stared out the window. 'Do you think she'll still be here?'

'Come again?'

'Gran. Will she still be with us when Hannah gives birth?'

Norman snorted. 'Course she will. She's strong as an ox, physically. It's just her head that's mixed up.'

Ryan recalled his dream. 'Aren't all of us a bit like that, now and again?'

Norman didn't reply.

To fill the silence, Ryan picked up a ragged rope toy and teased Kenzie with it. The dog leapt and snapped his jaws at fresh air. Ryan laughed. He tried again. This time, Kenzie caught a frayed knot, growled, and shook his head fiercely.

Ryan lost his grip on the rope and gave the German Shepherd a playful rub on his hind quarters. The dog's tail wagged feverishly and the other end set down the rope.

Ryan went to grab it just as Kenzie realised his mistake. The dog made a lunge for the rope but nipped the back of Jarrod's hand instead.

'Owww!' Ryan shouted.

Kenzie darted for refuge behind the sofa, tail between his legs.

Ryan brought his hand to his mouth and sucked it.

When he brought his hand away, he saw two puncture wounds, a sliver of blood trailing from each.

Two wounds.

Two trails of blood.

Two.

'I've got to go, Dad.'

**

Ryan marched onto the floorplate.

Gavin O'Hara stood in front of the crime board, staring at the photograph of his old friend. His murdered old friend.

Todd Robson edged past him, a wad of post-it notes in his hand. He began attaching them to the board. Names. Relationships. Dates. Times: the usual paraphernalia which the team hoped might stimulate a spark of inspiration.

Nigel Trebilcock stood slightly back from the board. His eyes moved from one corpse to the other. He sucked on his lip.

'Penny for them,' Ryan said from alongside him.

'You don't want to knows so I ain't telling you,' he said, his voice soft and lilting.

'Tell me about Cornish folklore.'

The Graveyard Shift

Trebilcock stared at him. 'And you won't be taking the piss?'

'No,' Ryan said, firmly.

'Alright,' Trebilcock nodded. 'Where you want me to start?'

Ryan checked no-one could eavesdrop.

'How about you tell me about vampires?'

**

'Ever goos, we calls 'em.'

They'd moved to the breakout area next to the conference suite.

'It don't mean anything. It's just our name for them, so it is.'

'Do you believe they exist? Vampires, I mean.' Ryan felt embarrassed asking the question.

'In the undead sense, no. Not in a frightened-of-garlic, cloak wearing sense, neither. But do I think there are people who act out a fantasy? Yes, I do.'

Ryan set down the sausage roll he'd been about to bite into. 'Why?'

Nigel Trebilcock stared into space for a moment. 'It were 2017. December, I think. I was a fresh-faced recruit, still in uniform. We get a call from a man. Henry Pascoe, his name. He were frantic. Screaming down the telephone. He said he'd been to a boozer and fallen asleep on his way home. He woke up in the morning and said the sun was burning him alive.'

'In December?'

'That's what I said, when I heard. Turns out he changed his story mid-call. He claimed it wasn't the sun; it was just the fact it was daylight. This Henry Pascoe, he said he was a vampire in need of rescue. Course, me being the new recruit, I gets sent out to find him.'

Ryan chuckled. 'Bloody hell, must be a quiet paper round being a copper doon those parts. Nobody would get sent out for that up here.'

'That's as maybe, but despatched I were.'

Ryan felt the strength to take a mouthful of Greggs. Looked at the pinkish meat inside and pushed it to one side. 'What happened?'

Nigel gazed over Ryan's head as he recalled the incident.

'I found him, alright. And I got the shock of my life, so I swear. Henry Pascoe hid in the shade of a park bandstand. His skin was red raw. Blistered. I was gorown, I was. Frightened, in your terms. Scared shitless.'

Ryan got the message. 'This Henry Pascoe bloke – he was a real vampire?'

Trebilcock half-smiled. 'I thought he was an ever goo at the time, but it turned out he'd just got back from a South African safari. He'd run out of sunscreen and got burnt to a crisp tracking rhino on his last day.'

Ryan laughed out loud. Trebilcock didn't join in.

'I took him home, so I did. Thought the sun had larded him. Or the drink, maybe. Anyways, when we got back, he offered me a drink. I were expecting the usual tea or coffee but no, that's not what he had in mind.'

Ryan had a horrible feeling he knew what was coming but encouraged Trebilcock to continue.

'He had one of those big fridges, like the ones you see on American TV shows. He opens the door, and there's rows and rows of little bottles.'

Trebilcock saw Ryan's face. 'I sees you ahead of me. Yes, they were filled with blood. Just like I'd drink cider, he drank blood.'

'Did you arrest him?'

'No. I couldn't. He showed me paperwork. The specimens were supplied voluntarily by like-minded weirdos.'

Ryan whistled. 'Bloody hell, man.'

Trebilcock smiled. 'Not sure about the hell bit, but bloody? Certainly.'

Ryan's sausage roll made its way into the bin.

The Graveyard Shift

'We's should be getting back,' Trebilcock urged.

'In a bit. What else do you know about vampires? I mean, if – and it's a big if, mind – I think we should mention it to the DCI, I need a bit more than this. He'll have us sectioned if I gan to him now.'

Trebilcock furrowed his brow. 'I'm not sayings this is an ever goo, you know. I just don't think we should ignore the possibility, that's all I'm saying.'

Ryan twisted his hair. 'Do you know anything more about them, these vampires or ever goos?'

Trebilcock shook his head. 'Not really. Straight after the Pascoe business, I did do a bit of research into it. All I remember - all I remember that's *relevant* - is there are three types of real vampires: sanguinarian, psychic, and hybrids.'

The words went over Ryan's head. 'It's relevant, how?'

Trebilcock held Ryan's gaze. 'The puncture wounds on Coulson's and Neill's throat: they were small. The photos show minimal blood leakage.'

Ryan looked at his hand where Kenzie had caught him. Two teeth marks. There'd been two trails of blood. 'I get that, but our victims only bled from one wound. Look,' he showed Nigel the back of his hand. 'Me dog caught us here. I bled from both.'

'Ryan, that's my point. Sanguinarians feed on very small amounts of human blood: a few drops is enough to satisfy them. They'd only need the blood from one wound to meet their needs.'

Nigel stood to signal the end of the conversation, but not before adding one final statement.

'I think our killer mays be a sanguine ever goo.'

FOURTEEN

John Kaye dashed into the bar area of the business bearing his name. Here, there was a chance someone may look through the window and witness the attack he knew was heading his way.

'How *dare* you!' Charles Proudlock's face was purple with rage, a stark contrast to his golden blond locks, as he chased after Kaye.

'I thought it was for the best. I thought it would keep them away from us,' John explained. He dodged behind a table; he and Proudlock circled it like judo players waiting to attack.

'You had no reason to bring my Sherry into it,' Charles countered. 'None at all, for Christ's sake!'

Kaye's foot caught on a chair and he stumbled slightly, spectacles slipping down his nose. He went to push them up again only to poke himself in the eye as Proudlock grabbed his arm.

Through watery eyes, John pleaded, 'I'm sorry, okay? They knew three of us were working. What else could I say?'

Charles hauled John towards him. 'You could have said anything. Anything at all. Sherry needs the money to pay off her debts. What happens if they report her?' The veins on Proudlock's neck stood out like exposed tree roots.

'And what about us, Charles? What about this place? If it got out she was a druggie and worked here, our reputation is down the pan. JayKay's might be shut down.'

With one hand, Proudlock hoisted John onto the table. Pushed him so he lay flat on his back.

'Do NOT call MY daughter a druggie!'

The Graveyard Shift

He pinned Kaye to the table with one hand around his neck, clenched his other fist and drew back his arm.

'Not the rings!' Kaye spluttered. 'Please. Not the rings. They'll mark me.'

Proudlock crashed down his fist. It rattled against the tabletop next to Kaye's head.

'Damn you!' he gasped through gritted teeth. 'Go to hell and back.'

He took the hand from John's throat and his partner sat up, gagging.

'Thank you,' Kaye whispered.

Proudlock took deep breaths. Gradually, the flush in his face receded. The knots in his jaw relaxed. The fury in his eyes died.

John Kaye knew the moment had passed, just as it always did. Eventually.

'Thank you, Charles,' he said again. 'I'm sorry.'

Charles offered John his hand and helped him off the table. 'No. I'm sorry,' he said. 'I over-reacted. It's just, after everything Sherry's been through, I don't want her involved in anything else. She's got a habit, but we both know why. Cut her some slack. Please.'

John smoothed himself down and ran his hand through Charles's long hair. 'I know, Charles. I shouldn't have called her that.'

'Okay. And I promise I won't lose my temper again, ever,' Proudlock said.

That's what he constantly said.

Until the next time.

**

The harsh white light came alive, illuminating the shroud and the outline of the cadaver beneath it.

Aaron Elliot tucked his straggly hair, once dark but now streaked with premature greyness, beneath his surgical cap. Rufus Cavanagh rinsed his hands and reached behind his head to wrap a band around his mousey hair.

'You should have done that before you washed your hands, Rufus.' Elliot wagged a gloved finger at him. 'Schoolboy error, my man. You'll need to avoid that when you're practicing without supervision.'

Suitably chastened, Rufus nudged on the tap with his elbow. 'Thank you, Dr Elliot,' he said in his perfunctory manner. 'I will.'

Aaron Elliot moved to the metallic table and pulled the shroud from Matthew Neill's face. 'It's been a pleasure to have you here, Rufus. Takes the pressure off me no end. And you've a good career ahead of you. You're the best intern I've dealt with.'

'I'm not an intern,' Rufus bristled. 'Haven't been for weeks. I'm fully qualified and I'm your *assistant*, please remember. Anyway, I'll soon be having interns of my own.' He removed the tools of the trade from the steriliser and set them up on a row of clean towels.

Aaron leant over the corpse and looked at the man's neck. 'Nantwich, I believe you told me you're off to. Nice neck of the woods.' He smiled at the ironic timing of his words.

'So I've been told. Three weeks and I'll be up and running.'

'Just don't forget to don your garb before washing your hands, old fruit.'

'Do you think we should ask the Detective Chief Inspector if he wants one of his officers to attend? Jarrod or O'Hara, perhaps?'

Elliot picked up a scalpel and saw it glint like a diamond ring in a jeweller's window. 'I think he'll want this done as soon as possible.'

'Yes, but last time...'

The Graveyard Shift

'Last time, we didn't know what we were looking for. With this chap, we know we're looking for nitrous oxide and, thanks to your astute observation, a possible cause of death.' He looked at Rufus and his eyes smiled behind the mask. 'I do think your prognosis could be correct, doctor. Proving it may be somewhat more difficult.'

Elliot returned to the table and folded the sheet down to the man's waist. He lay the blade against Neill's thorax.

'Anyway, we're about to find out.'

Aaron Elliot pressed down hard. The scalpel sliced into Matty Neill's remains, exposing layers of yellowish-grey fat.

**

Stephen Danskin had started the briefing by the time Ryan and Trebilcock returned to the floorplate.

'Good timing, Jarrod. You haven't missed anything. I was explaining to the guys we'd run through the similarities on the two killings to assure ourselves we are looking at the same perpetrator.'

Danskin used a ruler to point to the crime scene photographs.

'Both victims were white males in their thirties. They were, or appear to have been, homosexuals. William Coulson had indulged in anal intercourse shortly before his murder and we have footage of him in a known gay bar, whilst Matthew Neill is believed to have attended a same-sex party at a house known for hosting gay and lesbian gatherings. In addition, DC O'Hara has confirmed Neill was gay.'

Danskin paused for a moment to gather his thoughts, and to ensure Gavin appeared well enough to sit through the discussion.

'Both bodies were found in graveyards, both men had puncture wounds, possibly though not definitely caused by hypodermic needles, yet neither man was drugged. At least,

Coulson wasn't. We await the results of tox tests on Neill. We also know the victims were speared by implements, and this happened post-mortem.'

Out the corner of his eye, Danskin noticed Superintendent Maynard hovering in the background. 'Are we all agreed so far?' the DCI asked.

The question was met by a murmur of agreement.

'Looks clear-cut to me,' Todd Robson said.

'On top of all that, neither man had any living relatives or, at least, none that they'd had contact with for yonks.'

Gavin O'Hara's mouth twisted. 'I'm not sure about that, sir. Matty had a brother, a few years older. Keith, he was called.'

Lucy Dexter piped up. 'We checked that out, Gav. His brother was killed in an accident three years back.'

'Ah, Jeez, man,' O'Hara moaned. 'How did that happen?'

Dexter looked at Danskin who gave her a cautious nod.

'Keith Neill was an industrial painter by trade. Seems he was on a job when his ladder slipped.'

'Oh God.'

'Aye. He wouldn't know anything about it, if it's any consolation. He died instantly.'

'Broke his neck?'

Lucy swallowed. 'No. He fell onto metal railings outside the old Ashington railway station. I don't want to be too descriptive but...well, he was run through.'

The team let out a collective groan of despair.

Ryan exchanged glances with Trebilcock. 'Definitely an accident, was it?'

'Aye, Ryan. It was.'

'Sure?'

'Why would it be anything else?'

Ryan said nothing although Maynard noticed he shifted uncomfortably.

'Something on your mind, Ryan?' she asked.

He scratched his jaw. 'No. Let's see where this leads us to.'

The Graveyard Shift

Danskin picked up the mantra. 'Obviously, we await the post-mortem results so until we have a cause of death we can't reach a definitive conclusion. From what we do know, I strongly suspect we will find our killer is homophobic and, quite possibly, has a history of sadistic behaviour.'

Trebilcock considered the DCI's statement carefully, but an almost imperceptible headshake showed Ryan that his colleague dismissed the theory.

'Robson, I want you and Dexter to go through the records and pick out anyone who meets the profile. If you're up to it, O'Hara, you can help Sangar build a search parameter program for them.'

'I'm fine with that, sir,' Gavin confirmed.

'Anything else from anyone?'

Maynard stared at Ryan, who realised it was now or never.

'Sir, I'm a bit worried we're putting all our eggs in one basket.'

Danskin stroked the back of his head. 'I'm not sure we have any other baskets, have we?'

Ryan closed his eyes and took a deep breath.

'We might.'

Ryan felt the room drain of air as everyone looked towards him.

'I'm all ears, Jarrod.'

'Sir, I think I'd prefer to talk privately, in your office.'

'Bollocks, man. Spit it out. We're all one, here. Teamwork makes the dream work, and aal that.'

The vacuum of silence dragged on forever. Ryan fought back a blush before he'd even spoke. He was aware everyone in the room was looking at him, even some of Kinnear's team, including Hannah, had stopped what they were doing to watch.

'Get a grip, man,' he thought to himself. *'If I'm really DI material, I've got to have the courage of my convictions.'*

He opened his mouth to speak, only for Trebilcock to beat him to the punch.

'Have any of us considered the possibility of a vampire?'

Gasps of astonishment and disbelief filled the silence. Lucy Dexter's harsh laugh came out as a cross between a pig's snort and the bray of a donkey.

'What the fuck you been taking, Nigel?' Robson scoffed. 'I'll have some of it if you've any spare.'

'Can we bring this back to reality, folks?' Danskin said over the mockery. 'I know it's nearly Hallowe'en but, howay, man; divvent talk shite.'

Trebilcock didn't laugh, nor Ryan; something Sam Maynard noticed.

'Hold on,' she commanded. 'Let's not throw baby out with the bathwater. Let's at least hear what Ryan and Nigel have to say for themselves. After all, Stephen, you said yourself the circumstances in the case were weird.'

'Ma'am, with respect…'

'Wait. I think WE should show some respect and allow the men time to explain.'

Danskin stared at Ryan. Something in Jarrod's demeanour, the strength behind his eyes, the steely determination set in his rigid face muscles, made even the DCI have second thoughts.

'Okay. Aye, I'll buy you some time. Don't see what we expect to see, I always say.'

He stood aside and gestured for Ryan to step forward.

'Convince us, Jarrod. You've five minutes to make your case.'

FIFTEEN

'Let's get one thing straight,' Ryan began. 'I'm not talking about Christpher Lee, here. No creatures of the night emerging from dusty coffins, no Transylvanian castles or demonic organists hammering out doom-laden tunes. Get all that crap out your heeds before I start.'

He waited until he was sure the audience had taken his words on board before he continued.

'I'm talking about the cult of vampirism. Just like some people gan to the match, dress as Goths or Punks, become Trekkies or, even, attend church, there are some who act out vampiric fantasies. DC Trebilcock has first-hand experience of such things. Nigel, recount what you told me about Henry Pascoe, please.'

The silence on the floorplate was palpable as Trebilcock ran through his encounter with the blood-consuming Pascoe.

'Shut up!' Lucy Dexter scorned. 'He drank blood?'

'That he did, for sure,' Trebilcock asserted. 'They don't all drink blood, though. As Ryan says, it's a fashion or hobbyist thing for most ever goo followers.' He saw their blank faces. 'That's what we call 'em down Cornwall,' he explained, 'Ever goos.'

'Thanks for the background, lads, but can we get onto definite links to our murders?' Danskin urged.

'Aye, I will.' Ryan pointed to the photographs of the corpses. 'Both were found in graveyards which, for obvious reasons, are known to hold an attraction to vampire followers. The bodies were posed almost ritualistically on top of tombs. Again, the connection to vampire behaviour should be clear.'

He scanned the sea of faces. Took in their expressions. He thought he was winning over O'Hara and the Super, although Dexter and Robson found it hard to mask their scepticism. The jury was out on Danskin and Sangar's thoughts. At least Ryan felt he was making some headway.

'Both murders appear to have sexual elements to them. Sex plays an important role in vampire legends.'

'Aye, I've seen those owld films with Ingrid Pitt in. She always flashed her knockers.' Todd remembered Sam Maynard's presence. 'Sorry for interrupting,' he mumbled.

Again, Ryan was buoyed by the fact his colleagues didn't laugh at Todd's remark. Another sign he was making progress.

'Aye, and before you say it, there's not many virgins around these parts, neither,' Ryan added. Unlike Todd's, his riposte did attract laughter.

'Gents, your five minutes are passing quickly. Stick to the point, Ryan,' Maynard reminded him.

'Yes, ma'am. Now, we come to the wounds. Puncture wounds to the throat.'

'Puncture wounds is the key, Jarrod. Not bite marks.'

'Fair comment, sir. Remember, though, we aren't taking about fictitious vampires. We are talking about present day followers of a cult. Now, the wounds could have been caused by a syringe. It's possible – probable, even - our killer may take his victim's blood that way.'

Danskin remained silent this time so Ryan continued.

'Before anyone says it, I do know there were two wounds on each corpse and we only observed blood coming from one. I don't have an explanation for that. Hopefully, Aaron Elliot and Rufus Cavanagh will have an answer soon.'

Todd saw the others nod their heads. He wondered if he was the last sceptic standing. 'Reet. Assume what you say is true,' Todd said, 'What about the stake-through-the-heart bit?

It's the way vampires are killed, isn't it? That, or a silver bullet. It's not the victims who die that way.'

Todd had a point. 'True,' Ryan agreed. 'Perhaps it's just part of the fantasy; I honestly can't answer that.'

Trebilcock could. 'Do you know how the Dracula legend came about?' he asked.

'Whitby and Bram Stoker, isn't it?' Lucy offered.

'That be the recent incarnation, so it be. No, originally, vampires were based on Vlad the Impaler, or Vlad Dracul to give him his full family name.'

'And your point is?' Lucy persisted.

'The clue's in the name, Lucy. The vampire legend is based on Vlad the Impaler: the original vampire who DID impale his victims.'

Trebilcock's voice echoed in the stillness of the floorplate. Ryan noticed a couple of Kinnear's eavesdroppers nod their agreement. Even Todd Robson appeared less sceptical.

'Jarrod, I reckon that's aboot the best five minutes you've ever spent,' Danskin finally said. 'Mind, I still think it's less likely than our other theory but it's an avenue I'm prepared to let you and Trebilcock explore.'

'Thank you, sir.'

'Just for now, mind. You've the rest of today and tomorrow. Then, if you haven't come up with something substantial, you're back with the rest of us doing some proper coppering.'

Danskin clapped his hands.

'Okay everybody, briefing's over. Heads doon, arses up.'

**

Ryan and Nigel stepped out of the Forth Street station and headed off downhill. Jarrod wanted to talk tactics with his colleague out of earshot of the rest of the team. Having at least persuaded them that he wasn't worthy of a visit by men in white coats, Ryan was keen to avoid saying anything in their presence which might change their minds.

The two marched towards the quayside. A squall beat against the narrow passageway of the Long Stairs and Trebilcock fastened the hood of his coat tight over his head.

'You knows what, Ry – we forgot to mention the Thomas Raith connection to the first killing.'

Ryan smiled. 'I didn't forget. I chose to keep it to mesel' for now.'

'Why? Surely the more we tell the team, the better? I think it'd convince 'em, so I do.'

'We've got a day and a half to sort this before we're pulled back onto the mainstream enquiry. If we're running out of time, I'll hoy that little titbit into the mix. It might be enough for the DCI to grant us a bit more time.'

At the foot of the stairs, they stepped onto The Close and faced the brunt of the wind. Beneath the High Level Bridge, the Tyne lay still as death. Away from its shelter, the dark mass of water swirled and pulsed like a living being.

Ryan rubbed his hands together. 'By, it's Baltic doon here. Look, why don't you tell me more about this Raith bloke?'

Trebilcock gave a queer look. 'He isn't a real person, you know. He be a fictional character.'

'Aye, but the bloke in the grave Coulson was ditched on was real enough at one time. There might be some other connection we've missed.'

They were on Sandhill now and Ryan held open the door of The Little Coffee Shop Under the Bridge for Trebilcock to enter.

For a change, Ryan ordered a Bovril, the Cornishman a tea. Once they were seated, Nigel recounted what he knew.

'I'm not an expert, you know, but I have read The Dresden Files.'

'Is it a classic, like Bram Stoker and Shelley and such? I'm assuming it's set in Germany?'

The Graveyard Shift

Nigel took a noisy slurp. 'No. Wrong on all counts. The first book in the series was published around the turn of this century. And Dresden isn't a place; it's the name of the main character – Harry Dresden. He's a necromancer.'

'A what?'

'He's a, I dunno, a sorcerer, I be guessing. One who reanimates the dead.'

Ryan swirled the cup holding his meaty drink. 'Like vampires.'

'And zombies.'

'Howay man, don't go down that route. Vampires are enough for now. We'll deal with the zombie apocalypse later.'

Trebilcock grinned momentarily. 'Anyway, Thomas Raith is Dresden's brother. A vampire.' He stopped short. 'Ryan, maybe we got this wrong.'

Ryan's breath whistled through his teeth. 'I hope to hell we haven't. Me reputation's shot to shit if we have. What makes you say that, anyhow?'

'From what I remember, Raith didn't suck blood.'

'Fan-bloody-tastic. He's not a vampire at all, then.'

'He is, only he preys on human emotions and gets his strength from energies, not blood. Most often, he thrives on sexual energy.'

Ryan took time to consider Trebilcock's synopsis. 'That still sounds like our fella to me, apart from the blood thing. Owt else?

Nigel scratched the back of his neck. 'We're not wrong, Ryan. Not wrong at all.'

'What makes you change your mind?'

'Thomas Raith has the ability to slip in and out of his predatory behaviour.'

Ryan got it. 'Which means he can hide in plain sight. Blend into the background like any other bloke.'

'Do you think that's what our culprit does?'

'I'd bet my life on it, Nige. If you ask me, this Raith business was all planned. To our killer, this is just part of a game.'

He drained his cup, leaving a muddy sludge behind. 'Howay, we're off.'

'Where's we going?'

Ryan's face held no trace of emotion. 'I want you to go to the Lit and Phil.'

Trebilcock's face asked Ryan the question, not his voice.

'The Literary and Philosophical Society. It's the largest library outside London. It's up near the Central Station. Blag yersel' in and do more research.'

'What about you?'

'Me?' I'm going to talk to someone who I think can help us. Someone who knows all about cults and trends.'

His voice became quiet.

'They know a canny bit about games, too.'

SIXTEEN

Ryan was surprised she let him in. Most times, his brother's girlfriend didn't allow him over the threshold.

'Aal reet?' he enquired.

The girl pulled out her ear pods. 'Say again?'

'Doesn't matter.'

Germaine Shepherd, partner of James Jarrod, lay down the consul she'd been holding and disconnected it from the internet. The scroll of text down the side of the TV screen, most of it gibberish to Ryan's eyes, disappeared.

'Jam Jar's not in,' she said, referring to Ryan's brother by nickname, as she always did.

'That's a shame. I was gonna ask him if he wanted me to transfer me ticket for the Dortmund game to him. I'll be working.'

The girl tugged at a crucifix swinging from her earlobe. 'Football, you mean. That's not a game. Not a real game.' Subconsciously, she picked up the consul as if it held the magnetic attraction of Frodo's ring.

Ryan looked around the room. Walls of deep purple and dark red. A blue pentagram painted on one wall. A display case held models of dragons, goblins, Orcs – and bats.

'Germaine…'

'How many times? It's Muzzle to you and everyone else.'

Ryan continued without using her stupid gaming handle. 'What do you know about vampires?'

The girl studied him, eyes dead as a shark's. 'Why?'

'I'm interested, that's all.'

'Like fuck, you are,' she snickered.

Ryan took a deep breath. Met the gaze of the white-faced girl full-on. 'I'm after some help.'

'And I would know about them, would I?'

'Aye, I reckon you would.'

Muzzle sniffed. Tossed her violet-tinged black hair. 'Why?' she asked again.

'Because you Goths...' he saw her look daggers and corrected himself. 'Emos, some of you are into that sort of thing.'

Muzzle played with the hem of her long skirt as she tucked her legs beneath her. To Ryan, the dress looked like a black net curtain. 'Some are, yes,' she admitted.

'Look,' Ryan said, cutting to the chase, 'I'm working on a case that's got some odd qualities to it.'

The girl's eyes lit up. 'Like virgins and love bites gone deep, you mean? Oh wow. Tell me more.'

It was the first time he could recall Muzzle showing any degree of animation.

'I can't tell you more, and no – not like virgins.'

'Bites, then?' Muzzle sat forward on the edge of her seat.

'Hmmm. Not sure about that one. Not ruled out but probably not.'

'Aw shit. You little tease.' Muzzle came close to smiling.

Ryan suddenly felt ridiculous asking but ask he did. 'Is there much of that goes on around town?'

Muzzle considered the question. 'A bit, yeah.'

'Where?'

She sat back in her chair, invisible in the shadows and darkness. 'Are you sure you want to know?'

'I wouldn't have asked otherwise, man.'

'Okay.'

Ryan thought his brother's girlfriend had forgotten the question, so long the silence.

'There's a lot of different factions involved; you know? Mainly those on society's fringes.' She saw Ryan look at her.

The Graveyard Shift

'Like me, you're thinking, aren't you? Well, aye, I suppose so. Like me.'

'Goth-type, you mean?'

She didn't correct him this time. Instead, she nodded. The metal crosses and swastikas and stars slung around her neck jingled like sleigh bells. 'And others. Fetishists, sadomasochists, that sort of thing.'

Ryan tried to suppress a laugh. 'In the toon?'

'Yes. In the toon.' Her voice was authoritative. '*Club Purgatory*, for one.'

Ryan's mouth opened wide. 'For one?'

'Then there's *The Labyrinth*, and *Cellardom*, That's the one I went to.'

Ryan coughed and choked.

'I said *went*', she clarified. 'Only the once.'

Ryan shook his head. 'Does James know?'

'Probably not.'

'Shitting hell.' He shook his head again. 'Why would you gan there?'

She looked at him with genuine surprise. 'We only live once. I believe we should cram as many experiences as we can in the time we've got.'

'I'd rather stick safety pins in me gonads.'

'Ah – so you've been as well, then.' Muzzle laughed.

'No!'

'Only joking, man. Cool your piss.'

Ryan fought to bring his mind back onto the task. 'These sorts of places, that's where a vampire might meet a...' He almost said victim. 'A person with similar beliefs?'

'That's one of the ways. Or they could meet on-line. There's chatrooms and dating clubs.'

'What? For vampires?'

'Hell, aye. 'Course there is. Here, I'll get my laptop...'

Ryan's phone rang. *'Saved by the bell'*, he thought.

'Okay, sir. I'll be there in fifteen minutes. Yeah, no longer than that. I'm in Lemington so it's straight along Scotswood Road to Forth Street.'

He turned to Muzzle. 'I'm needed at the station. Tell James about the match ticket, yeah?'

'As if that's why you came,' she scoffed.

Ryan hurried to his car feeling he'd jumped from a parallel universe he never knew existed.

**

Three yellow awnings, angled towards the pavement, hid the windows of the Cullercoats Café Co from prying eyes. Not that anyone could see in anyway, so steamed up were the windows.

No-one sat outside, not in the biting nor' easterly which whipped the North Sea into a foaming frenzy. Inside, the café wasn't much busier.

A blonde woman sat at one table with her elderly mother who nursed a hot chocolate as frothy as the nearby ocean. Further in, against a wall of old brick, a young woman sat with her head almost hidden by a mug of turmeric latte held to her lips.

When she set the cup down, she lowered her gaze to the table and used a hand to sweep her long black hair in front of one eye. The other eye, hauntingly pale, flitted nervously. The coy, shy look was enhanced still further when she picked up a table menu and held it against her chest.

The blonde customer turned to speak to her. 'Excuse me, could we have a look at the menu? There isn't one on our table.'

In reluctant silence, the young woman took the menu to her fellow patron, then returned to her table without a word.

She was tall, almost six feet, and as painfully shy as her mannerisms indicated. She picked a leaflet from a rack on the wall behind her and buried her face in the reading material.

The Graveyard Shift

As she became engrossed in its contents, she forgot her self-consciousness.

She put the leaflet on the table and leafed through it.

'*Hallowe'en Howling,*' its cover announced.

Inside, details of the last open-air festival of the year – she thought the term 'festival' rather grand – included the band listing. The line-up consisted of an eclectic mix of has-beens, up-and-barely-comings, and tribute acts.

'*Not great,*' she thought, but it did offer something to fill a lonely evening.

'*Tickets reasonably priced,*' she observed. '*And local, too.*'

The event was scheduled for Tynemouth's Prior's Park, almost in the shadow of the ruins of the town's 12th century priory. The young woman folded the leaflet, slipped it into her pocket, and drained her mug.

All that remained was a decision on what to wear. She headed towards the exit; the leaflet poking from her pocket with the by-line left exposed.

'*Appropriate fancy dress encouraged.*'

**

Ryan's route from Lemington to the City and County CID HQ took him within spitting distance of JayKay's. If he'd had more time he'd have popped in, just to remind Kaye that he wasn't entirely off the hook yet, but he'd told Stephen Danskin he'd be fifteen minutes and the time was almost up.

He arrived in Danskin's office breathless after a dash from the car park. In the room with him were Sam Maynard, DCI Kinnear and the latter's DI, John Brownlee. In short, the leadership team in its entirety.

The wall monitor showed an image of a sterile room, with a digital clock counting down the seconds. It reached 21 seconds when a door to the room opened and Aaron Elliot stepped into picture, followed by Rufus Cavanagh.

He watched Elliot press a couple of buttons and Ryan saw the speaker icon on the screen go from *mute* to *live*.

Danskin made the unnecessary introductions before handing over to Aaron Elliot in the remote location.

'Thank you, DCI Danskin,' Aaron Elliot said. 'I take it you are all aware why we are here?'

Ryan spoke up. 'Hi Aaron. I've just this minute walked in the room so, for my sake, could you just remind me.'

'Certainly, Sherlock. Dr Cavanagh and I have conducted the post-mortem on Matthew Neill and we thought you'd want to hear the outcome.'

'Fire away,' Danskin urged.

'Well, there's good news and bad news. The good news is, we're looking at the same culprit. The details are too similar to the Coulson case – though not identical.'

'Do you have a cause of death?'

'Not specifically, no. The victim was indeed deceased prior to impalement. Also, the wounds on both victims' throats were identical. There was alcohol present in both corpses, significantly more in Mr Neill's case.'

'Any nitrous oxide?'

'No. I think the cylinders…what did you call them?'

'Whippets.'

'Ah yes, the nearby presence of whippets is a mere coincidence.'

Danskin hissed. 'No drugs, then.'

'We didn't say that,' Rufus interjected. 'Matthew Neill's toxicology tests revealed the presence of gamma-Hydroxybutyric acid. GHB, in layman's terms.'

Ryan spoke next. 'But not enough to kill him, right?'

'Quite right.'

Ryan thought for a moment. 'The second puncture wound: that's how the GHB got into his system. One to extract blood, one to inject a drug.'

The Graveyard Shift

'I think you're getting ahead of yourself, Sherlock,' Elliot rebuked. 'It's possible, but not certain, blood may have been removed via syringe. The GHB, however, was found in Neill's stomach, suggesting he'd ingested it rather than injected.'

It was Superintendent Maynard's turn to speak. 'Are the indications pointing towards a spiked drink?'

'I'd say so, yes.'

'Would it be important if we know what the drink was?'

Aaron Elliot's face wrinkled in smiles. 'I think you'd be interested, yes.'

'Okay, I'm interested.'

'Well, I – we – are confident the GHB was administered via a sucrose-infused consumption of blood.'

The room in Forth Street wrapped itself in silence. Slowly, all heads turned towards Ryan who tried his best to avert an 'I-told-you-so' look from his face.

'Doctors, are you sure? This links to a line of enquiry DS Jarrod is pursuing if correct.'

Rufus Cavanagh looked down the camera at Ryan. 'I'd swear to it,' he said.

Without knowing the nature of the deaths, a case of murder would be difficult to pursue. Danskin remained desperate to find one. 'Can you give us anything which might indicate how these men died? Anything at all?'

Elliot glanced towards Cavanagh. 'A theory, nothing more, but it's a plausible one. Dr Cavanagh proposed it. I'll let him explain.'

Rufus cleared his throat. 'You may have heard of a recent case where a nurse was convicted of killing numerous babies.'

The occupants of Mynard's room knew the case Cavanagh referred to, so they nodded.

'The theory put forward is that the nurse injected the victims with air, causing embolism and, ultimately, cardiac arrest. My theory is that the second puncture wound could be something similar. An injection of oxygen directly into the carotid artery would very likely lead to death, if administered correctly.'

Again, heads in Forth Street dipped in acknowledgement.

'Can you prove it?' Danskin asked, eagerly.

'Sadly not,' Cavanagh replied. 'Had we known to test for it immediately, we possibly could but not this long after death.'

Danskin billowed air from inflated cheeks.

'Now,' Aaron Elliot contributed, 'If a third victim turns up, we could test him...'

'Don't even joke about it!'

While the Forth Street end spoke at once about how difficult it would be to prove the theory in a court of law, Rufus Cavanagh gained there attention by tapping on his microphone.

'I do have some good news, though.'

'Thank Christ for that. We need a break, here. Go on, Dr Cavanagh.'

'If we assume this is how our killer murdered his victims, it takes a degree of skill and knowledge to know exactly how to do it.'

'You mean, he'll have had a keen interest in following the nurse's trial?'

'No, Detective Chief Inspector. I mean your killer has medical know-how.'

SEVENTEEN

The next few days passed without any substantial advances in the case. Despite the team accepting that the results on Matty Neill's post-mortem meant Ryan's theory was now the most likely lead, Jarrod remained downbeat.

The team's efforts focused on known homophobes with a penchant for violence and sociopathic sadists held on record, of which there were significantly more than anyone expected. None of them had a background in anatomy or medicine.

Danskin despatched an embarrassed squad of uniformed officers to the dodgy nightspots Muzzle had told Ryan about, only for them to be met by walls of silence. None of the establishments kept a list of members, much to Superintendent Maynard's chagrin.

Ryan's mood wasn't enhanced by missing the Borussia Dortmund Champions League match or its result, nor the news his Gran had contracted Covid despite the plethora of vaccinations she'd received. More especially, the fact Hannah attended her twenty-week scan without his knowledge really annoyed him.

He needed a break. A bit of man-time. Ryan invited Gavin for a pint at The Telegraph inn but O'Hara declined. Todd Robson was next in line but he feared another trip to the pink triangle and had a sudden pressing engagement. Trebilcock was on lates, Ravi didn't drink for religious reasons, and Danskin for the sake of his sobriety...which left Lucy Dexter.

Ryan almost asked her even though she quite clearly wasn't a man, but he wasn't convinced the torch she carried for him was out of battery power.

He settled for walking the hind legs off poor Kenzie. When the dog could take no more, Ryan had no other option but to ring Hannah.

'Out your huff yet, then?' she asked.

'Yes,' was his sharp reply.

'Good.'

'Looker, I don't want to go over old ground but you should have told me about the scan; at least give me the option of saying no.'

He heard her sigh. 'I told you everything was okay, didn't I? You were busy, Ry, and you, me, and little 'un need you to focus on your work. If we've an extra mouth to feed, we need the promotion for you.'

Ryan's turn to sigh. 'Aye, but *we* won't have an extra mouth to feed. *You* will. You've made that quite clear.'

'So much for not going over old ground,' she mumbled.

'Reet. Point taken. Listen, do you fancy going for some scran?'

'Yes, but I don't want to be late back.'

'How about the Jamdani or maybe Chutney's?'

'I like them both, but why don't you come over here? Florence on Osborne Road, maybe?'

'Good grief, I'll need that promotion to keep you in the lifestyle you're accustomed. Have you seen their prices?'

'The starters are pricey but the mains are okay and well-worth it. And, as a bonus, you get to stay over at mine, nudge-nudge wink-wink.'

Ryan considered the offer. 'I need to put this case to bed, love.'

'And you'd prefer that to putting *me* to bed? You've driven a stake through my heart, Ryan Jarrod,' she joked. After a moment's silence, Hannah realised what she'd said. 'Oh God. That was inappropriate, wasn't it?'

'Just a tad. Could be worse. You could have suggested we go to the steakhouse.'

Hannah sniggered. 'I take it from that last comment I'm properly forgiven now.'

'Are you paying?'

'Only in kind,' she teased.

'In that case, you're only kinda' forgiven.'

He ended the conversation, jumped in the shower, and packed an overnight bag. Within forty minutes, he was inside the Florence restaurant, Hannah by his side, ordering their food from a waiter in a blood-spattered surgeon Hallowe'en costume.

A witch brought Ryan's Moretti to him whilst Hannah sipped an eye-wateringly expensive soft drink. He, though, was pleasantly surprised at the cost of the food, especially when Hannah agreed to forego a first course.

'So,' she said, waving a fork in his direction, 'You've really bought into this vampire malarkey.'

'Aye. I have. More importantly, so has the rest of the team. If we suspend belief, it's the only logical conclusion.'

Hannah brushed a curl away from her eyes. 'I'm not sure *'logical'* and *'vampires'* belong in the same sentence, if I'm honest.'

He picked up a slice of pizza Bologna and took a large bite. He stared at the ragu on his fingers and licked them clean.

'Use a knife and fork, man,' Hannah urged, 'And a napkin.'

Ryan wriggled stained fingers at her. 'Now, if that were blood and I was a vampire, I'd be in ecstasy. You see, Hannah, a vampire just needs blood to maintain the fantasy, not to keep them young. That side of things is all bollocks. What's more, the blood doesn't have to come from a bite. If it's from a test-tube, syringe, goblet, or owt; it doesn't matter to them.'

'Okay, okay. Now, can we change the subject, please?'

He drank from his beer bottle. 'You brought the subject up,' he reminded her.

She mumbled something indecipherable through a mouthful of Italian meatball.

Ryan spoke, ignoring whatever Hannah had tried to say. 'How much do you know aboot sadomasochism?' he asked.

Hannah choked on her food. 'What the hell?' she spluttered through a coughing fit.

'Germaine, or Muzzle whatever you want to call her, she reckons that's where they meet. Vampires, like.'

'Oh aye, and she would know, how?'

He looked at her.

'No!!' she said. 'No way. Surely she doesn't?'

'Only once, so she said.'

'Does your James know?'

'Hadaway, man. Not likely.'

Hannah raised an eyebrow. 'Do you think they... you know?'

Ryan sat down a pizza slice. 'Don't even go there. I'm eating, man.'

A strange smile haunted Hannah's face.

'It's not funny,' Ryan said.

Still, she continued to stare straight ahead. Ryan felt her take his hand and pull it towards her. She lay it against her stomach.

Ryan's eyes opened wide, and he smiled, too.

'Is that our baby? Is it kicking?'

'Well, it's not indigestion, Ry.'

Ryan's face took on a look of beatific wonderment.

'Wow,' was all he could say.

'I'm pleased something took your mind off ghosties and ghoulies and things that go bump in the night.'

'Wow,' he said again.

Hannah and Ryan continued their meal in a lighter mood - small talk and laughter and whispered endearments across the table - until they left hand-in-hand.

They should have known peace wouldn't last.

The Graveyard Shift

**

'Trick or treat?'

'Fuck off.'

The man with coal black hair slammed the door shut in the kids' faces.

A fist hammered on the back of the door. 'How, man – they're only bairns. Watch your language.'

The man swung open the door and faced the children's father. 'Then you should keep them in the house. This is no night for them to be out.'

The father opened his mouth to speak, then stopped. Looked the man up and down. 'Bloody hell, you're a bit old for that costume, aren't you? Is that why you said kids shouldn't be dressing up tonight: in case they upstage you?'

The man sneered. 'This is no costume. I have work to do. Be gone with you.'

'*Be gone*? What sort of expression is that?' the father jibed.

The dark-haired man spoke with no malice in his voice, only a confident assurance as he added, 'In words you will understand, piss off along with your annoying brats.'

**

John Kaye was not in the bar which bore his monicker. In fact, there weren't many others, either. Kaye's gamble on NOT hosting a Hallowe'en event on the basis he would attract custom from those who preferred to avoid costumed events had fallen flat.

The Eagle, Bobby's, and The Yard were bursting at the seams with devils, zombies, Frankensteins, and mini-skirted witches. Jayjay's sat almost deserted and forlorn.

Kaye himself had left early, leaving Charles and Sherry Proudlock to cater for the few patrons who crossed the door.

Sherry pulled at her ebony-coloured pigtails. 'I hope I'm still getting paid for this.'

'You will,' her father assured her. 'John's never let you down.'

She continued to play with her hair as she looked around the premises. 'He should have done the place up. Ran a best costume competition or had a theme for the night. It's not exactly rocket science, is it?'

A middle-aged woman strolled to the bar and ordered a G&T and a white wine for her companion. 'You'd think the place was haunted,' she said while waiting on her drinks.

'Ha-bloody-ha,' Sherry replied, slamming the drinks on the bartop.

'Keep the change,' the woman replied after counting out the exact amount of coinage.

Sherry poked her tongue at the woman's back.

'I'm afraid I might be to blame for how quiet it is tonight,' Charles apologised. 'I wasn't sure...' he hesitated, 'I didn't know how you'd take it.'

'Seriously?'

Charles nodded.

'Dad, I might have my troubles...'

'PTSD, you mean.'

'All right. PTSD, and I might have dabbled more than a bit to forget things, but I can still think for myself. I can tell the difference between a few queens dressed up as Frank N Furter or body-painted werewolves and, well...what I saw.'

Charles Proudlock squinted at his daughter. 'You know, I'm proud of you. I don't say that often enough.'

Sherry spat a laugh. 'I haven't done anything to make you proud, apart from OD a couple of times and not get a proper job.'

Charles thought for a moment. 'Why don't I get you a proper job?'

'And where are you going to magic one of them up from?'

He looked directly into his daughter's eyes. 'I've got money. I'll buy John out. He's been, shall we say, 'distracted' lately so

The Graveyard Shift

I think he'll be willing to sell. Once he does, you can oversee marketing. Be an events manager, if you like.'

She shook her head. 'This place certainly needs something like that. I mean, look at it, man.' She gestured around the interior. 'But no; I can't do that. It'll finish you and John.'

Charles ran his fingers through his straggly blond curls.

'There's plenty more sharks in the sea,' he said, smiling like one.

Sherry shook her head, pigtails flying like knotted rope.

'Think about it. Please,' Charles said. 'And don't worry about John and me. We're already finished. We've been finished for months. He just doesn't know it, yet.'

**

Detective Constable Gavin O'Hara looked around the interior of the pub. It seemed vaguely familiar to him, with its lead-framed and stained-glass windows, dark wood wall panels, and old-fashioned beer barrel stools.

It dawned on him that Tynemouth's Cumberland Arms was reminiscent of a larger Crown Posada, his favourite bar in Newcastle.

Even the cask ales were similar. He'd arrived early and drained his pint of Breeches Buoy house ale. Once done, he began to relax.

He glanced at his watch. Five minutes until the appointed hour. He ordered another pint, remembered he didn't want to appear too pissed, so changed the order to a half which he tipped into the pint glass, spilling some onto the table as he did so.

Gavin placed a green Marks and Spencer carrier back in the centre of the table. Alongside it, he set down a flat cap. Prearranged signal set, he waited.

The door opened and closed, opened and closed, opened and closed. Each time, the Front Street noise and North Sea smell checked out the bar – but not the person Gavin awaited.

Twenty minutes later, his drink was empty. Folk in costume jostled at the bar, shouting for attention from the bar staff.

Gavin scanned their faces, checked for anyone looking his way. No-one did.

He fought his way to the bar, ordered a spiced rum, and returned to his table.

The carrier bag and cap were still there. So, too, were a couple: a woman dressed as Wednesday Addams, and a male in a Joker costume. Gavin offered them a wan smile but neither paid him any attention.

Gavin pulled out his phone, scrolled through a few messages, and snapped it shut with a sigh.

He stepped outside, the distant sound of music melding with the sound of the wind and the laughter of revellers moving from bar to bar.

'Sod it,' he said to himself. 'They're not coming. I've had enough of this.'

He dumped the carrier bag in a bin and pulled the cap tight on his head.

EIGHTEEN

Jordan Usher fingered the leaflet she'd picked up from Cullercoats Coffee and loitered by the entrance to Prior's Park; not the main entrance, the side one adjacent to the Haven car park.

She could hear the music clearly from where she stood and wondered whether it was worth putting herself through the agony of socialising with others.

In the end, she realised waiting by the park gates made her stand out like a turd in a fruit salad. She'd be less conspicuous mixed with the crowd. Jordan trailed her hair down one side of her face as a means of hiding herself and made her way into the darkened park.

She followed the footpath and the music through the trees until she disappeared from the view of those queuing for entry to the park, just as surely as if the Pied Piper had led her to the mountains.

**

The hospitality marquee filled up as one act finished and another set up their kit.

The man lurked in the background, drink in hand. For once, he didn't feel conspicuous in his long dark coat. Tonight, he had plenty of company. Although less than a third of the crowd opted for fancy dress, there were sufficient for him to blend in as if he wore an invisibility cloak. He smiled at the notion.

The throng at the bar dissipated as the first notes of 'Never Enough' struck up. The man glanced at the listings. Another tribute act – The Curious - had taken centre stage.

Whilst many left the marquee, he remained in the shadows, watching.

In the dimly lit tent, a duo of vampires lurked nearby; false fangs, blood-red contact lenses, and powder white faces. They sipped from plastic glasses of lager and black. He sneered at their feeble attempts to mimic reality.

The music, off key and slightly discordant, set an eerie tone for the night. The man took his eyes from the pathetic vampires and looked into a dark corner where mummy and zombie teased each other by unravelling their partner's bandages.

He sighed. Everyone seemed to be with a partner. He needed a sole mate to be his soulmate.

In a pause between songs, laughter pierced the air. A clown, scary make-up and rainbow afro hairdo, crept up on unsuspecting revellers. He touched them on one shoulder, hid behind them, then appeared at their other shoulder with an evil leer.

The clown was alone.

The man watched him like a cat watches a sparrow. Slowly, he edged towards the clown, keeping in the shadows at the edge of the tent. His breath came in short, sharp rasps. He felt in the pocket of his coat, fingers wrapping around the chalice.

'There you are!' a voice cried out.

The man jumped and turned to face the speaker.

'You could hardly miss me dressed like this, could you?' the clown said.

'Aye, but it's dark in here, man,' the voice said. 'Here – get your laughing tackle around that.' The clown's companion handed him a pint glass and sipped from his own. 'Sorry it took so long. Queue at the bar was a reet bugger.'

The dark-haired man hissed an obscenity and disappeared into recesses as dark as his mind.

**

The Graveyard Shift

The final notes of 'Love Cats' were drowned out by the applause of an appreciative audience as The Curious wrapped up their set.

Their Gothic appearance and haunting music fit the Hallowe'en mood to a tee. By common consensus, they'd been the best act of the night so far.

Jordan Usher shivered violently despite her thick coat once the crowd began to disperse. She squinted at her programme. Next up were a highly acclaimed band from Leeds, the programme told her.

The Happy Daggers were billed as 'funk rock to lighten the soul.' It was probably a good contrast to the sullen aura set by The Curious, but they weren't for her. Jordan preferred gloom to light.

Besides, she was cold and the relative warmth of the marquee beckoned her towards it.

She peeked inside. It was busy. Too busy for comfort. Outside, by the stage, Jordan knew no-one was watching her. Here, with no distractions, someone might notice her. Worse, they might try to speak to her. To Jordan Usher, attention was anathema and conversation her worst nightmare.

The marquee was adorned with cotton-wool cobwebs and flickering faux candles, and in the dim light she saw only the costumed festival goers. It was if those wearing normal attire didn't exist.

In the corner, she saw a group of pirates chatting with a man dressed as the Davy Jones octopus creature while a glamorous witch embraced a fortune teller complete with crystal ball (or balloon).

Jordan peered down through strands of hair at her own costume. She wore an old coat her grandfather told her was a Crombie. She'd fastened the top three buttons and let the rest hang open in the belief it might resemble a cloak. She'd turned up the colour and stitched a strip of red satin fabric to it, and smeared face-paint by her lips to mimic blood.

Compared to everyone else, her costume felt inadequate. Jordan Usher always felt inadequate.

With tears in her eyes, she shrunk against the back of the marquee.

The predator watched and waited. He stealthily inched towards her. He did nothing to draw attention to himself. He didn't look directly at her. More people entered the marquee. He became lost in numbers.

This was his moment.

'All alone?' he asked, softly.

Jordan whimpered at the closeness of his voice.

'I didn't see you,' she said, averting her eyes.

'Yes, it's very dark, isn't it?'

Stop asking questions, she thought. *I don't want to talk.*

'What's been your favourite so far?' He wasn't about to give up.

Jordan shrugged. 'Dunno.' She pulled more hair in front of her face.

'You've lovely eyes,' he said. 'Or, at least, eye. Let me see the other one.' He tenderly moved her hair aside. 'There. That's better, isn't it?'

She took a quick glance at the man then lowered her eyes. At least he'd been smiling. At least he'd been gentle.

'I like your costume,' he said. 'Unpretentious. Not like that lot over there, pretending they're *real* vampires.'

'It's not really a costume,' she stammered. 'I thought more people would be dressed up.'

The man's voice continued, composed and gentle. 'I think it's perfect,' he said.

'Thank you,' she said, and gave a shy smile.

'Nice smile, too. You should try it more often.'

Jordan smiled once more and looked at the man properly for the first time.

The Graveyard Shift

He was tall, not unattractive, with foppish black hair which may or may not have been a wig. He wore a long black coat or cape, she couldn't be sure in the darkness, and a crisp white shirt.

Her first thought was, '*Severus Snape.*'

'Who have you come as?' she asked, to be certain.

He smiled. 'Just me. I don't need to be anyone but me.'

His words resonated with her. 'I wish I felt the same,' she said.

He reached up and teased her hair back in front of her eye. 'You're perfect as you are.'

'Thank you.' Jordan looked away and blushed.

'Can I get you a drink?' the man asked.

She looked towards the bar, once again a throng of customers pushed against it. She shuddered. 'No. No, thanks. It's too busy.'

The man pulled something from beneath his cape. 'I've got my own,' he said. 'The prices are too expensive here.' He took a chug from a goblet-like flask and offered it to her.

She shook her head.

'Go on,' the Snape character encouraged.

Jordan hesitated. 'What's in it?'

The man smiled. 'A nice claret,' he said, licking his lips.

There was something repellent, almost reptilian, in the gesture, yet Jordan felt the man held an odd magnetism.

'I'll give it a miss, thanks.'

'Ah well. All the more for me.' He took another sip.

The Happy Daggers set ended and once again the huge space under the canvas became cramped.

Jordan felt herself break out in a cold sweat. She became claustrophobic. Unable to breathe. Too many people, too little air. She began to panic. She needed fresh air.

'Where are you going?' Snape asked.

'Outside. I need some air,' she said, rushing towards the exit.

'Wait. I'll come with you.'

The man felt the excitement build deep in his soul.

**

'It's a beautiful evening,' he said, staring up at the starlit sky.

'It is, now I'm out of that place,' Jordan agreed.

They sat on damp grass on the outfield of Prior's Park cricket pitch, the ruins of Tynemouth Priory standing proud atop the headland above them. Below, on the pier, the torch of a sole fisherman stood out against the blackness of the enveloping North Sea.

The Severus Snape lookalike stood suddenly. He offered her his hand. 'Come,' he commanded.

'Where to?'

'To where we belong.'

Jordan didn't know where or what he meant, yet something compelled her to take his hand.

He guided her up the steep gradient of Pier Road, the sailing club to their right.

'Slow down,' Jordan gasped. 'I can't keep up.'

'Yes you can.' He tugged her towards him.

'Where are you taking me?'

'Home,' he said.

'I don't live near…' Realisation dawned. 'No! I'm not going to your house. Let me go. I'll scream.'

The man gave an exaggerated eye-roll. 'I didn't say *my* home. No – it was a figure of speech. Come on. You'll enjoy it.' He looked her up and down. 'Especially in your costume. I promise you it'll be okay.'

Jordan laughed. She didn't know why but laugh she did. There was something about the man - a presence, a force, even. Was it because she thought of him as a character out of Harry Potter rather than an actual person? She neither knew nor cared. What Jordan did know was, for the first time in her life, she knew what carefree meant.

'Come on, climb over this fence and we're free as a bird,' the man said, as if he read her thoughts.

Her long legs easily reached over the short iron fence. She felt soft ground beneath her feet.

The man had stopped. 'Beautiful, isn't it?'

They gazed up at the skeletal ruins of the once great Tynemouth Priory, discretely floodlit to highlight the lancet windows in the presbytery's jagged remains.

'I've never seen it so beautiful,' Jordan whispered.

'Come on,' the man said. 'We're not done yet.'

He took her hand and they pressed on over sloping grassland like star-crossed lovers.

'Watch your step,' he said, stepping over an uprooted sign which once read *'Please Respect This Land.'*

'I can't go on anymore,' Jordan wheezed, collapsing to the floor.

The man's shadow fell over her. 'We need go no further.'

'Where are we?'

'The only place where a vampire and companion should be on Hallowe'en.'

'Which is, where?'

'A cemetery, of course.'

'Huh?' Jordan sat bolt upright.

Sure enough, they were surrounded by ancient headstones blackened and eroded by time and nature.

The man sat down next to Jordan. 'Isn't this a wonderful place to celebrate Hallowe'en?' he asked rhetorically.

'What's your name?' Jordan asked.

'What's yours?'

'Jordan,' she told him.

'That's all I need to know. Here, have some.' He brought out the flask again. She shook her head.

'Go on. It'll warm you up.'

He held it to her lips. She turned her head aside.

His hand moved to her chin. Turned her face towards him. He inched his face towards her. Hesitated. Then kissed her on the lips.

Jordan resisted at first, then yielded, then returned his kiss with passion.

The man moved his hand from the girl's cheek. Moved it slowly towards her breast. He took one in his hand. Squeezed gently.

She pulled away.

'Am I going too quickly?' the man panted.

'No. It's just…well, there's something you need to know, that's all.'

A dark light came on behind the man's yawning pupils. He smiled. Snarled, almost.

'You mean, you've never…?' His voice sparkled with delight, awe, and anticipation.

'No, I haven't. And…and, there's something else…'

The man wasn't listening. He'd climbed to his feet. Stepped behind Jordan. And lifted something from the ground.

Jordan didn't see what he what he'd picked up, but she felt it.

The wooden pole which once held the *'Respect'* sign thundered into the back of her skull like a baseball bat, sending her sprawling, bent double and semi-conscious, over a headstone.

Using his foot, he levered Jordan off the memorial.

She lay on her back, staring up at a silver moon and the blood-soaked face of her assailant.

'Where's all the blood from?' she wondered.

The Graveyard Shift

Her hands reached for her chest. They settled around the sharp, splintered pole, slick and warm with her blood, driven between her ribs.

Jordan Usher's screams fused with the burst of fireworks at the festival's finale.

NINETEEN

Hannah lay snuggled against Ryan, the fingers of one hand playing with the hair at the nape of his neck.

Ryan sighed contentedly. He reached behind him and stroked her belly.

'I think the bairn's asleep,' Hannah whispered.

'After what we've just been up to? Blimey, there's no chance of baby being a Ravi Sangar if it can sleep through that.'

Hannah laughed and slapped his backside. She was about to say something when Ryan's ringtone breached the peace of Hannah's bedroom.

'Ah hell,' Ryan exclaimed. 'Gotta be work at this time.'

Worse, Hannah's phone rang seconds later.

'Double hell,' she said. 'Must be something big if they're calling both of us.'

Ryan leapt out one side of the bed, Hannah swung her legs out the other. They took the calls facing one another.

'Sir?' Ryan answered.

'There's another body in another cemetery.'

'Shit. Where's this one?' He moved into the corridor to avoid the distraction of Hannah's conversation.

'Tynemouth Priory.'

'Same as the others, I'm guessing.'

'Seems to be. The body was found by a couple who'd been at a festival doon the road. They called it in and said they thought it was a Hallowe'en stunt at first.'

'What else do we know about it?' Ryan asked struggling to pull a sweater over his head.

'Body on a grave. Stake through the heart. Not much more than that.'

The Graveyard Shift

Ryan whistled. 'Yep, sounds the same.'

'We'll know better when we get there. Uniform should be on the scene about now. Aaron Elliot and co on their way, an' all.'

'I'm at Hannah's, sir. I'll get there as soon as.'

'I'll meet you there.'

'Sir.'

'Oh, one more thing, Jarrod.'

'Yes?'

'The couple who found them.'

'What about them?'

'They say we'll identify them cos they're dressed as vampires.'

**

Hannah told Ryan that DCI Kinnear had ordered her and DI Brownlee to meet him at Forth Street. Superintendent Maynard wanted them and Ravi Sangar to lead on things at the station while Danskin's crew supervised the crime scene.

They headed off in different directions in different cars but continued their conversation on hands-free until Hannah pulled into the HQ's car park.

A few moments later, Ryan turned right at the Tynemouth Castle Inn, sped along Grand Parade cursing at the cycle lane which narrowed the road, before screeching to a halt beneath the clock tower.

He climbed out the Peugeot and fought his way through a crowd clad in fancy dress until he reached the outer cordon.

A jobsworth PC blocked his way. 'You can't go any further, sir.'

'I think I can,' Ryan said, flashing his warrant card. 'You just focus on keeping this zombie hoard away. Where've they all come from anyway at this time of night?'

'Some concert-thingy in Prior's Park.'

'Is DCI Danskin here?'

'Aye. Got here fifteen minutes or so ago.'

'Any others?'

'He sent a blonde lassie down to the festival site along with a lanky bloke.'

Lucy Dexter and Nigel Trebilcock, Ryan guessed.

'And another big bloke to talk to the vampires who found her.'

'That'll be DC Robson,' Ryan said as he moved on. He moved on because he'd spotted Stephen Danskin looking down from the headland, seeking him out. When he caught sight of Ryan, the DCI beckoned him forward with a frantic wave.

Ryan broke into a sprint and was breathless by the time he scaled the grassy mound. He listened while Danskin briefed him on route to the priory graveyard.

'I'm not sure if this is the same guy, Jarrod.'

Ryan stopped momentarily. 'It's got to be, man.'

'I'm not sure,' Danskin repeated, marching on.

'Why?' Ryan panted as he caught up with the DCI.

'You'll see.'

They were heading downhill, now. In the near distance, they saw hastily erected spotlights pick out white clad figures glowing like fireflies as they went about their business.

'What do you mean by *'It's not the same guy'*?' Ryan asked. 'Sir? What do you mean?'

'It's not the same perp,' Danskin emphasised.

'There can't be another one.'

'I'll let you decide for yourself.' It was the DCI's turn to hesitate before he added, 'Just prepare yourself, son. It's not pretty.'

**

'Jesus!'

'I did warn you,' Danskin reminded him.

'Shit.'

The Graveyard Shift

'Aye. It's a messy one.'

Ryan Jarrod stood in the spotlight like an actor centre-stage. Everything around him was swallowed whole by a blackness of night neither moon nor stars could penetrate.

A lifeless body lay on the cold stone of an ancient grave. The victim was a tall young woman. *'A woman,'* Ryan noted. *'This IS different.'*

The headstone and surrounding grass were caked in thick, congealing blood. It reminded Ryan of mashed fruit he'd once seen on a supermarket floor.

'Lots of blood,' Ryan's brain computed.

The woman's hair flopped in front of one eye. The other eye, clouded in death, stared heavenwards. The look in her eye was one of frozen terror, and her facial muscles were contorted in agony.

'This wasn't a good death,' Ryan said.

Danskin nodded in silent agreement.

The girl's limbs were spread out at odd angles. 'She hasn't been posed,' Ryan added.

From the centre of the girl's chest, a wooden pole emerged, coated with layers of dark burgundy. Ryan noticed her clothing was drenched with the same material.

'She was alive,' Ryan whispered. 'My God.'

He stood up.

'Sir, this isn't the same killer.'

Danskin found no satisfaction in being proved right.

One of the white clad figures approached. Through a hazmat helmet, the muffled voice of Aaron Elliot greeted him with, 'A bit grim, isn't it?'

Ryan dragged his eyes away from the remains of Jordan Usher. 'It's not the same as the others.'

'Far from it, Sherlock; far from it, indeed.'

Ryan shivered as much at the thought of the cadaver at his feet than with the cold. 'I don't suppose we have an ID for her?'

'I believe we do. A travel pass was found a grave or two away. One of the forensics team bagged it up for evidence. They told me her name is Jordan Usher.'

'The killer made sure there were no clues to the identity of the other victims,' Ryan thought aloud. 'There's too many variations here, Aaron. It's a different killer, isn't it?'

Elliot hesitated. 'I can't give you an answer with any degree of certainty but, given the lack of puncture wounds to the neck and the fact our girl was alive and kicking – probably quite literally – would indicate not. I'll know more…'

'…When you get her to the lab. Yes, I know your spiel off by heart, Aaron.'

'For what it's worth, Dr Cavanagh's made his mind up already and he agrees with you.'

Ryan looked around the forensics team trying to spot Rufus. It was an impossible task. They all looked the same. 'Where is he?'

'There,' Elliot pointed to a figure standing apart from the rest of the team. He was shaking his covered head. Wringing his gloved hands. 'I've never seen him so upset.'

The figure in white saw them looking at him and stepped towards them.

'This is terrible. Awful,' Dr Cavanagh said from behind his mask.

'Thought you'd be used to it in your line of work,' Danskin commented.

'Doesn't stop me getting angry. Furious, even. This isn't right. Not right, at all.'

Although his face was covered, the angst in his voice was obvious.

'Dr Elliot says you think it's a different killer.'

The Graveyard Shift

Cavanagh gave a short, bitter laugh. 'Of course it is. Completely different method. Inhumane. Horrific.'

'Sorry, Dr Cavanagh but most murders are inhumane and horrific,' Danskin said. 'I've been in this job longer than I can care to remember and the day I stop thinking of murder as being horrific is the day I pack it all in.'

Rufus lowered his head. 'This shouldn't have happened. Not like this. It's appalling.'

Cavanagh turned away from the scene. Across the Tyne, the lights of South Shields twinkled brightly. Further down the coastline, Seaburn, Roker, as far south as Seaham, glowed like nebulous constellations. At their feet, the visible eye of Jordan Usher represented the void of a black hole.

'I'm livid,' Rufus Cavanagh said, his words lost in the wind whipping in from the North Sea.

**

Ryan, Danskin, Dexter and Trebilcock gathered by a police van. Someone had brought out a couple of flasks and the foursome cupped their hands around steaming mugs.

'We learnt nothing down at the festival site,' Lucy lisped. 'The organisers had security on site but no cameras, just manpower. Nige and me spoke to a few of the guys but there'd been little trouble.'

'I even asks 'em if they'd seen any vampires,' Trebilcock added. 'They says there were dozens of 'em, being Hallowe'en, loik.'

'Oh, and the press have been talking to them, an' all,' Lucy informed them. 'They'll have discovered less than we did but it won't stop them making stuff up.'

Danskin chewed on a lip. 'That's a point,' he said.

'What is?'

'The press. We haven't given them any details of the other two murders.'

'So?' Trebilcock asked.

It was Ryan who answered for the DCI. 'So, it can't be a copycat.'

'Exactly, Jarrod.'

'Which means we've either got two loony-tunes on the loose, which is highly unlikely,' Ryan concluded, 'Or...'

Danskin had second guessed him. 'Or we're looking for killers - plural -working together, and one's gone solo with this one.'

They considered the possibility in silence.

'Bloody 'ell,' Trebilcock cursed at length. 'It makes sense, so it does.'

Lucy agreed. 'What now?' she asked.

It was a question no-one could answer.

Or, it was until Ryan had a thought.

'We go back to the beginning.'

'What for?'

Ryan flicked his wrist and scattered the dregs of his coffee onto the grass.

'Let's get back to the station and I'll tell you.'

**

It was almost three in the morning yet the third floor of the City and County station was alive with activity.

Rick Kinnear, John Brownlee and Hannah were trawling through old casefiles and computer records while Ravi Sangar was developing a program to filter wheat from chaff.

'Ravi,' Ryan began.

'Sorry, Ry. Me hands are full here. I've no time to help.'

'It's okay. All I want is to know where the security footage from JayKay's is. You know, the night Coulson was killed?'

'Oh, that owld crap. It's in the tech room. Second cabinet on the left, third drawer down.'

Ryan was already halfway to the door, Danskin in hot pursuit.

Todd Robson had materialised from the ether and followed them. 'Owt I can do to help?'

'Can you remember the co-ordinates?' Ryan asked him.

'The what-ates?'

'The point where we first see Coulson and our suspect, man.'

'Oh, that. Nah but Ravi's edited the tape down so it'll be near the beginning somewhere.'

Ryan rifled through the drawer and produced the cassette tape. 'Cheers, Todd. Once you type up your interview with the vampire, give the others a hand, yeah? It doesn't need three of us in here.'

Ryan fed the tape into the player and pulled up a seat at the same time.

'Care to share?' Danskin asked.

'Well, it depends whether we're on the money about it being a tag-team of killers.' He pressed a button marked '>'. The screen came alive.

'I like your thinking. You mean the accomplice to our man in the shadow might be in the bar, too?'

'Exactly.'

The images on the screen flickered like a Roobarb and Custard cartoon.

'There!' Ryan paused the old video when he spotted Billy Coulson stepping through the door.

'Reet. Let's see if anybody shows any interest in him,' Danskin said peering intently at the screen.

They saw Coulson pick up a pint, drain it, and walk towards the gaming machine, just as he'd done every other time they watched the recording.

'Nobody's taking a blind bit of notice of him,' the DCI remarked.

'Not that we can see,' Ryan acknowledged.

'Had on: the bar staff aren't visible. We can't see what they're up to.'

'Aye, true enough.'

'Who did you say was on duty at the time?'

'John Kaye, his fella' – Charles Proudlock - and Proudlock's daughter. Shelly or Sherry or Cheryl, her name is.'

Danskin pulled at loose flesh beneath his Adam's apple. 'Let's follow this through until Coulson and Mr Nobody leave. If we see nowt else, we'll haul all three of the staff in.'

They waited until Coulson and his killer emerged from the toilet and walked to the door. They watched it open and close and the couple disappear into the night.

'Aw no. No, no.' Ryan's voice was almost a whimper.

'What is it, Jarrod?'

Ryan said nothing. He looked down at Ravi Sangar's keyboard and pressed a few buttons. The image enlarged so much it became heavily pixelated.

He tried again. This time, the image zoomed out: too far out to identify what he was after.

He touched the keypad again.

'There.' His finger lay against the screen where a figure sat on the periphery of the enhanced sector of the tape. 'I hope to God I'm wrong.'

Stephen Danskin's muttered 'Fuck' told him he wasn't.

The DCI's face was as white as the late William Coulson's hair.

'I want him brought in. NOW!'

TWENTY

The suspect was detained in a dimly lit holding cell in the bowels of Forth Street for almost three hours while Ryan and Danskin gathered evidence. They enlisted Ravi Sangar's help but left the rest of the team to plough their own furrow.

When the custody sergeant led the suspect into the interview room, the handcuffed man squinted and turned his face away from the harsh light in Interview Suite 5.

The custody sergeant ensured the man was seated before he retreated to the back wall.

Danskin switched on the recording device before going through the protocol of introducing himself and Ryan.

'For the purpose of the recording, what is your full name?' Danskin asked the suspect.

'Gavin Dermot O'Hara.'

'What is your position, Mr O'Hara?'

'I'm a Detective Constable.' O'Hara stared at a chip in the desk's surface as he spoke.

'Does the name William Coulson mean anything to you?'

Gavin nodded.

'For the benefit of the tape, Mr O'Hara has nodded his head,' Ryan said.

Danskin continued the questioning, as he'd pre-arranged with Ryan.

'Were you on duty the night Mr Coulson was murdered?'

O'Hara sighed. 'I was supposed to be on duty early the following morning.'

'You didn't show, though, did you?'

Ryan told the recording Mr O'Hara had shaken his head.

'Why didn't you turn up for duty?'

'You know why,' O'Hara said in monotone. 'I was pissed from the night before.'

Stephen Danskin scratched his bristled jaw to such an extent the recorder's sonograph spiked at the sound.

'And where did you get pissed?'

'You already know. I told you; it was The Traveller's Rest in Burradon.'

Danskin rubbed his forehead.

'I ask you again: where were you the night Mr Coulson was killed? Please, think carefully before you answer.'

Gavin raised his eyes fleetingly before they returned to study the desk once more. 'The Traveller's.'

Danskin let out an audible sigh. He stretched an arm towards Ryan who opened a folder and handed an A4 sheet to the DCI. Danskin turned the sheet so it faced Gavin.

'O'Hara, is this or is this not you?'

'For the tape,' Ryan explained, 'DCI Danskin has shown Mr O'Hara a still image taken from a recording made inside JayKay's bar.'

Gavin raised his eyes to meet those of his boss.

'No comment.'

Danskin vibrated his lips. 'You well-know that a *'No comment'* comment doesn't look good.'

'No comment.'

'...fuck's sake, man!' Danskin pushed his chair away as he stood. It rattled to the floor. 'Listen, I don't want this to be you,' he said, pointing at the photograph. 'I don't want to think you're capable of what's happened; but you need to talk, man.'

'No comment.'

Danskin picked up his chair and retook it.

'Okay. Moving on. The night a Matthew Neill was murdered in Gateshead. You're aware of the incident?'

'Yes.'

The Graveyard Shift

'Where were you?'

'At home. Before you ask, yes; I was steaming drunk.'

'Can anyone vouch for you?'

O'Hara made a noise. It could have been a bitter laugh; it could have been a sob. 'Me missus has left me, man. Of course there was no-one else there. There's never anyone there. That's why I was in JayKay's that first night. I needed to get out. Somewhere no-one knew me.'

Ryan and Danskin exchanged glances. Danskin's body relaxed, relieved he'd got O'Hara talking.

'Why didn't you tell us?' Stephen Danskin's tone was softer, more akin to the Danskin both Ryan and Gavin knew.

'Isn't it obvious? You know what sort of place that is, right? I could be labelled, you know? Bent copper, in more senses than one.'

Danskin took a deep breath.

'Did you meet anyone there?'

'What? No, of course not...'

'An accomplice, perhaps?'

'Hadaway, man.'

Danskin took a moment to reflect. Shifted through his notes.

'Okay. Back to Matthew Neill. He was known to you, I understand.'

'Yes. I told you. He is – was – an old friend of mine. Before you ask, you also know I haven't seen him for years.'

Danskin held a silence for a beat or two. 'Matthew Neill was gay. William Coulson was last seen in a gay bar. The same gay bar you were seen in.'

O'Hara sat back in his seat. 'Total co-incidence. And, in case you'd forgotten, the third victim was female, not a male homosexual.'

Danskin left the subject open, ready to come back to it.

'Now you've brought the topic up, let's move onto last night. October 31st. Hallowe'en. The night Jordan Usher was killed in Tynemouth…'

'I was working. You know I was.'

'Your shift had long since finished. I called you, and the rest of the team, hours later. So, between the end of your shift and my call, where were you?'

Gavin rolled his eyes. 'At home.'

'Try again.'

'Listen to the words, sir: I. Was. At. Home.'

Danskin snapped his fingers and Ryan handed over another printed sheet.

'O'Hara,' the DCI said softly, 'Your phone was pinged by a mast in Tynemouth Square, roughly ninety minutes before I called you – and around an hour before Jordan Usher's body was discovered.'

'I know when she was discovered!' Gavin barked. 'I interviewed the blokes who found her, remember?'

Danskin stared at O'Hara. 'I remember. I remember very well. I'm just curious why you don't recall already being in Tynemouth.'

Gavin sat back.

'No comment.'

Danskin's fist rapped the desk. 'Divvent start that shite again!'

O'Hara blinked back tears. Neither Stephen Danskin nor Ryan were far behind him. They took no pleasure interrogating one of their own.

'Mr O'Hara, do you recall a briefing where I explained one of the pathologists working the case believed the murderer had a degree of medical knowledge?'

O'Hara's eyes brightened. 'I do recall, yes. And I don't. Have medical experience, I mean. I'm a cop, pure and simple, and a bloody good and honest one at that.'

Danskin's tone mellowed again. 'As Detectives, we choose a topic to specialise in, should there be a need for additional expertise. Me, I chose Approaches to Major Enquiries. What was yours, Acting DI Jarrod?'

'Hostage and Crisis Negotiation.'

'What about you, DC O'Hara? What did you choose to study?'

'Sexual Assault,' Gavin whispered.

Danskin blurted out the next question, hoping to catch Gavin off-guard.

'Are you a sadomasochist?'

Gavin's eyes widened. 'Like fuck I am!'

'For the tape, that's a '*No*',' Ryan half-smiled.

Danskin stood again. Thrust his hands in his pockets and wandered back-and-forth.

'Are there any other tasks you undertake within the station?' he asked.

Gavin closed his eyes. He knew where this was leading.

'I'm a first-aid officer.'

'Yes, you are. What qualification do you hold?'

Gavin sighed. 'Level Four.'

Danskin leant over Ryan and picked a sheet of paper from the folder.

'Ah yes: Level Four.' He read out from the note. '*A Level 4 first aid qualification allows a person who has completed their basic subjects to gain a possible career in emergency services and high-risk work environments.*'

His eyes locked with O'Hara's.

'It goes on to say: '*This qualifies them for a career in ambulance services, medical response units, and other urgent care professions.*'

Gavin swore under his breath.

'I'd say,' Danskin continued, 'That gives you more than a tiny smidgeon of medical knowledge, wouldn't you?'

Before Gavin could continue, the interview room door opened without a knock.

The custody sergeant took a step forward to block the entrance, then stood back when he saw who it was.

'Stephen,' was all Superintendent Maynard said as her eyes ordered Danskin to step outside.

'Interview suspended,' he growled as he flicked off the recording.

In the corridor outside, Maynard slammed shut the door to the interview suite.

'What the hell do you think you're doing?'

'I'm interviewing our only identified suspect, ma'am.'

'Without his solicitor being present?'

Danskin shrugged.

'You did offer him one, didn't you?'

'He knows the drill.'

'But did you offer him one? On the tape?'

'No, ma'am. I didn't.'

She hissed a breath. 'I don't know where to start on this, I really don't. There's more cock-ups here than in a seventies porn movie.'

'Ma'am...'

'Don't *Ma'am* me, Stephen! Firstly, you shouldn't be conducting this interview. Not on such a serious allegation as this. You've a conflict of interest; a fucking almighty conflict. This must be an independent investigation.'

'Fair enough...'

'Secondly, without a solicitor present, anything he's told you is inadmissible. If it is O'Hara – and pray God it isn't – you've probably thrown the case down the toilet.'

Stephen smiled. 'Good.'

Maynard stared at him, dumbstruck.

'I don't think O'Hara's capable of these crimes but he's left himself wide open to accusations, especially as he's pretty vulnerable with stuff he's got going on,' Danskin explained.

'And I know there's a helluva lot of circumstantial evidence linking him to the crime scenes. Anyone else, and I'd say he was our man for sure. But I also say, *'Don't see what you expect to see'*.

'Are you sure the evidence is circumstantial?'

He hesitated. 'It is, but it's damning, all the same. I interviewed O'Hara to see how he'd stand up under questioning.'

'And did he?'

'To be honest, no. In fact, he was so shite, it can't possibly be him. A calculating killer would be far better under pressure than he was.'

Sam Maynard shook her head so violently her brain rattled. 'I don't believe I'm hearing this. If it is O'Hara, you've just given him a bloody dress rehearsal.'

'A risk worth taking, in my opinion.'

'What in that mixed-up head of yours leads you to that conclusion?'

'Well, if O'Hara is our man, we can make a winning case against him even if he performs better next time. And, if he isn't, we've ruled out one suspect. It lets us get back to proper coppering on other suspects.'

'Of which there are none.'

'I disagree. We've JayKay's bar staff, for three. Then there's the man who left JayKay's with Coulson 'cos, by heaven, I'm gonna track that bugger down. We'll talk to the vampire clones who found Usher's body, and I'll tear down those dodgy clubs brick-by-sodding-brick if I have to 'til I find every last one of the pervs who get their sad little kicks there.'

Maynard whistled. 'You'd better be right, Stephen. For all our sakes.'

'I think I am, ma'am.'

'Right. But you have NOTHING more to do with O'Hara. I'm calling in Jane Wilmott from North-West Borders to formally interview DC O'Hara.'

Stephen smiled. 'I'm pleased I gave him a rough time. She's a bit of a hard nut hersel', from what I've heard.'

'You'd better sort this out quickly, Stephen. Wilmott will slice through Gavin's defence like a knife through butter, solicitor or no solicitor, once she arrives.'

Maynard stared at Stephen with eyes as hard as Arctic ice. 'Gavin will be in custody until Wilmott gets here. I want this case nailed shut before she gets her claws into him.'

'Roger, ma'am.' Danskin gave a mock salute.

The Super sighed. 'Look, I'm sorry I was hard on you. You know that's not my style. But, Jeez, the damage you could have done…'

'Apology accepted. And, for what it's worth, you're right in everything you said.'

She offered him an apologetic smile. 'Thank you.'

Maynard reached for the interview suite door as Danskin started to speak.

'Oh, and ma'am?'

'Mm-huh?' She turned towards him.

'I like it when you're angry,' he winked.

TWENTY-ONE

'Listen up, everyone.'

Danskin clapped his hands to win attention. The hum of noise slowly faded to a silence broken only by the rain battering against the windows.

'Time's racing on. We've three victims now and at least one killer though, quite possibly, we're looking at two. We all know the first forty-eight hours are crucial. We lost that advantage with the first two victims. It's not happening with the third.'

He removed the crime scene photograph of Jordan Usher from the board and held it aloft.

'This lass gives us an opportunity we didn't have with the first two. Now, Aaron Elliot has promised to fast-track the post-mortem and tox tests. He's looking for similarities with the first two murders. Any major differences – and there appear to be plenty from my perspective - point to the latest killing,' he waved Jordan's photograph above his head, 'Being the work of one man, not two.'

He looked from face-to-face so they understood the significance. 'If it is a sole killer, find him and squeeze him 'til his balls come out his gob. He'll give us his accomplice on a silver platter.'

'And if we don't find him?' Lucy dared ask.

'That isn't an option. You lot,' he moved his arm in a semi-circle until his extended finger picked out everyone, 'Are the best. Dexter, you go and talk to the blokes who found her.'

'Again?'

'Yes, *'again'*. Trebilcock and Sangar, continue searching for similar cases. Go wide, if needs be. As for you, Robson, I want you trawling through every statement we've got from folk who were at the festival. Anything odd, you highlight it. Understand?'

'Sir.'

'Jarrod and me are going to talk to the JayKay lot. I think there's more gannin' on there than they're telling us.'

'What aboot Gavin?' Todd asked.

Ravi Sangar looked to the floor. Ryan shifted his weight from right foot to left. 'O'Hara's on a separate task for the Super,' he lied.

Danskin moved on before anyone had time to question him further.

'Right, you've DCI Kinnear's team at your disposal to help with anything you need. By the time Jarrod and I get back, I want answers.'

**

The clouds wept a torrent of tears. Rain speared down, straight and silvery, like a hail of arrows. Despite the city setting, lava-red leaves and others of burnished brown lay prostrate in pooling water on the footpath.

Danskin and Jarrod bowed their heads in deference to the elements as they sploshed towards JayKay's. Once inside, they shook themselves like a pair of soaked spaniels.

The interior was warm and, more importantly, dry. Although JayKay's had been open less than an hour, it had attracted a goodly number of customers.

Behind the bar, John Kaye and Charles Proudlock stood at opposite ends of the counter. Kaye was hunched over a chalkboard updating a list of cask ales while Proudlock chatted to a punter as he poured the man a pint.

Danskin made himself familiar with the set-up: the gaming machine Coulson had sat at, the position of the security camera, and the shadow their killer had hidden in.

He also surveyed the customers. He dismissed the females and focused on the men. Three were elderly and grey-haired; two of whom so frail they looked barely able to lift a chopstick let alone a wooden stake.

A flamboyantly dressed young man caressed the thigh of an effeminate looking guy. At the neighbouring table, another young man typed studiously on a laptop.

By the window, a man with a shaven and tattooed head drank at a table alongside a gaunt looking man while, by the bar, a red-haired man with a grey-tinged beard garnered the attention of Charles Proudlock.

Although the security footage had revealed almost nothing of their suspect, Danskin was confident their man wasn't one of this lot.

Ryan spoke quietly. 'Should I take Kaye and you Proudlock?'

The DCI considered the prospect. Both he and Jarrod craved sleep. They'd been at it all day and night and halfway through another day. This was when mistakes were most likely to creep in.

'Nah, we'll do them both so we don't miss owt.'

'And do we see them together or separately?'

'Normally, I'd say separately. But y'knaa what, I'd like to see how they bounce off each other. Let's talk to them at the same time.'

Ryan approached Kaye. His shadow fell over the publican's chalkboard, which he pushed aside and said, 'What can I get you... oh, it's you again,' as he looked up. 'Quite the regular these days.'

Ryan tried to judge whether the man's smile was forced or natural. The jury was out. 'We'd just like to ask you a couple more questions.'

'We?'

Ryan glanced in the direction of Danskin who was having the same conversation with Charles Proudlock. 'Yes, my DCI and me.'

Kaye hid the chalkboard beneath the counter. 'Okey-dokey, then. Who first?'

'Both of you together.'

'I'm sorry, that's not possible. I mean, I know our customers are loyal but even they'd help themselves if we left the bar unattended.'

'I'll cover if you've got summat on.' The voice came from the room which housed the old VCR equipment. A young, pale-faced woman with pig tails and wearing a black sweatshirt emblazoned with *'Stranger Things'* appeared in the doorway.

'No,' John Kaye said, hurriedly. 'We'll manage.'

'Sherry Proudlock?' Ryan asked.

'The very same.' Her words were jovial but vocalised in a downbeat manner.

Ryan studied her. She was attractive in an understated way despite the dark shadows beneath her eyes and her insipid manner. She was the polar opposite of her bleached blond, tanned father.

'Good. Thank you, Miss Proudlock. I think that's settled, then, Mr Kaye, don't you?'

Kaye had no option but to comply.

'I'd like a word with you, Sherry, after we've spoken to your father and Mr Kaye.' He saw her face sag. 'Don't worry,' Ryan smiled, 'It's purely routine.'

'That's what they always say,' she smiled.

This time, Ryan was sure the smile was forced.

**

In the shabby-chic lounge of the flat above JayKay's, Danskin did most of the talking.

'Mr Proudlock, if I could begin with you, you were working the night William Coulson was killed, I believe.'

'Yes.'

'Did you spot anything unusual?'

Proudlock glanced towards Kaye. 'Not that I can recall. It was a very busy night. I was concentrating on serving our patrons.'

'Ah yes. Your regulars, I believe Mr Kaye described them as to Acting DI Jarrod.'

'We have a committed following, you could say,' Proudlock said, twisting a chunky ring on his middle finger.

'So you'd spot someone who wasn't a regular?'

Proudlock took another look towards his partner. 'Not necessarily. I mean, we were busy.'

Danskin asked Kaye the next question. 'Yet, you immediately knew Coulson was a stranger. How come, if the bar was so busy?'

Kaye rolled his eyes. 'As I told your young colleague here the first time we spoke, it's my name above the door. It's my responsibility to look out for troublemakers.'

Danskin folded his arms. 'Did you notice any other strangers that night?'

Without pausing for thought, Kaye told him he hadn't.

Ryan produced a photograph of Gavin O'Hara. 'Have either of you ever seen this man?'

Both detectives held their breath, praying they got the answer they wanted, as Kaye and Proudlock studied the photograph. Ryan noticed the picture shook slightly. One of those holding it was nervous. He couldn't tell which.

'I don't know him,' Kaye said.

'Not one of our regulars,' Proudlock added. 'Who is he?'

'He was in the bar the night Coulson died.'

'Do you suspect him, now? Not the bloke who left with Coulson?'

Danskin shook his head. 'We're just checking how observant you are. You've told us you have your regular customers, that you watch out for strangers, yet neither of you saw this man nor recognised the man who left with Coulson.'

John Kaye startled them by jumping to his feet. 'I resent your insinuations. I think you need to remember it was me who came forward to say I'd seen the poor man who was killed, it was me who was able to describe the other man to your sketch art...'

'You didn't, though, did you?' Ryan interrupted.

'Didn't what?'

'Describe the man. You described yourself to her, didn't you? We've already had this conversation.'

Kaye removed his glasses and rubbed his eyes. 'That's not fair. I've done everything to help your enquiry. Everything. And now, you're treating as me a suspect.'

Danskin's eyes narrowed. 'Where were you on Hallowe'en?'

'What? Where did that come from?'

'Answer the question, please.'

'I was working. Here. With Charles and Sherry.'

'All night?'

'Yes.'

Ryan observed Proudlock glance to the carpet. 'Can you vouch for that, Mr Proudlock?'

'Of course I can.'

'So, you don't mind if we look at more of your security footage, then?'

Kaye and Proudlock stared at one another. 'We don't have any.'

Ryan through his arms up in mock surprise. 'Oh really. Very convenient.'

John Kaye sat down. Took the hand of Charles Proudlock. Stared at the floor as he said, 'I went out for a while.'

'Anywhere special?'

Kaye shook his head.

'Where, then?'

Tears welled in Kaye's eyes. 'To meet a friend.' He glanced at Proudlock but quickly averted his eyes. 'I'm sorry, Charles. Really, I am.'

Proudlock clenched his fist until his knuckles bleached white. 'And here's me thinking you were distracted by money troubles. Who the hell is it?'

'I'd rather like to know that, too,' Danskin added.

'He's called Tim. He lives in Heaton, but we weren't at his. We went to a concert.'

Danskin gave an ironic smile. 'Where was this?' He already knew but Kaye had to say it.

'Tynemouth.'

Ryan and Stephen Danskin led John Kaye out through the bar, as subtly as they could. It seemed every customer was waiting for service.

They soon realised why.

The bar was unattended.

Sherry Proudlock was nowhere to be seen.

TWENTY-TWO

With a second suspect now in custody, Sam Maynard ordered Ryan and the DCI to get some sleep. She delegated responsibility for interviewing Kaye under caution to Rick Kinnear, who brought in Hannah Graves to assist.

Maynard told Todd Robson and Lucy Dexter to take a break before coming back to relieve Trebilcock for his powernap. To no-one's surprise, Ravi Sangar refused the offer of a break.

With the operation running like a well-oiled machine, Superintendent Maynard messaged both the DCI and Jarrod, telling them she didn't want to see them back on duty until the next day.

When the next day dawned, Ryan was in for a shock.

'I hear I've got masel' a wee bit of competition,' Lyall Parker smiled, teeth gleaming from beneath a suntan.

'I wasn't expecting you back yet.'

'Aye, well, when the Super called me, I thought I'd best get masel' in rather than skulk aboot at home.'

'Right. So, where does that leave me?'

'Don't worry, laddie. I'm just an extra pair o' hands on this case. You keep doing what you're doing, which is bloody well, I'm told. I won't be back properly until this is all sorted.'

Danskin walked across and shook Lyall warmly by the hand. 'Good break?'

'It was good to get some sun, I can tell ye. And I gather sun is the last thing our killer would want to see, if I'm hearing right.'

Ryan agreed. 'Aye, it's an odd one, for sure. You're probably in a better position to fill us in on our vampire or otherwise.

The Graveyard Shift

You'll have a more up-to-date picture than us two. What's the latest?'

Lyall gestured towards the crime board where John Kaye's picture had joined the other images on the board.

'We've released this bugger.'

'What?'

'We've nae evidence. We spoke to the man he was with on Hallowe'en. He showed us a couple of selfies of him and Kaye all touchy-feely in front of the stage at Prior's Park. He also showed us some even more touchy-feely photos, if you ken what I mean, back in his hoose in Heaton.'

'He said they weren't Heaton.'

'He's been economical wi' the truth. The second photographs clearly show the clock above the bed. They were taken around the same time as the lassie was killed.'

Danskin swore. 'Kaye didn't want to tell us in case it upset precious Charles even more, I suppose.'

'Aye. And Ravi has rerun the security footage from the night Coulson was killed. Kaye – or at least his hands – were there all neet.'

Ryan sighed. 'I still can't get me heed around why he'd describe himself for the identikit session.'

'I agree it looks like him but, until we find the real culprit, we won't know. Perhaps he has a doppelganger.'

'Or a twin?' Ryan asked more in hope than expectation.

'Sorry, lad: no siblings. If it's any consolation, we released him under investigation so you can call him back anytime you want.'

Ryan stared out the window at weather as miserable as his mood. 'I'll have a word with Hannah. She was in on the interview.'

'Don't think she'll have much to add,' Lyall warned him.

'We could have a chat with Proudlock's daughter. Find out why she did a runner before we could talk to her, like.'

Danskin rested a hand on his shoulder. 'Let it go, Jarrod. We've got to move on and find the bugger who walked out of JayKay's with Coulson.'

Ryan glanced at his watch. 'Shit! I forgot. The woman from North-West Borders is due today, isn't she?' It dawned on him what he'd said. Glanced towards Lyall Parker.

'I know about Gavin,' he whispered.

'What else do you know?' Ryan urged. 'What have we missed? We've got to find our killer or else Gavin's the only one in the frame.'

What Lyall told them filled neither Jarrod nor Danskin with much hope. There was still no word about the post-mortem. No-one had come up with a theory why the killer (or killers) would turn their attention to a female victim, or why he'd change methods.

Ravi hadn't found any remotely similar case in the city, Northumberland, Durham, or Teesside, dating back the fifteen years he checked. He'd only begun to widen the parameters to take in neighbouring regions.

Nigel Trebilcock had undertaken an eye-opening tour of torture chambers, punishment cells, and witnessed all manner of unfathomable hoists and pulleys, masks and chains, whips and collars, hosted by, and housed in, the three SM clubs.

He found all those things, but no murderous vampires. When he'd returned to Forth Street, an ashen Trebilcock had told Lyall, 'I'll stick with ever goos and the faes from now on, if you's don't mind.'

In short, they had diddley-squat.

'What now, sir?' Ryan asked.

Danskin shrugged his shoulders. 'The only thing we CAN do. Go over everything again. And bloody quickly. We haven't much time.'

The Graveyard Shift

Lucy Dexter bustled over to them. 'Dr Elliot's doing the post-mortem, sir. He's asking who's attending for us.'

'We haven't time, man. Can't he just tell us what he finds? I mean, we know how this one died. She had a stake through her heart. All I need to know is, if she was drugged.'

'I'll tell him, sir.' She hurried back to her desk.

'Sangar,' Danskin shouted. 'Where are we on similar cases?'

'I've made a start on southern Scotland and I'm running a program to interrogate Yorkshire's crime history database. I thought it made sense to start nearby and move outwards.'

'Sound thinking. What is it now, Dexter?' Danskin said as Lucy appeared at his shoulder.

'It's Dr Elliot. He says there's something you really should see.'

'I'm too busy to trail halfway across toon.' He glanced around. Caught the eye of the nearest DC. 'Robson, get your ugly mug ower to the mortuary. You're needed at a post-mortem.'

'*I'm* needed, am I? Me? Nobody else, like?'

'Yes, Robson. You. Now, go.'

Robson went.

'Sir,' Ryan said, 'I've had a thought. I know you told us to go over everything afresh. Have you enough resource to let me check something new out?'

Danskin looked at him with a cocked eyebrow. 'Onto something?'

'It's a longshot, but if we're right in thinking we're looking for two murderers, I might be.'

'Then what are you waiting for, man? Piss off and do it. And keep me informed, yeah?'

**

'Do you never do any work?' she said.

'I am working, man.'

Muzzle gave what passed for a smile. 'Am I assisting you with your enquiries, officer?'

'Look, I'm freezing me nuts off here. Can I just come in?' Ryan urged.

Muzzle looked up and down the terrace. 'What's the password?'

'Just let me in, yeah?'

She kept him waiting on the doorstep, watched as a cold wind swirled a scattering of sodden leaves discarded by the trees at the top end of Hulne Terrace. A DPD truck turned into the lower end from Lemington Road. Muzzle watched it approach until she saw it continue beyond her house.

'Bollocks. I thought it was my new gaming chair.'

'Sod your sodding gaming chair. Let me in, man, woman!'

Satisfied she'd left him hanging long enough, she stood aside with a smirk.

Ryan's brother didn't look up from the sofa until the consul in his hands brought a nasty end to several orcs and a shadowy ring-wraith on the wall mounted screen.

Gorefest complete, James paused the game. 'Aal reet, Ry? Thanks for the ticket, by the way.'

'Never again, though. You're a bloody jinx, do you know that?' He felt bad but had to add, 'Do you mind leaving me and your lass together for, like, ten minutes?'

James turned to look at his brother. 'Aye, nee bother. What's up?'

'Nowt, really. I just want to pick her brains on summat for a minute.'

James pushed himself up from the sofa. 'Just make sure she doesn't handcuff you and string you from the ceiling,' he smiled.

Ryan hoped it was just a turn of phrase but, after what he'd discovered about Muzzle on his last visit, he couldn't be sure.

Once James had left the room, his girlfriend spoke. 'Let me guess: we're going to talk vampires again?'

The Graveyard Shift

'Kind of, aye. Boot that laptop up, will you?'

While she retrieved the device from beneath a pile of vinyl records by a host of bands Ryan hoped never to hear, he explained what help he needed.

'Last time I was here, you mentioned chatrooms and such like.'

'For vampires? Yes, I remember.' She flipped up the laptop lid and entered the string of nonsense which was her password.

'I'm guessing you know how to get into the dark web?' Ryan asked.

She looked at him, her facial piercings squirming this way and that as her face contorted. 'No comment,' she said.

It made Ryan think of Gavin O'Hara's interview and spurred him on. 'If you don't know the dark web, tell me now. If you do, get on it and show me one of these chatrooms.'

Muzzle threw back her head and cackled like a witch. 'You really have no idea, do you?'

'No, I don't. That's why I'm here, man.'

'You don't need go on the dark web for that kind of thing.'

'Seriously? It's all above board?'

She hesitated. 'Sort of. Here, I'll show you.'

Her fingers flew over the keyboard. She'd typed in *'Websites for vampires'* 'Which one would you like?'

Ryan gawped at the screen. He blinked rapidly. The top of the screen read *'3.5 million hits.'*

'Bloody hell! Millions? Hadawayandshite. Never,' Ryan exclaimed, once he'd rediscovered his voice.

The first line read, *'Vampire Rave is the social networking website for vampires and goths. We are a home for real vampires around the globe.'*

Beneath it, a description of a second website: *This is a unique Real Vampire website for vampires as well as the curious. It has valuable information for all us real vampires.'*

Another: *Real vampire website: for real vampires and people wanting to learn or meet about real vampires.*

And so the list went on.

'I can't get me heed round this,' he whispered.

She chuckled. 'Let's narrow it down a bit.' She searched for *'Vampire chatrooms'*, before adding *'UK'* as an afterthought.

'Great,' Ryan moaned. 'Only five-hundred thousand hits.'

She put speech marks either side of the search quote and tried again.

'Twenty-two thousand. Howay, man: that's still crazy.'

Ryan looked down the list, ordered by most relevant.

Vampirechat.co.uk
Vampirechatcity.net
Vampirechatcity.com
Vampiresingleschat.com.

'Try that last one,' Ryan demanded.

Muzzle opened the screen and Ryan's jaw almost dislocated.

'Bloody hell, they've got actual photos on! Why would you?' Then, he realised what a bonus that was - they could find their man!

Of course, there were no names alongside the photographs. Just nicknames.

'Ah, man. It's like your lot,' he proclaimed. 'All handles and such shit.'

'You didn't expect owt else, surely?'

He looked at some of the names. 'Blood Lust,' 'Diabolo,' 'Bat 69,' 'Morticia', 'Return to Darkness,' 'Nosferatu.'

Thirty pages, each with thirty profiles. And that was just one site. Ravi Sangar was going to have his work cut out with this.

Ryan made a note of the search terms Muzzle had used. 'Cheers, Germaine...'

The Graveyard Shift

'Muzzle.'

'Aye, her an' all. I need to get back to the station.'

He stood to leave. Spoke over his shoulder.

'I had absolutely no idea. None, at all.'

'You've never lived,' Muzzle smirked.

**

Todd Robson trudged towards the mortuary with the enthusiasm of a man on his way to watch a Steve Bruce team.

The sight of a corpse didn't bother him. He'd seen more than a few in his time and he wasn't especially squeamish. It was the smell he couldn't abide, the chemicals, the stench of decomposition, the lingering odour of excrement; the whole nine yards.

He wasn't a regular presence at post-mortems but, when called upon, he always had a nose clip to hand. Except for today.

'Bloody great,' Todd mumbled as a search of his pockets found nothing but small change and his mobile. He peered through the window of Aaron Elliot's lab and was relieved to see he'd missed the main event.

The remains of Jordan Usher were covered by a green sheet, apart from those bits of her stored in jars of formaldehyde on a metal bench.

Todd shrugged into a protective suit two-sizes too small and tapped on the glass. He saw Elliot's eyes narrow with a frown until the pathologist recognised Robson. Aaron Elliot beckoned Todd to enter.

'Here goes nowt,' he said to himself as he slipped the loops of a facemask around his ears.

'DC Robson, isn't it? I'd shake hands but, well…you know.' Elliot held out bloodied gloved hands in demonstration.

'Nee bother,' Todd assured him, shrinking away. 'Listen, doc – I've got a shedload of stuff on back at the station so can we get this over with sharpish?'

'Of course, of course. I understand.'

Todd dove straight in. 'So, was the lass drugged?'

'We need to run more extensive tests but, the ones we've tested for such as excessive alcohol, nitrous oxide, and GHB; no. Also, there's no trace of the usual Class A substances we'd expect to see in a habitual user.'

Todd kept Elliot between himself and the smelly bits of Jordan Usher suspended in the specimen jars. 'What about the injection of air Cavanagh suspected?'

Elliot shook his head. 'No injections or extractions of any kind, as far as we can ascertain.'

Todd sighed. 'Aal reet, then. In that case, what's so urgent for us to be here?'

Robson was sure he saw Dr Elliot's eyes smile as he said, 'Come here. There's something I'd like to show you.'

He moved towards the green shroud. Todd followed.

'Tell me what you make of this.'

Aaron carefully and neatly folded the sheet in on itself until Jordan Elliot's face was exposed, her hair carefully arranged over one eye, the other open and opaque.

Elliot folded the covering down once more, revealing Jordan's breasts – small, immature, even – and the ragged cavern between them. With the stake removed, the hole appeared much larger, the damage caused to her organs barely imaginable.

Todd swallowed hard and tried his best NOT to imagine, or to look at the pickled organs on the bench.

Elliot put another fold in the shroud.

His eyes never left Todd Robson as he made one final fold.

Aaron Elliot saw Robson's pupils widen, then dilate as they subconsciously tried to unsee what they'd seen.

'Holy shit!' Todd gasped.

TWENTY-THREE

For the first time in years, Ryan felt uncomfortable leading the update meeting. It wasn't the subject matter, weird though it was to have dating websites for vampires as the headline topic.

No, it was the fact DI Lyall Parker was in the huddle. Deep down, Ryan knew Parker wouldn't mind, he'd all but given Ryan his blessing - yet it didn't sit well with him; didn't feel right.

When Ryan told the squad the facts and figures about the on-line vampire presence, they were as astonished he was when he'd first seen them. As a team, they wondered how they could possibly trawl through all the data in the time they had.

'Is there any chance the Super will let us have Gavin back to help with this?' Lucy asked.

Ryan managed to avoid looking even more uncomfortable as he told her there was no chance.

Lucy's gaze wandered to Ravi Sangar.

'Divvent look at me,' Ravi said. 'I've enough on me plate searching the records for anything resembling our killer's methods.'

'No luck, I take it,' Ryan assumed.

'None. What I was thinking, rather than spread the net even wider at this stage, I might look at cold cases. Check if there's owt similar that hasn't resulted in a conviction.'

Ryan pursed his lips. 'Good call, Rav.' He didn't add, '*You should have thought of that earlier.*' 'Really, though, we could do with you looking at both aspects.'

'I'm only one man, Ry. Give us a break, man.'

Ryan looked towards Danskin for support, but it came from Parker.

'I'll give you a hand.'

'You? With respect, sir, your less tech-savvy than Todd,' an exasperated Sangar said.

'Aye, that's as maybe but you said you'd set a program running, didn't you? Evena technological luddite like me can monitor the outputs to see if it comes up trumps,' Parker said, before adding with a wink, 'Assuming you've got your programming right, of course.'

The door to the floorplate opened. A desk-sergeant appeared with a grey-haired woman in tweed skirt and sensible shoes walking by his side. She carried a battered attaché case in her right hand.

'Bollocks,' Danskin whispered to himself as his team's eyes followed the woman. It gave Ryan a chance to mouth, '*Jane Wilmott?*' in the DCI's direction.

Danskin nodded in the affirmative.

'Okay,' Ryan said, recapturing attention, 'This gets more urgent by the minute. We need answers NOW. Let's focus on the job, people. Briefing over.'

'Not yet, it's not,' Todd Robson panted as he stumbled onto the floorplate and belatedly joined the group.

'Are you okay, Robson?' Danskin asked.

Todd didn't answer. 'Elliot's finished the post-mortem. No drugs in the victim's system.'

'That's no bad thing, I suppose. Indicates we're on the right lines in believing it's a separate killer.'

'Had on, though,' Robson continued. 'Unfortunately, the PM also brought to light a similarity we thought didn't exist between this and the previous cases.'

'Enlighten us all, Robson.'

Todd hesitated. Fought for the right words. None came.

'Well,' he said eventually, 'Jordan Usher's not who we thought.'

The Graveyard Shift

'Stop being bloody cryptic, man.'

'Okay, then.' Another pause. 'Let's just say it's not *Jordan* as in Katie Price, more like *Jordan* as in '*Short Arms*' Pickford.'

Some understood, some didn't. To make sure they all got the point, Todd clarified things.

'Jordan Usher: she's all cock and balls.'

**

In the ensuing hubbub, they missed the sight of Sam Maynard shepherding Jane Wilmott towards a lift destined for the interview suite where Gavin's Spanish Inquisition would begin.

Instead, they tried to reassess the Jordan Usher case.

'I'm not sure it makes a huge difference,' Ryan contested.

'Course it does,' Lucy Dexter countered. 'We ruled out the gay connection…'

'Hang on. Don't display your ignorance, here. There's a helluva difference between being gay and being transexual. Let's not go down the stereotype route.'

'Perhaps there is a difference, I admit I'm not well up on these things,' Lucy confessed. 'Regardless, though, we looked at this case differently because we thought we had two male deaths and a female. If it's now three males, we might need to think again.'

Ryan fought to bring his exasperation under control. 'DC Dexter. Jordan Usher *IS* a woman. She mightn't have finished her re-assignment, but she's a woman, nonetheless.'

'What if the killer didn't know? Would it even make a difference?' Trebilcock wondered aloud.

Ryan scratched his head. He was losing the briefing, in danger of losing the team, he might lose the case and, worst of all, he'd possibly already lost Gavin O'Hara to Fraulein Wilmott of Stalag Luft iii.

Fortunately for him, Lyall Parker had his wits about him. He'd watched Maynard and Wilmott leave the floorplate, and now he was seeing a warning light flash on a computer in his peripheral vision.

'Which piece o' kit is your program running on, Ravi?'

'The one next to Lucy's desk,' he said continuing to dispute the significance of Jordan Usher's sexuality.

'You mean the one with the light flashing on it?'

Ravi's head spun towards the kit.

'Sir, we might have something!' he shouted to Danskin.

'I'm reet next to you, man. No need to yell.'

'It looks like we might have a case match. If that's not worth shouting about, I don't know what is.'

Stephen Danskin was long enough in the tooth not to get as excited as Sangar.

'Let's have a look, then, should we? The rest of you get on with your duties. This might be a red herring and we can't afford us all to be sidetracked if it is.'

**

Neither Danskin nor Jarrod thought it was a red herring. Not once they'd read the case notes.

The file belonged to the East Yorkshire and Humber force. A lot of the facts matched the MO of their own cases, especially the Jordan Usher one.

The file was opened on November 3rd, 2015 - two days after the conclusion of Goth weekend in the town of Whitby. The corpse of a man, Bryan Swaine, was discovered in the shadow of Whitby Abbey. He was dressed all in black, wore long false eyelashes and white make up. On his head was what appeared to be the headwear of a World War Two spitfire pilot. He was thirty years of age, single, and a loner.

Most compelling of all, a six-foot pole had been hammered clean through him.

'Bring the post-mortem results up,' Ryan asked.

Ravi obliged. The report detailed the fact Swaine had no underlying medical conditions. No drugs were found in his system. His stomach contents revealed a quantity of whisky and rum, but not sufficient to render him drunk, never mind incapable.

The report made no mention of puncture wounds or bloodletting, apart from the fountain which had erupted from his chest and covered the ground all around him.

The electronic file contained several images. One taken from above, showing the corpse lying on blood-soaked grass between the pillars of the abbey, mirrored the images lifted from Jordan Usher's casefile.

'What do you think?' Danskin almost whispered.

'I think we've got him. Or, if not, if someone saw this happen, they've decided to replicate what they witnessed and settled on our patch to do it.'

'Unlikely to be the latter. This was eight years ago, remember. Why wait until now?'

Ryan shrugged. 'Lack of opportunity, lack of desire, who knows?' He thought for a moment. 'Now, this is a bit of a giant leap of imagination, but what if our man had his fire reignited. Say, by someone he'd met on-line?'

Danskin sucked in breath. 'Don't get ahead of yersel', Jarrod. Mind, it's possible. I'd also ask, what if they've been inside for eight years and only recently released?'

'I'd say either is the best lead we've got.'

'Was that a thank you I heard for my programming expertise?' Ravi asked.

'Nah, not yet. I'll save that 'til we catch the bugger.' Danskin checked his watch. 'On that note, O'Hara's probably getting electrodes attached to his bollocks as we speak. Let's not rest on our laurels. Before we press on, did the Yorkies have anyone in the frame for it?'

Ravi hit a few tabs on the PC and a list appeared.

'What's this?' Ryan asked.

'All those who were interviewed,' Ravi explained.

'There's bloody hundreds of them.'

'Just a minute.' Ravi weaved his magic again.

Three names appeared.

'Who's this?'

'The three main suspects.'

They studied the men's names, and the scant headline details.

'JOHN TOBINS. *Self-employed courier. Forty-two. Unsubstantiated alibi. Insufficient evidence to proceed.*'

'YVES FAVRE. *French national. Thirty-four. Abattoir worker. Allegedly working alone at time of crime. Alibi partially verified. Insufficient evidence to proceed.*'

'JACKSON WEBB. *Construction worker. Ex-forces. Thirty-three. Unsubstantiated alibi. Insufficient evidence to proceed.*'

Danskin swore. 'Is that all we've got?'

'Give us a minute, man,' Ravi complained. 'I've just sat down to this myself.'

He scrolled down a screed of text, speed-reading as he went.

'Have we any photos of the suspects?' Danskin asked.

Ravi raised his eyes to the ceiling and tutted. He stopped what he was doing and opened another window. Three images, standard police mugshots showing the men face-on and in profile, appeared on screen.

Two - Favre and Webb – had dark hair. Tobins was balding.

'One down, two to go,' Danskin smiled. 'Our man, assuming he's the one who left the bar with Coulson, had dark hair on the JayKay security footage.'

'Hang on, though,' Ryan said. 'These photos are eight years old. They could look different now.'

'Aye, but this Tobins bloke isn't going to develop a full head of hair, is he?'

The Graveyard Shift

'The man we saw in the JayKay's recording could be wearing a wig, sir.'

'Bollocks. True enough, Jarrod.'

Danskin scribbled the names on a sheet of notepaper. Looked around the floorplate. 'Dexter,' he called. 'Check these names out, will you? See if there's any of them living in our area.'

'They've quite probably changed their names, sir.'

'Look on the bright side, why don't you?'

Ryan studied the images with the intensity of a big cat stalking a gazelle. 'It's impossible to link any of them to the JayKay video. It's not clear enough.'

Danskin rubbed at an already bloodshot eye. 'Do any of them look remotely like the description Kaye gave?'

'The description of himself, you mean? Nah. I suppose Webb's the closest likeness but that's just off the shape of his face more than owt.'

'Look, I know we're keen to pin this down but let's think it through,' Ravi cautioned. 'We're assuming there's two killers involved in the Coulson and Neill cases, one of whom went rogue with the Usher killing. We've also assumed whoever killed Usher is also responsible for the Whitby murder.'

'Divvent tell us you're doubting your own program, Ravi.'

'No. Not at all. What I'm getting at is, we don't which one of the two we suspect of being involved in our murders is the man leaving with Coulson. It might be the other fella who's the rogue. The one who, if he exists, we've no description. He might be bald,' Ravi pointed at Tobins, 'He might look like, or even be, John Kaye; or he could resemble might look like Li'll Wayne, Fu Manchu, or Mr Blobby. We haven't a clue, have we?'

Stephen Danskin let out air. Ryan thumped the desk.

'You're bloody right again, Sangar.'

'I take it I don't get a thank you for that, either?'

Nobody was in the mood for Ravi's sarcasm. They were all tetchy, worn out – and desperate.

'What else does the file tell us?' Ryan urged.

Ravi sighed and resumed the task of reviewing the Yorkies' report.

'It says here, there was a witness, of sorts.'

'If there was a witness, how come they couldn't press charges?' Ryan wondered.

'I'll get there in a sec.' Ravi speed-read the report, going through a page before Ryan and Danskin managed a paragraph. 'Ah, that explains it. Seemingly, the witness was blind drunk at the time. Had gone up to look for UFOs, would you believe?'

'Given what we know so far, aye; I would,' Ryan commented.

'Okay,' Ravi resumed. 'It seems the witness heard a commotion in the distance. Headed towards it and saw a bloke dashing off. They didn't catch a good look at him.'

Ryan paused for thought. 'So, how did the Yorkies come up with these three as suspects?'

The screen rolled up under the control of Sangar's finger.

'They were spotted on CCTV around the area and around the same time.' The text continued to scroll. 'All three were in an ID parade but the witness failed to pick any of them out.'

'And they didn't pursue things further?'

'The report says the witness was considered unreliable. At fifteen years old, the witness was considered a minor and was already dealing with alcohol issues. It seems the story given didn't entirely add up either, apparently.'

Ravi called up another window over the larger one. The box was too small for Ryan and Danskin to read.

'What are you looking at?' Danskin asked.

Ravi breathed out. His fingers stopped the dance with his keyboard.

'Sir, we've assumed it's two men involved in the case. What if one was female?'

Ryan and Danskin looked at one another. 'I suppose it's possible, if she wasn't the one to wield the stake. What makes you suggest that?'

'Well, the witness was also the person who found the body, which is always suspicious.'

'Is that the best you can come up with?'

'No. It's more who the witness is.'

Ravi Sangar magnified the report so they could all see the script.

Ryan whistled. 'Of all the gin joints in the all the world…' he quoted.

They were staring at a footnote to the report; a footnote which contained details of the 'unreliable witness.'

The name was familiar to them.

Sherilyn Proudlock.

TWENTY-FOUR

Jane Wilmott plopped a sugar cube into a teacup and stirred slowly.

'Samantha, I have to be honest with you, I have absolutely no doubt that your Detective Constable is a guilty man.' She took a sip from the cup, her eyebrows shooting upwards as the hot liquid entered her mouth. 'His solicitor is playing hardball. She's insisting we either release him or charge him.'

'If we don't have the evidence, there's only one thing we can do,' Superintendent Maynard said.

'Oh, we've a few hours yet. Besides, on balance, I think we have more than sufficient evidence. Just not the silver bullet. Not yet.'

Sam Maynard poured bottled water into a glass and took a long drink. 'I've got my team working flat out exploring other lines of enquiry.'

'I think you're wasting resources, Samantha. You already have the murderer in custody. They'd be better employed trying to find said silver bullet,' Wilmott simpered.

Superintendent Maynard's eyes narrowed. 'I have every confidence in my team, thank you very much.'

Wilmott dipped a ginger snap into her tea. She wagged it at Maynard. 'Even DC O'Hara?' she said as she took a bite.

'Innocent until proven guilty, I shouldn't need remind you.'

Wilmott's eyes hardened. 'Which he will be, soon enough.' She drained her cup. 'Thank you for the tea, Samantha. I must press on because time is ticking and I assure you I'll prove O'Hara is as guilty as the sins he's committed.'

Maynard was about to reply when the door opened. It was Hannah Graves. 'Ma'am, Acting DI Jarrod says there's something you need see. We've a major breakthrough, with several names in the frame,' she glanced at Wilmott, 'And none of them are Gavin O'Hara.'

Maynard barely suppressed her satisfaction. 'Thank you, DS Graves, I'll be with you imminently.' She turned to Jane Wilmott. 'It looks like your silver bullet has turned out to be one made of tin foil. Now, if you don't mind, I'll leave you with that thought.'

Wilmott's face darkened. 'We'll see about that,' she said to Sam Maynard's empty office.

**

Danskin left Lyall Parker and Hannah to brief Maynard while the DCI and Ryan beat the familiar route to JayKay's. It wasn't late but it was already dark and the lights inside JayKay's offered the promise of a welcoming warmth within.

A warm welcome was not what they got.

John Kaye had his back to them, fitting spirit bottles to optics, but he caught sight of them courtesy of the mirrored panels behind the dispensers.

'If I didn't know any better, I'd call this harassment,' he said. 'I hope you have a damn good reason for being here.'

Danskin ran a finger along the bar top and inspected it for dust as Ryan spoke. 'It's a public house, Mr Kaye. I'd assumed we'd be welcome anytime.'

'As a customer, perhaps. On duty, definitely not.'

He turned to face them, displaying an eye ringed by blues and purples.

'Bit of a shiner you've got,' Danskin said. 'One of the regulars not so pleasant?'

'Oh, this,' he waved dismissively. 'I walked into a door. A bit of man product will cover it until it fades.'

'I see. Charles not around?' Danskin asked pointedly.

'No. He's out. I have to go soon, too, so what can I do for you this time?'

Ryan took over the baton from Danskin. 'If Mr Proudlock is out, and you're soon to follow, who's looking after the shop?'

'I am,' Sherry said, emerging from the back.

'All by yourself?'

'She'll manage 'til Charles is back. He won't be long,' Kaye said.

'Actually, it's Miss Proudlock we're here to see,' Danskin said.

Kaye took a deep breath and relaxed. Sherry exhaled and stiffened.

'I take it you have no objection?' the DCI asked Kaye.

'As long as it's not here and now, I don't.'

'It doesn't have to be here but it does have to be now.'

'Gentlemen,' Kaye protested, 'We'll be busy soon and, as I've said, I have to go out.'

'Ah, but you also said Mr Proudlock would be back soon,' Ryan pointed out. 'I'm sure you can manage until then.'

Backed into a corner of his own making, John Kaye relented.

'What do you want me for?' Sherry asked.

'Firstly, I presume your full name is Sherilyn, is it?'

'Never been called that for years,' Sherry said as she flicked one pigtail behind her shoulder, 'But yes. That's me.'

Ryan looked around the bar. There weren't many customers but enough so it was a little uncomfortable to talk. 'We've a car waiting outside. I think this is better done at the station.'

'What? Seriously?' she said, blanching.

'Without her father? I don't think so.'

'Mr Kaye, Miss Proudlock doesn't need her father present. She isn't a minor.' Ryan met her gaze. 'Not this time.'

Sherry's eyes told them she knew what was coming.

'I'll be okay, John,' she said without conviction. 'Don't tell my dad. Not yet, anyway.'

The Graveyard Shift

Kaye's hand automatically went to his eye. Sherry's words were the most comforting thing he'd heard all day.

**

'I was working. You know I was,' a defensive Sherilyn Proudlock told Ryan.

'How would we know that?'

She snorted a laugh. 'Because you've got the recording of the night the man was killed.'

'Billy Coulson, you mean. That was his name.'

'Whatever.'

Ryan sat back in his chair. 'We saw three pairs of hands. One of which could belong to you, or they could have been Taylor Swift's, for all we could see.'

She shrugged. 'Not my fault.'

'What about Hallowe'en? Were you working then, too?'

'Aye, me and dad. It was dead as a dodo, mind.'

'But busy enough for us to have witnesses who can say they saw you working?'

Sherry began tapping her foot on the floor. 'Yes.'

'Were you working all night?'

'I got off about, I dunno, half-ten or so.'

Danskin suddenly joined the conversation, the change in voice making Sherry jump.

'Have you ever been to Goth weekend? The one in Whitby?'

There was a slight tremor in Sherry's voice as she replied, 'Couple of times. When I was a kid.'

'Define *'a kid'*?'

'Teenager, I suppose.'

'How about a fifteen-year-old teenager?'

Ryan and Danskin saw a shudder run down Sherry, from head to foot. 'Yes.'

'How about the night of November third, 2015?'

Sherry's foot tapped so quickly the table began to shake.

'Can I have a drink, please?' she said, looking at the jug on the desk.

She used two hands to pour the water yet still some missed the plastic cup.

'I was only a kid. Well, a rebel, really. I'd found out dad was gay a few months before. It really messed with my head, you know? Attitudes have changed a lot in eight years but, at the time, I thought my world had come to an end.'

She took a sip from the cup and moistened her lips with her tongue.

'I was stupid but felt I had to prove something to myself. I started drinking. Cheap cider at first. Then, lager. Soon I was downing vodka like this water.'

Danskin and Ryan were conscious of Gavin O'Hara's clock ticking down but they waited patiently for Sherry to continue.

'Something still wasn't right with me, though. My dad was gay, y'know? I wondered if I might be, too. I mean, I hadn't been with anyone.'

Her eyes took on a faraway look.

'So, that weekend, I kinda' went a bit OTT. Whitby was rammed with folk. They were all a bit weird but I didn't care. I'd come to terms with the fact I was a bit weird, as well. I met this lad, a lanky streak of misery, and he'd been touching me up. I thought what the hell; let's go for it. So, I made a grab for his nuts and, guess what? He ran a fucking mile,' she smiled. 'Turns out he was as naïve as me and I scared him off. He did have a mate, though. A few years older. He'd seen all this and thought I was easy pickings. I suppose I was. Anyway, before he went chasing after the lanky kid, he said he'd meet me the next night at the bottom of the stairs leading to the Abbey.'

Sherry stopped talking. Looked at Ryan and Danskin. 'Before I go on, I'm not under caution or anything, am I?'

The Graveyard Shift

Ryan let Danskin answer. 'No. You've no need for representation. All we want is a better picture of what happened that night.'

She looked between the two of them. Satisfied, she continued. 'I hung about at the bottom of the steps for ages. He was a no-show so I wondered if I'd got it wrong. I started climbing the stairs, which isn't an easy task sober never mind as pissed as I was at the time.'

'Once you got to the top?'

'I sat down on the grass. Lay down, more like, staring at the sky 'til I got my breath back.'

'Is that why you told the police you were looking for UFOs?' Ryan asked.

She gave him a peculiar look.

'Yes,' he said, 'We know you were interviewed as a key witness.'

'That's not what I'm wondering about. It's the UFO bit I don't understand.'

Ryan shrugged. 'Like I say, you told the investigating officers you went up to the Abbey to look for UFOs.'

'Did I?' She paused for thought then burst out laughing at the memory. 'Yes, I remember now. I did. You see, the lad never told me his name so I was looking for an Unidentified Fuck Object.' Sherry laughed again. 'I think I was quite clever coming up with that at the time.'

Danskin rolled his eyes. 'What did you do next?'

'I heard something. I couldn't – still can't – describe the sound. It was…well, spooky, I suppose. I looked up and saw a bloke running in the opposite direction, about fifty yards or so away. It was dark, of course. Almost pitch black, in fact. I couldn't really see who it was. I went over to where I saw him run from. And that's when…' she reached for her cup.

Sherry's hands trembled so much she dropped it. Spilt water over the desk.

'Shit. I'm sorry,' she apologised through tear-filled eyes.

Ryan dug in his pockets and produced a tissue. 'It's okay,' he said, mopping up the spillage.

'Sherry,' Danskin said, 'We're going to show you some photographs. Tell me if you recognise any of these men.'

'It was dark. It was eight years ago. I couldn't describe them then so I certainly won't now.'

Danskin smiled. 'Then, just humour, please. I have to go through the motions.'

'Okay.' She didn't sound enthusiastic.

Ryan slid across an altered image of the Frenchman, Favre. It'd been altered to show the man with dark hair.

Sherry studied it and shook her head.

Next, John Tobins.

'Never seen him in my life, as far as I can tell.'

'Are you sure?'

'As sure as I can be, yes.'

Danskin's hand stopped Ryan pulling out the third photograph. Instead, the DCI produced the sketch Kaye had drawn.

'John told me he'd done it.'

Danskin and Ryan's heartrate leapt.

'John Kaye told you he did it?' Ryan sought clarity.

She nodded. Looked at the detectives. Saw the look on their faces. 'Oh, no. Not that. He didn't kill anyone. I meant he told me he'd described himself to you.'

Danskin deflated.

'Did he tell you why?' Ryan asked.

She nodded. 'John's a nice man. He was trying to protect me.'

'I'm sorry, Sherry; you're not making sense.'

'He told me you'd wanted a description of the suspect. The one who left with...'

The Graveyard Shift

'Billy Coulson.'

'Yes. Well, John knew you'd be back again and again if he didn't come up with something. He didn't really notice the bloke in any detail, but he wanted to stop you coming to the bar. So, he came up with the first description he could think of. Himself. He didn't think you'd cotton on it was him and thought you'd spend your time elsewhere looking for a man who didn't exist rather than pester me and Dad.'

Danskin puffed out his cheeks. Ryan asked, 'Why did Mr Kaye think you needed protecting?'

She looked away.

'Sherry?' he persisted.

'After what I saw that night, alcohol didn't do it for me anymore. I needed something else to dowse the memories.'

'Drugs,' the DCI realised.

'Yes,' she nodded. 'Lots of them. They don't work, though. I still get the memories. The flashbacks. In here,' she poked a finger at her temple. 'All the time. I'll never forget what I saw. John didn't want you to bother me in case you found I was on drugs. That's the sort of protection he was offering me.'

Ryan and Danskin gave Sherry time to collect herself. They realised how traumatic the sight of the skewered man must have been to an already troubled teen.

The silence was interrupted by a knock on the interview room door. Hannah Graves opened it.

'We have something,' she said.

Danskin nodded for Ryan to continue while he stepped outside to hear what his team had uncovered.

'We've discovered the whereabouts of the three Whitby suspects. Yves Favre's out the frame. He's working in a slaughterhouse in the Rhone Valley. Tobins is living in Robin Hood's Bay. We've got the Yorkies onto it as I speak.'

'What aboot Webb?'

'What about him, indeed. Turns out he's from Newton Aycliffe.'

Danskin nodded. 'Close enough,' he said.

'Aye, but there's more. Seemingly his employer's a sub-contractor and Jackson Webb's out on a building job. Guess where?'

'The toon.'

'Right in one. He's working on the development of the new office complex down Pilgrim Street.'

Danskin was on his way back into the interview room before Hannah finished the sentence.

Inside, Sherry was chuckling at the sight of an unmasked Yves Favre, telling Ryan the fake hair he'd put on Favre had been a pathetic disguise.

'Show her Webb!' Danskin demanded.

Ryan pulled the last picture from the folder. Sherry took it from him. Held it up and studied it.

'I don't recognise him...'

'Ah hell. Are you positive?' Danskin pressed.

'If you'd wait for me to finish,' she chastised. 'I don't recognise him from Whitby. I couldn't possibly tell if it's the bloke I saw that night or not, but I do recognise him.'

Danskin gave a contented smile. 'Where do you know him from, Sherry?'

'From JayKay's. He's not a regular, but I've seen him a couple of times.'

She picked up the photograph again.

'Yep, that's definitely where I know him from.'

TWENTY-FIVE

They made sure Sherry Proudlock was okay to return to JayKay's so she could cover for the proprietor's 'urgent appointment' elsewhere. Ryan arranged transportation for her while Danskin stepped outside. Once he'd sorted things for Sherry, he joined his DCI.

'Howay, Jarrod: we've a million things to do. We must find Webb and bring him in. He's probably going under an alias. He might be renting a property, or in a hotel, or a B&B. He might even be in a caravan. He could be bloody anywhere. Right, we'll go over forensic reports for all the crimes. See if there's any DNA, blood, prints, owt at all.'

'Sir, we've done forensics to death…'

Danskin jabbered on, his mind working overtime. 'It makes sense, y'know. What Proudlock's just told us. We said whoever took Coulson had prior knowledge of the security cameras in JayKay's. If Webb's been there a couple of times, he'll have had ample opportunity to scout 'em out. Angles, coverage; the works.'

Danskin stopped talking. Swayed slightly. 'Whoa,' he said. 'I think I've just hit the proverbial wall. I'm exhausted.'

'So am I, the way you've been rabbiting on. Listen, tomorrow's going to be full-on. Why not call it quits for tonight? Uniform can do all the donkey work on Webb. Then, you'll be bright as a button to start grilling him once they haul him in.'

Stephen Danskin hated being defeated but he knew Ryan was right. He remembered what he'd said to Ryan earlier: *'This is when mistakes happen.'*

'Aye, son. You're right. In fact, I'll ring upstairs and tell Lyall what we want from uniform, then the whole lot of us can get off. That includes you, Jarrod. And I want you home for a good night's sleep. No kipping at Hannah's, or her yours. Got it?'

Danskin gave Lyall the order to stand down for the night after running through his better-ordered thoughts.

'Right. That's all sorted. Lyall's telling uniform what's needed from them, and he's instructing Aaron Elliot to review the forensics. I wanted Cavanagh to chase up medical information on Jackson Webb but he's off duty. That'll keep 'til tomorrow, I guess.'

Danskin bent forward and lay his hands on his knees. 'You'd think I'd been hit by a freight train.'

'Get yourself home, sir.'

'In a minute. I want to give O'Hara the good news first. He's free to go.'

'I'll see to Gavin; you get off. That's an order,' Ryan smiled, and was surprised when Danskin didn't object.

Ryan collected O'Hara's belongings from the locker and, with a spring in his step, marched to Gavin's holding cell.

'Christ, mate, you look like shit,' Ryan said when he saw the gaunt, unshaven face of his former mentor. 'You look aboot sixty.'

The comment didn't raise a smile. 'Hardly a surprise, is it?'

'Nah, mate; it's not. Anyway, do you want the good news or the bad news?'

'Ry, man. I can't be arsed.'

'The good news,' he said, holding up the package containing Gavin's belongings, 'Is you're free to go.'

Gavin's mouth curled in disdain. 'And I suppose the bad news, you're going to follow it up with a *'For now'*, aren't you?'

Ryan smiled and tore open the sealed flap on the package. 'Nope. We know who the killer is. A bloke called Jackson

The Graveyard Shift

Webb. Once we get him in custody, we'll soon find his partner in crime, assuming there is one.'

Gavin would have smiled if his face hadn't forgotten how to.

'The only bad news, you have to go back to that shitty house of yours,' Ryan joked.

'Better than this dump, I assure you.'

O'Hara checked through his personal items. Keys, phone, wallet, belt: everything seemed to be in order. He signed to acknowledge receipt. He checked his phone was in working order and, while it loaded, looked towards Ryan.

'Nobody thinks I did it, do they? The team, I mean?'

'No Gav; not a single one of us. And, in case you're wondering, that includes the guv'nor and the Super. She gave that Wilmott bitch a dose of her own medicine, from what I hear.'

O'Hara sniffed a laugh, before the tears started. 'Ry, there's something I need to say…'

Gavin's phone connected to the service and a series of messages; six, seven, eight; signalled their arrival with a succession of wolf-whistles. He shoved the phone into his pocket.

'You don't need to say anything, Gav. It's my pleasure.'

'No, you don't understand. There's something I NEED to tell you.'

'Not tonight, yeah? It'll keep 'til tomorrow. I'm off to kip so I can help the gaffer catch this bastard tomorrow.'

Gavin opened his mouth, but was halted by Ryan's, 'No buts, okay?'

Reluctantly, Gavin nodded his agreement.

'Reet,' Ryan announced. 'I'm off yem. I suggest that's what you do, as well.'

As Ryan left the cell with his arm over Gavin's shoulder, a muffled ping came from the depths of O'Hara's pocket.

'There's no way I'm going home,' Gavin thought.

**

Jackson Webb, for the first time, felt uneasy. Not with what was about to happen – his appetite remained unquenched; his primordial need close to the surface once more.

No, he was more concerned about *where* it was happening. It felt too close and too soon.

In the dimly lit corners of The Fluid Fountain, a popular upmarket bar in the Grainger Town area of the city not far from the Centre for Life, shadows danced and secrets lurked.

The air was drowned in a cocktail of scents: aged whisky, fragrant perfumes, musky aftershaves. The rhythmic pulse of music reverberated through the crowd, drowning out whispered conversations and providing cover for the shy, bashful, and curious.

Webb knew he was underdressed for the setting, yet no-one seemed to notice him. Not like him, who already had eyes on a man who flitted from table to table, flirting with people he seemed to know well, and those he didn't know at all.

A second likely target sought solace in the soft glow of the neon signs and the promise of anonymity the crowded bar offered. This, Webb thought, was a more likely candidate.

Webb watched him with an unsettling intensity, eyes the shade of obsidian following his every movement. The target wore a leather jacket the colour of the whisky in his glass. He seemed uncomfortable. Vulnerable, even.

'The weakest of the herd,' Webb thought as he blended seamlessly with the low hum of conversation and clinking glasses.

The man engaged in light banter with the bartender as he sipped his drink. Webb saw him shiver and look around, as if he sensed the eyes on him. Webb didn't care: the man

The Graveyard Shift

wouldn't see him. He'd mastered the art of remaining unseen whilst in plain sight.

As each moment passed, he moved closer to his prey. He positioned himself at a nearby table, never too close to arouse suspicion, yet near enough to maintain an unbroken line of sight.

The prey became more relaxed in the lively ambiance of The Fluid Fountain. As he did so, his guard began to drop. He engaged in conversation with a couple of well-dressed gentlemen, laughed at their jokes, smiled when they smiled.

The couple finished their drinks and left without him.

Webb moved closer to him. Brushed against him. Apologised for spilling his drink. Asked if he could buy him another.

They began talking. Webb discovered the man's name was Eli and he was here on business. Webb smiled. Not at the conversation, but at the fact it meant the man's identity would go unknown for some time, even after his body was discovered in the cemetery.

When Eli nipped to the washroom, Jackson Webb followed.

**

The moon cast a hazy, eerie glow through the bony fingers of naked trees, their discarded clothing scattered along the worn path as a carpet of brown and rust.

The air hung heavy with the ominous odour of moss and decay as the accomplice paced between the tombstones of Westgate Hill cemetery. He checked his watch for the umpteenth time, the ticking echoing in the desolate silence. He'd ordered Webb to be there with the next one by midnight, and the graveyard seemed to hold its breath in anticipation.

He scanned the surroundings, his eyes darting from one crumbling tombstone to the next. He'd selected the oldest section of the cemetery as the rendezvous point, where time had blurred the names and dates into indecipherable etchings.

The wind whispered through the gnarled branches, carrying tales of the long-forgotten souls resting beneath the soil.

Webb's accomplice briefly illuminated the torch he carried with him to ensure he was at the right spot. It was a place veiled in secrecy and shadows; the result of a pact forged in the crucible of their shared history.

As the chimes from a distant church signalled the arrival of midnight, the man extinguished his light and waited.

**

When Eli and Webb returned from the Gents, Eli reflected on their conversation. He didn't know why, but he had a growing sense of unease. There was something about the subtle shift in Webb's behaviour which alarmed him. He felt a knot tighten in his stomach.

'Thank you for the drink,' Eli said. 'It's been a pleasure meeting you but I'd better go.'

'Already?' he saw a look of alarm in the man's eyes so pulled himself back. 'I'll see you home. If you like.' Webb hoped he sounded casual.

'No, it's okay. My hotel's nearby.'

'Honestly, it's no problem,' Webb felt the panic of a lost kill well inside him. He followed Eli out of The Fluid Fountain into the neon lights of the city.

Eli increased his pace. Jackson Webb kept up with him.

'I'm sorry if you think I've led you on,' Eli said in a shaky voice, 'But I'm not interested. Nothing personal; it's not you - I'm just not after sex. I just wanted a night out.'

'Well, that's a shame.' He made a grab for Eli's arm, 'Because I am. Sex, and more.'

'I'll scream,' Eli threatened. 'Don't think I won't.'

The Graveyard Shift

Eli tried to tell himself he held the advantage. That the man didn't know where his hotel was. He'd find sanctuary there. Soon. Very soon.

But not soon enough.

Webb grabbed the man by the throat. Rammed him against a wall. 'You're going to get fucked, my friend. Well and truly fucked.'

Eli brought his knee up into Webb's groin. He gasped for air and released his grip on Eli.

In fewer than twenty paces, Eli was inside the lobby of the Holiday Inn Express, the spell cast over him by The Fluid Fountain and the man with the Devil's eyes well-and-truly broken.

Eli shouted for Reception. 'Call the police. Now!'

He saw the night receptionist's eyes widen. She reached for the phone and began dialling 999.

Eli toyed with his wedding ring. Thought of his wife. His children. The consequences.

'Sorry, no. Don't. It's my mistake. Forget it.'

**

In Westgate Hill Cemetery, Webb's accomplice – or puppeteer, as he preferred to think of himself – checked his watch.

Twelve-twenty.

He strained to hear. Imagined the sound of soft footsteps shuffling through shrivelled leaves, pretended to hear the whispers and giggles of an unsuspecting victim lured towards him, imagined the urgent breathing of an aroused Jackson Webb.

Instead, the only noise was the muffled crunch of gravel beneath his own worn-out boots - until a gust of wind swept through the cemetery, carrying with it the distant wail of a siren.

Distant, but closing.

'Fuck it!'

As the man hurried towards the exit, the gravestones loomed all around him like silent witnesses to a reunion missed.

TWENTY-SIX

A heavy police presence descended on the site of the proposed new Government office complex in Newcastle city centre.

They police vehicles outnumbered the longreach excavators patiently demolishing the interior of the old Carliol House building whilst ensuring its listed façade remained intact.

Huge cranes, so tall they seemed to pierce the clouds, hoisted heavy girders skywards and manoeuvred them into position on the tall structure already taking shape to the south of the Carliol building.

The rumble from the machinery and the roar of traffic disguised the police vehicles approach as they brought their own form of chaos to the normal morning rush hour madness.

With access to and from the Tyne Bridge as well as the city centre itself blocked off, Superintendent Maynard knew she had limited time to apprehend Jackson Webb.

Although uniform hadn't found where Webb was staying overnight, they confirmed where he was working. And his presence on site was easily established. To the astonishment of everyone in the City and County squad, Webb wasn't hiding behind an alias. The site manager knew who Webb was, and where he'd be.

Within ten minutes of arrival, Ryan and Stephen Danskin were shielding their eyes from a silver sunrise, gazing up at the platform of a pale green scissor lift on which four men, identical in Hi-Viz jackets, grubby safety boots, and brightly coloured hard hats, stood.

One of the men turned to lean against the scissor lift railings. He removed his hat and ran a hand through longish vantablack hair.

Ryan was catching his first glimpse of Jackson Webb.

While the lift operator collapsed its layers, a posse of uniformed officers surrounded the platform. It didn't need them all. In fact, one officer would have been sufficient.

As he stepped from the lift into the arms of the constabulary, Jackson Webb remained calm, composed, and completely unflustered. He carried an aura, one which seemed to come with a century of knowledge and the foresight of Nostradamus.

His black eyes settled on Ryan and Danskin as if he knew who they were, and a smile formed on his lips.

'Cocky bastard, isn't he?' Danskin said out the corner of his mouth.

'He doesn't look bothered,' Ryan said, perplexed.

'Aye. Considering he's oot in daylight, it sort of ruins his reputation, though.'

Ryan's eyes were riveted by the man's mesmeric qualities. 'Mebbe. He still gives us the creeps, like.'

'He won't be half as cocky or creepy when I've finished with him. Howay back to the station with us, Jarrod. I take it you'll want to sit in on the interview?'

'Hell, yeah,' Ryan whispered. 'Interview with the vampire's what they call it, isn't it?'

'Don't worry, son. I'll fit him with a Hannibal Lecter mask if you're worried he might take a chunk out of your neck.'

**

Danskin arranged for the lux levels in the interview room to be turned up to max. He wanted to psyche out the creep across the table and if Webb did believe he was a vampire, he wanted him to be as uncomfortable as possible.

The Graveyard Shift

Jackson Webb massaged his wrists where the handcuffs had bruised them. Apart from that, he appeared self-assured and unworried.

'Do you know a William Coulson?' Danskin began.

Back came the expected and standard response to such questions. 'Who?'

'What about a Matthew Neill?' Ryan asked.

Webb studied his fingernails and smiled benignly.

'Have you ever been to a public house called JayKay's?' Danskin asked.

'Do you think I'm homosexual, Detective Chief Inspector?'

'I'd say if you tell me whether you've been to JayKay's or not, I'd be able to answer your question. Now, will you answer mine?'

Onyx eyes searched Danskin's face. 'I'm sexual,' Webb replied, 'Not one particular type.'

'Where were you on Hallowe'en?' Ryan asked.

Webb's eyes blinked slowly, like a crocodile's, as he shifted his gaze to Ryan.

'You're pretty,' he said.

Ryan shivered. 'Answer the question, Mr Webb.'

'I will answer when you ask me the right question.'

Ryan rubbed his top lip. 'Are you a vampire?'

Webb laughed with such malevolence even Stephen Danskin winced. 'That, my sweet, is the right question. Yes. I am a vampire.'

He said it proudly, as if telling someone he'd received a Knighthood.

Ryan stared at him. 'I'd say you were of the sanquinarian type.'

Danskin shot Ryan a quizzical look.

Webb eased himself against the back of his chair. Steepled his fingers.

'My, you are good. I like you, sweetie,' Webb smiled. 'If only things were different, we could have such fun together.'

Webb's tongue flicked against his lips. Ryan's stomach flipped. DCI Danskin squirmed in his chair.

'Do you know William Coulson?' Danskin repeated, 'Or, Matthew Neill.'

'Of course, I do. I had fun with them. Shagged them. They turned me on. A bit like you do,' he said, eyes on Ryan, 'But I didn't kill them.'

Ryan knew Maynard was watching from behind the mirrored glass of the interview room wall. He wondered what was going through her mind, and he felt relief Hannah wasn't watching a killer vampire flirt with the father of her child.

'Have you any children?' Webb asked.

Ryan couldn't help but blurt out, 'How the fuck…?'

Webb nodded. 'I see. You aren't homosexual, then. But are you sexual, my dear; just like I am?'

'Enough of this bollocks, you creepy little arsehole!' Danskin screamed, slamming the desk with his fists.

Webb didn't even blink. Just smiled as if he'd won the battle.

'Whitby November 2015. Tell me about it.'

Webb put a finger against the corner of his mouth in mock thought as if he were Dr Evil. 'That was such a long time ago…'

'Cut the shit and answer me.'

'My first. My very first. They say you always remember your first time, don't they?'

Ryan and Danskin were shocked at the man's candour and indifference.

'Why didn't you admit it to the police at the time?'

'Oh, a couple of reasons. Firstly, they weren't as nice as you,' he leered at Ryan. 'More importantly, I hadn't had enough fun.'

The Graveyard Shift

Danskin let the silence stretch to the horizon. The air in the room was frigid. He couldn't decide if it was the heating turned down or the presence of the man.

'Jordan Usher. Tell me about her.'

'Oh, Usher. Was that her second name? Now, that was something really special.'

'You reverted to the technique you used in Whitby. Why?'

'Because, like the first, it was completely unplanned. The Whitby one, it was the very first time I'd taken drugs. It was Goth weekend. We started talking about vampires, me and this guy I hooked up with, and I thought it appropriate. We were fooling around and there was a stick nearby. I wondered, *'What if?'* So, I found out. You know what? It was the greatest high of my life. I've never touched drugs since. Blood, yes: lots of it in small doses, but not drugs.'

'And Jordan Usher?'

Somewhere in the black holes of his eyes, something changed. He beamed a smile. Shifted in his seat. His hands moved beneath the table. From Ryan's position, he could see Webb trying to hide an erection.

'Dear Jordan. I hadn't planned anything that night but my hunger got the better of me. Then, when she told me she was a virgin,' his eyes rolled back in ecstasy for a second, 'I knew what I had to do.'

Danskin stared at Webb. 'You do know Jordan Usher was transsexual?'

He didn't know what he expected Webb's reaction to be, but it wasn't what he got.

'How interesting.' Then, he snapped his fingers. 'Of course! She said there was something else she wanted to tell me. Oh wow. I love that girl, you know.'

'Jesus Christ. You are one sick sod.'

'Thank you, Detective Chief Inspector. That's very kind of you.'

Danskin forced his arms to remain by his side rather than throttle the last breath out of the creature opposite.

Ryan saw Danskin's struggles so he picked up the interview.

'You told us earlier you didn't confess to our colleagues in Yorkshire because you hadn't had enough fun. Does that mean you've had your fill now? Is that why you're coming clean?'

Webb smiled at Ryan, a lascivious, unsettling sneer. 'Let's just say I've thought of a much better way to have fun. And lots of it.'

'Meaning?'

'You'll see, my pretty one. All in good time.'

Danskin stood. 'I've had enough of this...'

Ryan held out a hand to silence him.

'Why did you change methods with Coulson and Neill? And why wait eight years?'

'You're confusing me, pretty boy. That's two questions. As for the first, I told you: I didn't kill them; just toyed with them a little.'

Ryan stared at Webb. 'And why wait eight years?'

'Because, throughout those eight years, the feelings were building in me.' He rolled up his sleeve to reveal a series of scars. 'I tried to quench my thirst in my own way, but that was never going to be enough. Recycling, if you like, didn't cut it.'

Ryan waited for Webb to continue. In time, he did.

'The lust. The desire. The yearning...you have no idea what it's like. It's a NEED, nothing less.'

'Yet, you restrained yourself for all those years. What made you start again?'

Webb rediscovered the faraway look.

'I met my soulmate, that's why. The one I'd been looking for all my life. My fire was reignited and, now it is, I can't stop. I'll never stop.'

TWENTY-SEVEN

Stephen Danskin called for a short break.

From the outset, he'd ensured Webb had been offered the services of a solicitor, which the man had turned down with disdain. After the O'Hara ticking off, Danskin wanted to confer with Superintendent Maynard to ensure she'd noted the offer but, more importantly, whether she felt the need to change tack.

He found her in the adjoining room, looking more disturbed than he'd ever seen her.

'You okay, Ma'am?'

'Not really. He's a monster, isn't he? Figuratively and in real terms.'

'He certainly is.'

Maynard took a sip of cold coffee, her hands trembling. 'Ryan seems to be holding up well, given the fact Webb clearly fancies the pants off him.'

'Aye. I'd have knocked the bastard's non-existent fangs doon his throat if he'd tried it on with me.'

Maynard held the thought. 'Perhaps that's Webb's intention. Wind one of you up so he can play the brutality card, try to get off that way. He knows it'll all be on camera.'

'Truth be told, he doesn't want to get off with it. It's almost as if he wants to go down for it. I mean, he's admitted everything so far.'

Maynard considered Danskin's words. 'Perhaps there's a smidgeon of remorse, a touch of guilt, for what he's done somewhere inside him.'

'Nah. Like you say, he's a monster. He feels nothing for his victims. It's more like he's got a plan of some sort.'

The Graveyard Shift

Sam Maynard winced. 'So, I suggest when you reconvene, you suss out his accomplice.'

Danskin dipped his head in agreement. 'We're on the same page there.'

'Good. Right, you've another ten minutes until you get back at it. I suggest you go upstairs, grab a coffee, and calm down. The last thing I need is for you to lose your cool in there.'

**

What Ryan really wanted was to hold Hannah, take comfort from her and, daft though it sounded, ensure the child she carried was safe from the monsters under the bed.

Instead, Ryan used the break as an opportunity to get some fresh air.

He turned left out of the Forth Street station and headed up Forth Banks, stooping into a headwind.

Ironically, when he lifted his head, he found himself trudging past Hatchet Harry's Axe Throwing emporium. For a moment, he considered if he should add this to the list of potential vampire meeting haunts. He dismissed the idea but sighed with the realisation that the case, and Jackson Webb, remained embedded in his thoughts.

Unable to rid his memory of the way Jackson Webb looked at him licentiously, he accepted the fresh air wasn't going to clear his mind.

He decided to check in on Gavin O'Hara. Make sure he was recovering from his ordeal at the hands of Jane Wilmott. He pulled his phone from his pocket and dialled.

Just when he was about to hang up, O'Hara answered.

'Yeah?' Gavin said through an obvious yawn.

'It's me, mate. Just wonderin' how you're doing.'

'I was doing okay 'til you woke me up.'

'You still in bed?'

'What? It sounds like you're in a wind tunnel. I can't hear you.'

'Aye, it's a bit breezy, like.'

'I wouldn't know. I'm still in bed.'

Ryan laughed. 'That answers my question.'

'What question?'

'Bloody hell, man: the question you didn't… oh, never mind. Sleepless night was it?' Ryan turned right at a fork in the road, not really aware of where he was going.

'You could say that. My fault, really. I went out last night. Thought it'd do me good.'

'Ah man, you didn't get pissed again, did you?'

'Nah. I just wanted some fresh air. Just walked and walked. It was way after midnight when I turned in.'

Ryan stopped to gather his breath after walking uphill against the wind. 'You're okay, though?'

The delay in reply was telling. 'It'll take a while, but not bad, I guess.'

'Hmm. I'm not convinced…'

'Gotta go, Ry. Someone's trying to ring me. Catch up soon, yeah?'

Ryan was left holding a dead phone.

He took a deep breath and looked around, unsure where he was. The street sign above his head read, 'Churchill Street'; the building next to him, 'The Yard Bar.'

He knew where he was. Less than a hundred yards further on, Ryan found himself outside JayKay's. He checked his watch. He had ten minutes.

Ryan looked through the window. He was in luck. Sherry Proudlock was behind the bar.

'Morning,' he breezed.

Sherry looked at the clock on the wall. 'Afternoon, technically. Anyway, what do you want, this time?'

'I just wanted to check on you. You know, after reliving things yesterday.'

The Graveyard Shift

For the first time, Ryan saw the girl give a smile of genuine warmth.

'Wow. Thanks. Yeah, I'm good, thanks. Working helps.' She looked around the empty bar. Not that there's any work to do, mind.'

A thought hit Ryan. 'Mr Kaye said you only worked when things got busy. You seem to be here a lot, these days.'

Sherry's smile faded to sadness. 'Aye, well. There's a lot of *'These days'*, these days.'

'I haven't got long, but if you want to talk…'

Sherry studied him. Tilted her head to one side. 'Is this your way of asking me out?'

'What? No, I mean…' he blushed. 'I just meant if there's something you want to get off your chest..'

Sherry grabbed her breasts and laughed when she saw Ryan's mouth open. 'I'm only joking, man. I don't get many offers working in a place like this. Well, not off men, anyway.'

'Right. I'd better be off,' Ryan said, not knowing what else there was to say.

As he turned to leave, Sherry spoke again.

'I'm worried about John,' she said. 'If anything happens, can I give you a ring?'

'What sort of *'anything'* are you thinking of?'

'I don't really know. He's just…not himself. Dad says they had a big argument last night. ANOTHER big argument. John didn't get back 'til yon time, Dad says. There's something not right.'

Ryan knew what wasn't right. Tim in Heaton is what wasn't right. He decided to leave well alone.

'Yeah. If anything happens, let me know. Anything serious, I mean. Criminal, like. I'm too busy for general counselling.'

Sherry gave another impish smile. 'That's a pity. You're good at it.'

**

Ryan was almost ten minutes late arriving back at his Forth Street HQ but both the Super and the DCI were relaxed about it.

'It'll do no harm to let him sweat for a while,' Danskin commented.

'I'm not sure vampires do sweat, sir,' Ryan joked.

'That's not vampires, man. You're thinking of Prince Andrew. There again, mind...'

Maynard quickly moved the conversation on. 'Okay, let's get back to it. I want to learn about his partner in crime; his 'soulmate', as Webb put it. We've got number one in the box. It's time we found number two.'

'Ma'am,' Ryan said, 'If the DCI's got no objections, I'd like to lead this session.'

'Stephen?' Maynard asked.

'Hey, it's fine by me. I'm not sure I could control me temper much longer, anyway.'

'Okay, guys. Go get 'em.'

The temperature in the interview suite seemed to have reached a new low. The lighting appeared subdued, too. Not so Jackson Webb.

'Ah. Welcome back. I was beginning to miss you,' he said.

They ignored him as Ryan went through the introductions for the tape and repeated Webb's right to representation. Once more, he declined the offer.

'Mr Webb,' Ryan began, 'Before we broke, you mentioned finding your soulmate.'

'Yes, that's right.'

'Where did you meet him?'

'Him? What makes you so sure it's a 'him'?'

The reply threw Ryan. It also threw everything they suspected out the window, and Danskin's face let Webb know.

'Tell me about this soulmate of yours,' Ryan recovered.

'My soulmate is precisely that. The one who understands me. The one who recognises my need. Most importantly, they share the need. Perhaps in a different way, but their need is the same.'

Jarrod, Danskin, and Maynard in the adjoining room, convulsed.

Ryan steadied his hand before taking a sip of water.

'Have you ever visited a website called Vampire Rave?'

Webb didn't answer, but his eyes turned a darker shade of black.

'Or how about Vampirechat.co.uk?'

A look of glee spread over Webb's face. 'My darling,' he trilled, 'You truly are one of us, aren't you?'

'Don't get ower excited.'

Webb's eyes drilled into Ryan's being. 'One day, I'd love to show you just how excited you make me.'

Ryan flinched.

Danskin had heard enough. 'Stand up!' he yelled.

'Rude.'

'Do it. NOW!'

Slowly, without taking his eyes from the DCI, he rose.

'Look over there,' Danskin demanded, pointing to the mirrored window in the wall. 'What do you see?'

'I see you, and my dear friend.'

'Who else?'

'Me, of course.'

'Ha!' Danskin gave a yell of triumph, 'If you can see yourself, you're no fucking vampire, are you? Now, cut the crappy ham actor-bit and talk some sense.'

Webb gave Danskin a look of genuine sympathy. 'You've been reading too many books, Detective Chief Inspector. That side of things is all fiction. Me? I'm real. Oh, and to prove it, I can clearly see your colleague on the other side of that mirror.'

He wiggled his fingers in an effeminate wave. 'You've got gorgeous eyes, my dear,' he said to the mirror.

Sam Maynard shrunk into the corner of the darkened adjacent room. A lucky guess? Had he noticed her when they arrested him on the construction site? Read something about her in the papers? Or could he really be...

She heard Danskin order Webb to sit down and the spell was broken. Still, Maynard felt she could do with the stiffest of drinks.

'Those websites – is that where you met him?'

'My dear, you're making the same assumption.'

'Tell me: is my assumption wrong?'

'I've had enough of this game,' Webb declared. 'No, you're assumption is not wrong. My soulmate is a man. Of course he is.'

'Thank you...'

'There again, I was wrong about Jordan Usher, wasn't I?' Webb teased.

Even Ryan had to fight down the urge to swear.

'Did you find *HIM* on either of those websites?'

'Not those ones, no.'

'One like it?'

Webb leant towards Ryan. 'I want to taste your blood,' he whispered. 'I want it now,' before he shot back in his seat and answered the question as if nothing had happened. 'Yes, one like it.'

'Interview suspended,' Ryan said. He switched off the tape and marched out the room, leaving a bemused Danskin wondering what the hell he'd just witnessed.

**

'What the hell have I just witnessed in there?' he asked, vocalising his thoughts to Sam Maynard.

'I have absolutely no idea, Stephen. I really don't. This Webb character has some weird shit going on inside that head of his, that's for sure.'

The Graveyard Shift

They stood in the lobby of the Forth Street station, neither giving voice to the ludicrous notion that Webb, somehow, could see and hear the events of the adjoining room.

'There you are,' said Ryan as he stepped into the lobby from the Gents. His face still held the tell-tale sheen of a man who'd recently rinsed it. 'What do you make of it all?'

Danskin snorted. 'To use the Super's words, it's all weird shit.'

'Are you okay, Ryan?' Sam Maynard asked, picking up on his unease.

'Yeah. I can't help but feel he's invading me, somehow. I know it doesn't make sense, but there's something not normal with him.'

Maynard lightly took his hand. 'You did right in calling for a break,' she said.

'That's not why I did it. Ma'am, I'd like Ravi Sangar to join me for the next session. I want to get into these websites and chatrooms he uses. If he doesn't give us the name of his soulmate, I think Ravi will help us navigate through them.'

Danskin made a sucking noise. 'Just you and Sangar in there with him, you mean?'

Maynard jumped in before the DCI could raise an objection. 'I think it's an excellent idea. Providing you're sure you can handle his snidey chat-up techniques, you've clearly got a rapport with Webb. Sorry, my bad. He's got a rapport with you. He might open up to you and, if he doesn't, I agree DC Sangar will offer great technology support. Stephen, you get Sangar then join me behind the mirror.'

'There's not much point. He seems to know everything that's gannin' on anyway. We might as well just stand out in the open.'

TWENTY-EIGHT

'For the benefit of the tape, Acting Detective Inspector Ryan Jarrod is now joined by DC Ravinder Sangar.'

Jackson Webb cocked his head to one side as he studied Sangar. He gave a sharp nod then said, 'You enjoy the night, don't you, Mr Sangar?'

Ryan felt the shockwave run through Ravi so he stepped in with, 'I'll ask the questions, Mr Webb.'

'Okay,' Webb said, still smiling at Ravi with a knowing look in the cavernous depths of his dark eyes. 'Fire away.' He dragged his eyes back to Ryan.

'Who is your accomplice? And, before you start with the *'Soulmate'* nonsense, I want a name.'

'I don't have a name for him.'

'You seriously expect me to believe that?'

Webb's laugh rolled like distant thunder. 'You've seen the websites. You know how they work.'

Ryan smiled. 'I know enough to know they use names.'

'I'm disappointed in you. You've looked at the wrong ones.' He looked at the closed laptop Ravi had with him. 'May I?'

Ravi looked at Ryan, who nodded his assent. Ryan raised the lid of the laptop and passed it over the desk.

Webb quickly typed in a site name, then a personal password, and turned the laptop to face them with an, 'Et voila.'

Ryan and Ravi were staring at the homepage of *PrimaDaemon*. Webb watched the faces of the two detectives with growing amusement as they read its descriptor.

'*PrimaDaemon and its sub-domains is a piggyback to the standard internet. Its primary use is for communication between like-minded members of the Nosferatu.*

It may also be used to share secrets and information, plans and goals, and allows for integration with other social networks dedicated to the vampire community.

Restricted areas are available at a premium and come with bespoke, guaranteed encryption.'

Ryan glanced towards Sangar. 'Legit?'

Ravi shook his head but his words contradicted the action. 'Seems to be.'

'It is, gentleman. And it's completely unhackable.'

'No such thing,' Ravi said.

Webb through down the gauntlet. 'Try it.'

'We haven't time. At least, not yet. DC Sangar will prove you wrong, trust me.'

'He won't.' Webb said it with such confidence even Ravi believed him.

'Moving on,' Ryan said, 'You met your accomplice on this…this thing here?'

'PrimaDaemon. Yes, I did.'

'How?'

Webb looked towards Sangar for permission before taking control of the laptop. In seconds, he'd brought up another screen containing profiles and interests, ages and locations, gender if important, and photographs.

Except, the photographs were either Avatars or folk wearing masks. And the names were nonsense handles, like those used by Muzzle, Jam Jar and the rest of their gaming community.

Ryan swallowed down both his curiosity and desire to browse as he pressed on. 'You're on here?'

Webb reached forward, typed something in, and up he popped. Or, at least, the image of someone wearing a demonic prosthetic mask appeared under the name of The Vampire Queen.

'That could be anyone,' Ravi scoffed.

'No. It's him.' Ryan assured. The mask exposed Webb's eyes and they left Ryan in no doubt who was behind the disguise.

'Can I show you my friend?' Webb said, almost taunting them.

'That's what we're here for.'

Again, Webb knew precisely where to find his 'soulmate.'

Ryan stared at the image. The profile, he ignored. The man could say anything about himself. No, it was the photograph Ryan wanted.

It was impossible to tell the man's height from the headshot. He wore a skullcap which disguised his hair and a black and white phantom of the opera mask covered his face. It could be anyone.

Ryan groaned. 'Describe him to me.'

'He looks like this,' Jackson Webb said, pointing to the screen.

'Behind the mask, fool.'

'I don't know. Whenever we've met, in the graveyards, he's always worn the mask.'

'What about outside the cemeteries?'

Webb locked his fingers in front of his stomach. 'I've never seen him in the realm of the living so I wouldn't know.'

Ryan was getting nowhere. He thought for a moment, then changed tack once he noticed the legend alongside Webb's co-conspirator's image.

It read, '*Morticia.*'

Ryan thought for a moment. 'You confirmed your friend is a man, earlier.'

'I did.'

'So why is he calling himself Morticia, the matriarch from the Addams family?'

Webb looked at Ryan with disappointment. 'Don't say you've forgotten about Jordan Usher?'

'That's different. The name Jordan is unisex.'

The Graveyard Shift

Webb shrugged. 'You'll have to ask him why he chose that nickname.'

Ryan dug his tongue into his cheek. Looked to the ceiling. 'I would if I knew where to find him.' Ryan quickly brought his eyes back to Webb. 'Bring up your chats with him.'

'Impossible.'

'Why?'

'They don't exist.'

'Telepathic now, are we?'

'No.'

'Show me your chats.'

Webb tutted sarcastically. He repeat a statement from the PrimaDaemon website. *'Restricted areas are available at a premium and come with bespoke, guaranteed encryption.'* All chats are part of the premium service.'

'So, enter it.'

'There's no point. It says it on the tin. It's encrypted . The messages are deleted automatically as soon as a message has been read.'

Ryan put his arms behind his head. 'Ravi?'

'It's probable, yes.'

Ryan puffed out air. Thought for several moments. 'Tell me about Thomas Raith.'

Webb's smile spread from ear to ear. 'Clever AND pretty. I think I'm falling in love with you, my sweet.'

'Raith – what made you come up with that one?'

Behind the wall, Stephen Danskin and Sam Maynard shared bemused looks. They had no idea who Thomas Raith was or what he had to do with the case. Then, Danskin remembered. 'The grave Billy Coulson was found on. It was Thomas Raith's.'

'I understand,' she said, turning her attention back to Webb's response.

'It won't come as a surprise to you to learn I spend a lot of time in graveyards,' Webb was saying. 'It just so happened I saw Raith's grave around the time I met Morticia. I mentioned it to him, and we hatched a plan. Or, rather, he did. You see, while my interests lie in the carnal and symbolic sphere, his is in the realm of death. He has such a dark side to him. That's what attracted me to him. Coulson and dear Matthew were all his idea. I didn't lie when I said I hadn't killed them. I didn't. That was Morticia's doing – and what better place to do it than on the grave of someone bearing the name of a vampire? Such sweet symmetry.'

Jackson Webb's face bore the contented look of one who had found his destiny.

Ryan leant towards Webb. 'Where do I find Morticia?'

Webb leant in, too. 'You don't.'

He blew Ryan a kiss and sat back in his chair.

'How do YOU meet him?'

'On here, of course.' He pointed to the laptop.

Ryan had thought of something. A plan which might just work. If it didn't, it would be catastrophic.

He knew his idea needed approval. He didn't seek it.

'Mr Webb, I want you to set up a fake killing. In a cemetery, like all the others. Only, we'll be there, waiting.'

In the other room, Danskin and Maynard went into meltdown.

'What the hell's he doing?' Maynard wondered.

'I've nee idea but I don't like it.'

'We've got to stop it, Stephen.'

'Aye. Let's go.'

They were too late. Webb had considered Ryan's words and the Super and Stephen Danskin saw a smirk twitch Webb's lips. 'Tell me more.'

'Firstly, you do NOT touch this laptop. WE input the message, YOU tell us what to say. No codewords, no tip-offs; Morticia mustn't have a clue what we're doing.'

Webb laughed. 'This is such fun. I do like games.'

'Secondly, don't think it's a chance for you to escape. Wherever we choose, we'll have men all over the place. Undercover, and armed. You won't see them, but they'll be there.'

Jackson Webb looked genuinely affronted. 'Why would I want to escape? I've already told you that isn't part of my plan.'

'Okay. As long as that's understood, my team will sort out the details. Until then, you're locked up.'

Webb set back. Stared at Ryan, longingly.

'I do have a condition, though.'

Ryan's forehead wrinkled. He realised what Webb meant. 'No, I can't make any promises that it will get you a lighter sentence. That's totally out of my control.'

Webb's voice remained calm and cogent. 'That wasn't my condition.'

'Go on, then; what is your condition?'

Jackson Webb smiled, revealing glistening white teeth contrasting with the inky depths of his eyes. He narrowed his eyes as he spoke to Ryan in a whisper.

'My condition, darling, is that you, and only you, play the role of our victim.'

TWENTY-NINE

Ryan, sandwiched between Stephen Danskin and Sam Maynard, strode onto the third floor of the Forth Street station and through the floorplate to the accompaniment of absolute silence.

Every eye in the room locked on the threesome as if they were a wedding party marching down the aisle. Maynard's command were long enough in the tooth to know when something was up – and they sensed this was as far 'up' as the International Space Station.

Danskin slammed the door of Maynard's office behind them with so much force the windows rattled. Once inside, Ryan's senior officers let rip.

'What the hell possessed you to suggest that?' the Super demanded. 'I absolutely forbid it.'

'I think it's a good idea.'

'A good idea? Are you mad? Ryan, Webb's a maniac. If you think I'm going to leave you in the hands of that monster, you're as crazy as him.'

'Please, give me a chance to explain. You don't know what my plan is yet.'

Sam Maynard's face had turned the colour of a plum. 'Perhaps not, but I suspect it involves cemeteries in the middle of the night, with at least two nutters of the highest order.'

Ryan took a deep breath. 'How else do you propose we catch Webb's accomplice?'

Maynard hesitated. 'We let Ravi loose on the crazies' website, for one.'

'Ma'am, Ravi's already as good as confirmed it's as secure as the Bank of England.'

The Graveyard Shift

'He hasn't had time to check it yet, for Christ's sake!'

'We don't have time. If the second man tries to contact Webb without success, he'll guess something's up.'

'In that case, we chase up Elliot and Cavanagh. Get them to go over the forensics again and again until they find something. The man can't be foolproof. He must have left a trace of himself somewhere.'

'The medics won't have missed anything. In your heart, you already know that, don't you?'

'Uuugh!' Maynard uttered, tossing her head and stamping a foot. 'Stephen, what do you think? Tell him.'

The DCI moved towards Ryan. Danskin's face was impassive. He raised a finger and aimed it inches from Ryan's eyes. 'If you think I'm prepared to risk my grandchild growing up without a father, you don't know me at all.'

Stephen's voice broke with emotion as he spoke.

Ryan gulped down an overwhelming sense of guilt. 'I have two questions for you: realistically, what are our chances of finding the second culprit without doing what I suggest? And, what other suggestions do you have?'

Maynard and Danskin stared at each other.

'…fuck's sake!' Danskin exclaimed, spinning away.

'Ryan,' Maynard said, more gently, 'You'll be there alone, apart from one man with a bloody great sharpened pole and another with a shitload of syringes and God knows what else.'

'Ma'am, I won't be alone. We'll have men hidden nearby. Armed men, if you give the order. Nothing can go wrong.'

Maynard inhaled through her nostrils, but the fact she didn't instantly shoot him down in flames offered Ryan encouragement. Even Danskin mellowed a little.

'I'm being selfish here but if – and it's a humongous if – we agree to this insane plan of yours, does it have to be you?'

'Who else do you suggest? Trebilcock's so wary of ever goos and the supernatural, they'll hear his knees knocking in Sunderland. We can't risk using Sangar because the victims we know of are all white – that could be part of the criteria. Gavin's on a R&R break, and he might be recognised 'cos we know he's been to JayKay's. Lyall's too old to fit the profile, and as for Todd; well, he's scarier than owt there is in horror movies. They'll run a mile. No, it's got to be me.'

Stephen Danskin gazed out the window and down to the River Tyne, its colour the grey of a decaying cadaver.

'Seeing as you brought the name up, what if it is John Kaye?' the DCI mused. 'He knows you. He'll recognise you. In a word, you'll be fucked.'

The thought was one Ryan hadn't considered. Not fully. It flummoxed him for a moment. All he came back with was, 'It'll be dark. I'll take my chances.'

Danskin swore again. Moved to the door of the Super's office. Flung it open.

'DS Graves!' he bellowed.

Moments later, a confused-looking Hannah entered the room.

'You called for me, sir?'

'Aye. I did. Have you heard what this nob of a boyfriend of yours is suggesting now? Huh? No, you won't, because he won't have dared mention it to you. Go on, Jarrod: tell the mother of your child what you're up to.'

Ryan couldn't look her in the eye but, tell her he did – in a flat, mumbled monotone.

Hannah's face said it all. She was mortified. Was about to tell Ryan he was as mad a box of frogs. Then, she remembered.

The whole point of her excluding Ryan from their unborn's upbringing, of not moving in with the man she loved, of keeping her distance from him, was because she'd promised herself she wouldn't allow herself to affect Ryan's career.

The Graveyard Shift

Hannah recalled a conversation she'd had in her head, the one in which she told herself she couldn't stop Ryan taking the risks which would further his career.

'I think it's a good idea,' she said.

**

'Dad, I've got something to tell you.'

'You're not gay, are you?'

'Divvent be daft. Now, shut up and listen. You know the case I've been on?'

'The one with the graveyards and such like? Aye, I do.'

Ryan remained standing in his father's kitchen, Kenzie failing to understand why Ryan wasn't interacting with him.

'I can't say much, but we're planning an undercover operation. A set-up, if you like.'

Norman Jarrod crossed his arms. 'Gan on,' he encouraged, wondering where this was leading.

'Well, we need a location. One that I know summat about.'

Norman said nothing.

'And, I was thinking about Blaydon. You know, the cemetery, an' all.'

His father's eyes narrowed. 'What's this got to do with me?'

'It's where Rhianne's memorial is, man. I don't know how you feel about me working where my sister's headstone is.'

'Are you planning on using her plot?'

'What? Good grief, no. But she's still there, isn't she?'

Norman unfolded his arms and looked at the kitchen floor. 'No, she's not, son. It's just a headstone, isn't it?'

'You sure you don't mind?'

'I've just said so,' Norman Jarrod said with some irritation. 'You do what you have to do. Just don't tell me too much aboot it until it's over, okay?'

'Deal?'

'Deal,' Norman said, turning down Ryan's offer of one of those stupid gangsta' hip-hop handshake things.

Instead, Ryan gave Norman Jarrod a hug before leaving a dispirited dog and a bemused father to their own devices.

**

'Why are churches always so bloody cold?' Ryan thought as he blew on his hands to warm them.

He looked up at the arched window, its coloured glazing depicting cherubim and seraphim, doves, a winged angel, and a bowing Jesus. For once, the colours were dull rather than radiant, the scene morose and not uplifting.

Perhaps it was the grey sky outside or the morbid subject matter he was about to discuss, but things seemed different, even to a non-believer like Ryan.

The clip-clop of approaching footfall echoed from the stone floor and brought Ryan back to the present.

'Mr Jarrod, Ryan – good to see you again.'

Reverend Murray Appleby smiled benignly, looking for all the world like a cherub lifted from the stained glass. He took Ryan's right hand in his and placed his left hand on both.

'And you, Reverend. Thank you for agreeing to see me.'

'What an odd thing to say, young man. That's what I'm here for; to see people. I just wish there were more of them to fill this place,' he said, gesturing at row upon row of wooden pews.

'I'll be quick,' Ryan promised. 'I need a favour.'

Without any sense of judgement, Murray Appleby said, 'Another one? I pushed the boat out for you last time. The church elders would be mad if they knew I'd let you place a memorial headstone in our cemetery without the accompaniment of your dear departed sister.'

He saw Ryan's face drop.

'Sorry. A joke. Bad taste. I apologise.'

The Graveyard Shift

Ryan's face lightened. 'No offence taken, Reverend. Mind you, I think the elders would completely lose the plot if they knew what I was about to ask of you.'

They perched themselves on the end of pews facing each other. Ryan explained he needed a setting for an undercover operation, apologised for being unable to share the details, and kept any mention of vampires and the Dark Arts out of the conversation.

When he finished, he waited for Appleby's response. And waited. And waited some more while the clergyman lowered his head and steepled his fingers against his chin.

'I don't know, Ryan. I really don't. I'd like to help, you know I would, but this? I really don't know.'

Ryan could see Appleby was still contemplating so he thought it best not to interrupt his thoughts.

'This is Holy ground. Consecrated land. I'm very uncomfortable, I really am.'

Again, Ryan remained silent as the last few words of Murray Appleby's statement repeated themselves in the concrete chamber.

Appleby stood, abruptly. 'Follow me,' he said.

Ryan trailed behind the Reverend as they left the church, walked a hundred yards along Shibdon Road towards Blaydon Cemetery, and into the graveyard itself.

The first thing Ryan saw was his sister's memorial, and the stalks of long dead flowers protruding from the vase.

'I'm sorry, Rhianne. I'll be back to see you soon,' he thought.

Murray headed uphill, passing old graves, recent graves, and a couple of freshly dug plots waiting to swallow their occupants.

Still they marched uphill until they reached a part of the cemetery not yet used. It was a patch of land no bigger than a large back garden.

'Will this do you?' Appleby asked. 'You won't impose on any souls here. Feel free to do what you will but, please, you must not intrude on any part of the cemetery where the departed already lie. I beg you. Do I have your word?'

Ryan looked around. The land was far from the entry point to the graveyard. Whilst there was housing in sight, they were distant enough not to afford an easy escape route. There was a path leading to a narrow gate little more than the length of two cricket pitches from the offered land, but Ryan felt this wasn't an obstacle to his plan.

'This is perfect, Reverend. Thank you so much.'

'Do I have your word?' Appleby persisted.

'You do,' Ryan smiled.

'Then I'm delighted to say it's all yours, dear boy.'

At that moment, the sun burst through the grey clouds and bathed the cemetery in a heavenly glow.

'I think we have God's blessing,' Murray Appleby smiled.

THIRTY

Jackson Webb sat in the interview suite in the company of two uniformed officers who shifted uncomfortably under the dark-eyed stare of their suspect. Webb's eyes only moved from them when the door opened.

'My darling,' he smiled as Ryan entered.

'I think he fancies you,' Ryan said to Ravi.

'You know only too well who I'm addressing, and it's not the one who goes without sleep.'

'The sod should be on BGT with his mindreading act,' Ryan thought as Ravi opened the laptop browser to the PrimaDaemon site.

'Clever boy,' Webb smiled. 'You managed to enter the site but you couldn't hack into it, could you? Go on – admit it.'

Ravi said nothing. Instead, Ryan spoke.

'You know what you have to do. Contact this Morticia person…'

'Entity, not person,'

'Contact him and tell him you're in need of blood.'

'That's no lie. I am always in need of blood. Where do we meet?'

'One step at a time. Access the chat.'

Webb looked up at a red light on the ceiling. 'Switch off the camera. No-one sees how this is done.'

Ryan had to give the man credit. He was a smart bugger.

Webb waited until the light extinguished. 'These two behind me – I want them out the room.'

The PCs looked towards Ryan. He gave them a cautious nod. 'Give us two minutes. No more.'

They left Ryan, Ravi, and Jackson Webb alone.

Satisfied, Webb shielded the movements of his fingers as he logged into the secure area. A few seconds later, he raised his eyes from the screen. 'I'm in,' he said.

Ravi took the laptop from him and poised his fingers above the keypad.

'This has to look like it's coming from you so you tell Ravi what to type.'

Webb smirked. 'Okie-dokie. First, in upper case, type 'NEEDLES AND PINS.'

Ryan put his hand on top of Sangar's. 'Hold on a minute, Ravi.' He moved his eyes onto Webb. 'I told you no code words. That sounds remarkably like a code to me.'

Jackson Webb laughed. 'Of course it's code. It's OUR code, Morticia's and mine. It has two purposes. It satisfies Morticia that it is me speaking. It also lets him know I need a kill.'

'How does it do that?'

'Needles. Morticia brings them to the event. He uses them to draw blood for me and injects them for his kicks.'

'What does he inject them with?'

Webb shrugged. 'Who knows and who cares? Certainly not me.'

Ryan turned to Ravi. 'Looks like Rufus Cavanagh was on the money with his theory.'

'He was, aye.'

'What's the significance of the pins?'

'Oh come on, my love. You're better than that. The pin is code for my stake, of course. Once I've had my way with the victim,' he looked into Ryan's soul, 'Which, this time, is you, I pin them to the ground. Clever, no?

'Sick as fuck, yes,' Sangar answered.

'What do I do next?'

Ryan scratched his knee. 'You use whatever phrases you normally use to describe the location, time, and anything else you tell him.'

'Where's my little mystery tour taking me?'

'Blaydon Cemetery.'

'Oh, that's a new one for me. Good. When?'

'Tomorrow night.'

'That's short notice.'

Ryan grimaced. 'How much notice do you normally give each other?'

'Forty-eight hours.'

'Shit. We'd better tell Maynard to delay the firearms deployment.'

'We have given each other short notice before, though. Only, it went wrong.'

Ryan and Ravi exchanged glances. 'Wrong?'

'Yes. Recently. Very recently, actually. Morticia might be angry it went wrong. He may not wish to participate again so soon.'

'What do we do now?' Ravi asked Jarrod.

'We don't have a choice. We risk it.'

Webb leered once more. 'Oh the jeopardy of it all. I just luurv it!'

'Never mind *'just luurving it'*, just tell DC Sangar what to type.'

Ravi input Webb's words to the letter, even included a grammatical error which Webb explained was a weakness of his.

'Shit,' Ravi exclaimed.

'What's the matter?'

'Me screen's gone blank.'

Ryan swore, too.

'That's good,' Webb said.

'What in that sick mind of yours makes this any kind of good.'

'It means Morticia's seen it already. I told you the chat disappeared once messages were received.'

'Impressive,' Ravi said, like Mr Spock praising a piece of alien technology.

'What do we do now?'

'We wait for darling Morticia to consider it.'

The detectives stared at a screen as black as Webb's eyes for what seemed like an age.

'What will he say if it's a no-go?'

'He'll say *'I had to run away.'*

The wait went on. Ryan and Ravi called for a coffee for themselves, water for Webb. By the time it was delivered, Morticia still hadn't replied.

Ten long minutes passed.

With no warning, the screen blinked awake.

The Phantom of the Opera mask appeared above a message box. It contained the next line of the old Searchers song.

'Get down on my knees and pray they'll go away.'

Webb clapped his hands.

'Looks like we're in business,' Ryan whispered.

**

The following twenty-four hours passed in a blur of planning and preparation.

Maynard mobilised an armed response unit and ensured they were discretely despatched to Blaydon Cemetery. Lyall Parker and Stephen Danskin pored over a detailed map of the graveyard, highlighting specific points where men could be deployed with minimal chance of being spotted.

Rick Kinnear's team searched for weak points in both planning and site security. Sam Maynard sucked up to the powers-that-be and gave repeated assurances up the chain of command, persuading them the general public were at no risk because the mission would be undertaken at midnight.

Hannah Graves wandered back and forth, talking comfortingly to her baby who kicked like a boxing kangaroo.

As darkness set in, Ryan prepared for his mission. He put in phone calls to James, Norman, and his grandmother's care home. He assured them he'd be okay but made a point of letting them know they were loved.

He shared a brief hug with Lucy Dexter, shook hands with Lyall Parker, high-fived Ravi Sangar, and got caught in Todd Robson's bearhug.

He left Nigel Trebilcock to his own devices, twirling with worry beads and any other superstitious routine the Cornishman thought might help.

Twenty minutes before he was due to leave, Ryan and Hannah spent a private moment alone in Stephen Danskin's office, professing their love for one another and both promising the other that they'd be fine.

The DCI knocked lightly on the door. 'We're ready, Ryan.'

'Bloody hell. You must be worried if you're calling me Ryan,' he joked.

No-one laughed.

'Come here, son,' Danskin said. He opened his arms and welcomed Ryan into his embrace. 'We'll look after you. You won't see us, but we'll be there.'

The DCI turned to leave. 'Be careful with Webb. You know what he's capable of, and he's probably got summat even worse somewhere in that soul of his. Don't trust him as far as you can hoy him.'

'See you on the other side, sir.'

**

Ryan travelled in the back seat of an unmarked car. Webb followed in another vehicle, handcuffed to a uniformed officer and tailed by two unmarked vans.

Ryan felt his phone vibrate in his pocket. He opened it and looked at the picture message Hannah had sent him.

It was an image of her twenty-week scan, their child curled up inside her. The baby looked to be smiling.

Hannah's legend beneath it read, *'Good luck, Daddy. Love from your little boy xxx'*

Ryan released a guttural sob. *'A boy. I'm going to have a son. WE are going to have a son,'* he corrected. He brought the screen to his lips and kissed the photograph.

'I'll be with you soon, little one,' he whispered.

The car switchbacked around the tight curve of the Scotswood Bridge approach, the river broody as ever beneath it. Ryan shivered.

'Ah man.' He'd forgotten someone. He picked up his phone and dialled. 'Hey, mate, how's things?'

The reply came back breathless. 'Not you again. Will you not leave us alone, man?'

'I just wanted to say thank you, Gavin.'

'What for?'

'For being me mentor, like. I wouldn't be where I am today without you. I just thought you should know.'

'Give ower, you soft shite. Where are you, anyway?'

'I'm just crossing Scotswood Bridge. Just on me way to see wor Rhianne, you know. It's been a while. I don't want her to feel neglected.'

'You really are a softer shite than you were two minutes ago.'

Ryan gave a nervous laugh. He thought he heard the sound of traffic coming over the phone.

'Are you out again?'

'Aye. Don't worry. I'm not at the pub. Just having a walk. I'm well into it these days.'

'Okay, mate. Watch what you're doing, yeah?'

'You too, Ry.'

He returned the phone to his pocket, unaware he'd received a message while he'd talked to O'Hara.

Still unread, the message said, *'It's Sherry. I think something's happened to John. He's gone missing. Call me when you can.'*

**

The Graveyard Shift

The car carrying Ryan parked up near Shibdon Pond. He made his way to the cemetery gates with a plain clothes cop in tow, casually chatting as if they were mates out for a stroll.

In the small turning circle outside the cemetery gateway, Jackson Webb was being uncuffed inside his car. 'Remember, we've got men aal roond the place. Armed men,' his escort said. 'They're wearing night vision goggles. They'll be up trees, behind walls, anywhere you look, they'll be there.'

'So?' Webb said, shaking his wrists to get the circulation flowing.

'So don't try any funny business. In fact, don't even THINK of any funny business. We're watching, we'll know, and you'll be dead.'

Webb laughed. 'Only if they're using silver bullets.'

The PC didn't know if he was joking or not.

Ryan and Webb joined up just inside the gates.

'After you,' Webb said. 'You know where we're going. I don't.'

'Does Morticia?'

'He'll be watching.'

They began the uphill climb into an increasingly mizzley night and a fate worse than death.

'You need to stagger a bit,' Webb whispered.

'Why?'

'Pretend you're pissed. It'll seem more natural to Morticia.'

Ryan feigned a stagger, then staggered for real.

The clammy hand of Jackson Webb had taken hold of Ryan's. It was like holding death itself.

'You want this to look real, don't you?' Webb explained as they wound their way along a curving uphill path between trees and hedges.

'I suppose so,' Ryan admitted.

'Good.' Still clutching Ryan's hand, Webb stepped in front of him, walking backwards. He tipped his head towards Ryan.

'In that case, kiss me like you mean it.'

'Like fuck I will,' a repulsed Ryan said.

He had no choice. Jackson Webb did as he pleased, and Ryan felt a cold, wet, reptilian sliver probe deep inside his mouth.

THIRTY-ONE

In the upper reaches of the desolate cemetery, Danskin, Parker, and Robson huddled in an unmarked van which had been placed there the previous day alongside numerous genuine pieces of graveyard machinery.

The intention was to use the van as a communications hub from which they'd monitor feeds from hidden cameras and microphones secreted at various intervals amongst bushes, memorials, and stone buildings throughout the main routes through the cemetery.

Mother nature had her own ideas. Despite a waning gibbous moon, a swirling mist and low dank clouds shrouded its eerie light, adding to the otherworldly atmosphere.

'Christ, this is bloody scary as fuck,' was Todd's considered opinion.

'Aye, I cannae say you're wrong,' Lyall Parker whispered.

Danskin whispered even more quietly. 'If anyone can see anything, tap your earpiece. I'll hear it. I want no other form of communication. None at all.'

His voice crackled in the earpieces of those officers tucked behind tombstones and up trees. They clearly hadn't got Murray Appleby's message to stay on the path.

Nothing came back.

'Christ, we might as well be on the moon,' he cursed.

They waited in silence.

An owl hooted.

'Jesus, man. Can this get any more like a John Carpenter filmset?' Danskin muttered to himself.

He heard a rustling in his ear.

'If it's safe to do so, tell me what you see.'

'Two figures, sir. About halfway to you. I can't tell if it's Ryan and Webb or not.'

'It's got to be,' Parker mused.

'We'll know soon enough.'

They heard the drip-drip of light rain patter against the side of the van as they waited in a cocoon of silence.

'I've another sighting,' a second voice whispered. 'They've just walked by the toilet block I'm behind. They didn't see a thing. ETA at site, approx. 4 minutes.'

Danskin's breath came in spurts. 'Armed response, they are heading our way. Be ready on my word.'

Four minutes passed like four hours. Danskin watched the monitors but the cameras showed nothing but mist and the blur of raindrops. He went over everything in his mind for the umpteenth time.

Then, a microphone picked up a sound. Unclear at first, then the unmistakeable sound of footsteps on a gravel path.

'Where's that?'

'About two minutes away, sir.' Robson said. 'Just entering the last part of the graveyard proper.'

'Still two minutes? Bollocks.'

Another microphone picked up the sound of singing.

'That's not Jarrod, is it?'

'I think it is.'

Next came laughter. The jokey, teasing laughter of a seductive lover.

Danskin shivered. 'Christ. This is bloody awful.'

The voices became distinct as they approached the hit zone. The talk was flirty, sexual, and uncouth.'

'What the hell?'

'I think they're hamming it up, sir. Making it up for the sake of the accomplice in case he can hear.'

'Jarrod had better be acting, that's for sure.'

'Ssshhh!' Parker urged. He mouthed, *'They're outside.'*

The Graveyard Shift

All three occupants held their breath until the sounds outside ceased.

'I can just about see them,' Danskin pointed to a monitor. 'They're at the fake grave.'

In the mist and drizzle, a sodden Ryan was wishing this was over. He'd had enough of holding hands with a madman, talking dirty with him. He could tell Webb thought it was more than a fantasy. He was pretty sure Webb had a hard-on but he certainly wasn't going to check.

Webb manoeuvred Ryan over rolling ground blanketed with wet leaves and snapped twigs. Ryan caught site of the stake and swallowed hard. Six foot long, tip sharpened like a giant pencil, he reminded himself it was the real thing, not a prop.

'Lie down next to me,' Webb murmured.

Ryan closed his eyes. Felt Webb's cold hand caress the side of his face. His lips feathered against Ryan, who swallowed down bile.

Jackson Webb's hand moved lower.

'Don't push your lick, pal,' Ryan hissed.

'Don't tease me,' Webb sneered. He put his lips to Ryan's ear. 'He's here. I can sense him.'

Inside the van, Danskin listened with mounting fear. 'I can't see the other fucker. Can anybody see him?'

No response came.

'Shit. Where is he?'

'Och, I see him. God, what's he wearing?'

The DCI stared at the monitor. 'That's Morticia, aal reet. It's his Phantom disguise.'

He flicked on his microphone. 'Armed response ready. On my word.' He thought of something. 'But, if you see him with a syringe in his hand, just shoot the bastard.'

252

Ryan felt a shadow fall over him. This was it. Morticia was here.

He felt Webb roll away from him, to be replaced by someone else. Ryan saw a hand reach into a pocket, then the dead rose from the grave.

The ground around them shifted. Figures emerged, slowly at first, then rapidly, as the armed response unit threw off the camouflaged netting and its leaves and grass cuttings.

'Armed police!'

'Do NOT move!'

In the van, Danskin flew towards the door. 'Got the bastard!' he yelled. As the door opened, he shouted, 'Hold him. Wait 'til I get there!'

He was *there* in seconds.

Webb was back in handcuffs, Ryan one side of him, Todd the other. Morticia faced them, his chest heaving, breath rattling behind his mask.

Ryan started laughing.

Danskin looked at him, wide-eyed. 'Are you okay, Jarrod?'

'Yes,' he said through peals of laughter. 'I just find it funny.'

'What is?'

'Well, think about it, man. We're in a graveyard. Mist all around us, with a vampire in handcuffs and another saddo in a mask in front of us.'

Danskin still didn't get.

'All we need is Fred or Velma to unmask the villain and Shaggy to toss some Scooby snacks around.

Danskin gave a brief laugh. 'Aye, well. Should I be Velma or you?'

'I'll let you have the honour, sir.'

Stephen stepped forward, took hold of the man's disguise. And pulled it from his face.

He gasped.

They were staring at a face every one of them recognised.

Then, all hell broke loose.

The Graveyard Shift

**

In the shock of the moment, Jackson Webb used the pause to his own advantage.

He looked towards Robson on his left, who was staring open-mouthed at the second killer. His eyes moved to Ryan. He waited for the moment.

Ryan tipped his head back. Muttered 'Bloody hell, no.'

This *was* the moment.

Webb lunged at Ryan. Clamped his jaws around Ryan's throat and shook him like a dog with a soft toy.

Ryan screamed, eyes wide in shock. Blood spurted skywards yet still Webb chomped away.

Todd Robson hit Webb twice. Kicked him in the groin. Poked him in the eye.

Webb continued his feast.

It took three men to haul him off, even after he'd been shocked with a taser.

Ryan fell to the ground, clutching his throat.

And the one known as Morticia bolted for the gateway forty yards away.

In the maelstrom, he soon reached the metal gate. He fumbled with it. Looked behind him to make sure he wasn't being followed.

He wasn't.

He hurdled the gate.

And ran straight into the extended fist of Gavin O'Hara.

**

Maynard and Danskin ordered Morticia to be held until Ryan returned from hospital.

When he did, he wore a wad of padding taped to his neck, hiding a dozen stitches and a hickey the size of a chrysanthemum head.

'Was that him or wor Hannah?' Stephen Danskin teased.

'Pretty much one and the same, aren't they? Divvent tell her I said that, mind,' he laughed.

'No lasting damage?' Sam Maynard asked.

'Nah. They reckon I'll have a pretty ugly scar for a while yet so Todd and Lucy have a bit of competition. He caught a few blood vessels but nowt major. The sod mainly got his pound of flesh. Oh, me arse is a tad sore from the tetanus shot but me neck will be okay.'

Maynard bit the bullet. 'HIV?'

'Negative according to the finger-prick. I'll have to wait a bit longer for the full test but they reckon the finger-test is canny reliable.'

They remained silent for a while, both Maynard and Danskin staring at Ryan in admiration.

'What, man?' he said, embarrassed.

'I dare say you'll want a word with Morticia.'

'Oh hell, yeah.'

On the lift down, Ryan suggested they should have worked it out before now.

Danskin disagreed, saying it was never easy bringing the pieces of a puzzle together.

'I just want to know why the hell he did it,' Ryan said as they approached the custody suite.

'You sure you're up to it, Jarrod?'

'Let's do it.'

Stephen Danskin swung open the heavy door.

THIRTY-TWO

'I have Asperger's Syndrome,' Rufus Cavanagh said, staring at his feet.

'So do thousands of others. They live perfectly normal lives. They don't go around meeting vampires and killing people. If you even think of using that as your defence, you can forget it.'

'Morticia' continued to look down. 'It's not a defence. Not even a reason. I just thought you should know.'

Ryan battled to remain patient, to understand why Cavanagh would do what he did. Webb was a raving nutcase. He, though, was far from that.

'You must think it's significant or you wouldn't have mentioned it.'

'I'm just explaining,' he said, his voice flat.

'You're not explaining very well.'

'Listen, I have trouble forming friendships. Relationships always turn out wrong. Life's not easy.'

Ryan laughed sarcastically. 'Tell me about it,' he said, patting the protective strapping on his neck.

'I suppose,' Rufus continued, 'That's why I do what I do.'

'Do you mean your, shall we call it, *'hobby'*, or what you do for a living?'

'Both, I suppose.'

For the first time, he'd said something that made sense to Ryan.

Rufus raised his eyes. They were glazed and hollow as he began his explanation.

'I can't understand the living, so I deal with the dead. I don't have to talk to those who have passed on. I mean, I do, sometimes; when I'm alone with them. Never when Dr Elliot is around. They don't answer back, though. I don't have to talk WITH them.'

Ryan squirmed in his seat. 'Dr Cavanagh, it's one thing not talking to the living, it's quite another turning the living into the dead.'

Cavanagh looked at Ryan with something akin to pity.

'I disagree. We all come and go and, in the infinite time of the cosmos, our time amongst the living amounts to less than...' he snapped his fingers. 'A few relative milliseconds stripped from it means nothing.'

'Try telling that to William Coulson. Or Matthew Neill.'

Rufus Cavanagh shrugged and looked downwards.

'Why do it, Rufus?'

'I exist among those who live, who remain a mystery to me. I work with the dead, who I understand. I wanted to see what changes as they move from one realm to the other; what happens in the very moment they switch from a puzzle to something I understand. Acting Detective Inspector, I am interested in the moment of death.'

Ryan felt a chill run through him. 'Did you find what you wanted?'

'No. No, I didn't. Because you stopped me.'

Ryan took a sip of lukewarm coffee to gather his thoughts. 'Why did you tell us how you did it? The injection of air?'

'I don't know. Perhaps I wanted to prove myself to Dr Elliot; to gain his respect. There again, just because I have Asperger's doesn't mean I'm entirely without empathy. Perhaps something in me wanted me to get caught.'

Ryan rocked back and forward in his chair. 'Okay,' he said. 'How did you meet Webb?'

'You already know. Via a website.'

'Why that one?'

Cavanagh rolled his eyes. 'Have you listened to anything I've said? I need to be around people, whether I like it or not.

I can't avoid them. So, I thought if I had to befriend someone, why not make it one of the half-dead?'

Ryan swore. 'For a clever bloke, you're really not very sensible. Webb's still a person. He's just a man, warped though he is.'

'I don't know I'm any less sensible than you. You didn't see through my other clue; Morticia the mortician, did you?'

Ryan ignored him. 'Why pick Webb, though?'

'Simple, really. He was local. I didn't realise he was quite as sick in the head until it was too late.'

Ryan leant forward. 'Dr. Cavanagh, you're the one who instigated the killings.'

'True, but I only killed them.'

'Ha!' Ryan spat, '*Only* killed them? Are you for real?'

Cavanagh managed to meet Ryan's stare once more. 'Perhaps I did kill them, but my experiment brought them a calm, peaceful end. As for Webb, he did unspeakable things. Horrid things. And that girl, the one from the festival, how DARE he do that. It was so sick, so awful.' Cavanagh shook his head.

'Rufus, listen to me. You and Webb are two cheeks of the same arse. Understand?'

Ryan took another drink, the coffee as cold as Jackson Webb's touch. 'You were first to the scene of the crimes because you were already nearby. Am I correct?'

Cavanagh nodded.

'And the footprints on Coulson's grave – they were there not because you took crime scene photographs but because you were the one who posed the body.'

'No. That was Webb.' He looked away. 'He asked me to help. I didn't want to lose his companionship so I did as he asked.'

Ryan stood. Moved towards the door.

'Before I go, you told me you wanted Aaron Elliot's respect. I've just spoken to him. You had his respect, Dr Cavanagh. In bucket loads. I just thought I should tell you that your actions have left him a broken man. Please remember that when you're rotting in hell.'

**

Back upstairs, Ryan was delighted Gavin O'Hara had joined the team after giving his statement. They shook hands warmly.

'How did you know where I'd be?' Ryan asked.

'I'm a cop,' he laughed. 'No, you told me where you were, I just put two and two together to work out WHY you were there.'

Gavin's eyes flicked downwards. 'Ry, I was going to tell you summat a while ago, when you were at my house, but the moment passed. Can we do it now?'

'Sure. Fire away.'

'Not here. In the caff, aye?'

'Ok, sure.'

Half-an-hour later, Gavin and Ryan re-entered the floorplate.

'Can I have your attention, please? Gavin would like to say something.'

Ryan stood aside as the team gathered around, all smiles at the successful conclusion to the case. Jarrod gave him an encouraging nod.

'As you know,' Gavin began quietly. 'I'm not one for grand announcements. I like to keep myself to myself, y'know?'

He cleared his throat and spoke with more confidence.

'Me and Di, the missus, we've split up, like. I think most of you know. Anyway, that was my fault as well, and it's also the reason I'm a closed book.'

The team wondered where this was leading. 'Get a move on, Gav. There's a pint waiting for me on a bar, somewhere.'

The Graveyard Shift

'Sorry, Todd. Anyway, since me and the missus split, like, I've gone a bit off the rails. Joined a few dating sites and such like. Wanted a bit of company, I guess.'

'No shame there, Gav,' Nigel Trebilcock said to a chorus of 'Here, here's.'

'Yeah, but it's not what you think. I wanted you all to hear this together.'

He looked around the assembled crowd and took a deep breath.

'Thing is, they weren't ordinary dating sites. They were gay dating sites. Yes, I'm gay. That's why I was in JayKay's that night, it's why I was in Tynemouth waiting for someone who never showed.'

He looked around, trying to gauge their reaction. He couldn't.

'So, that's it, really. I'm in a better place now I've admitted it to myself. I hope you won't look on me badly.'

No-one spoke. Slowly, Todd Robson stepped forward until his shadow cast Gavin into the shade.

'Oh God,' Ryan whispered to himself, 'Please don't go all Gene Hunt.'

Robson moved to within an inch of Gavin's face.

He pointed a finger at him.

'Don't. You. Ever. EVER. Say. You're gay, again.'

He grabbed Gavin by the ears and planted a slobbery kiss on Gavin's forehead.

'You'll always be wor Gav to us. Howay, then it's your roond,' Todd concluded to raucous cheers.

The squad filed out the floorplate. Hannah slipped her arm around Ryan. 'You coming?'

'Aye. I'll be there soon. Just give me a minute to finish summat first, yeah? You go on ahead.'

'Okay,' she said. She stood on tiptoe and kissed his cheek. 'Love you to insanity and beyond,' she laughed.

Once he was left alone on the floorplate, Ryan felt his phone vibrate. It was a message from Sherry Proudlock. It didn't make sense until he read her previous one; the one he'd missed. The new message read, *'False alarm. John's back. He was just building him up to something. Guess what? He's just proposed to Dad! All's good.'*

Ryan moved to the lift lobby and pressed the call button. The lift made the journey to the basement, uninterrupted.

When the doors opened, Ryan walked along the corridor. He stopped outside the door and waited for a split second before unlocking it and stepping inside.

'What a lovely surprise,' Jackson Webb said. 'I've missed you so much.'

'Don't even think about moving. Stay seated.'

'You have the most gorgeous blood, you know. We must do it again, sometime.'

'Not for at least thirty years, we won't. You'll be lucky if you don't get longer.'

Webb smiled. 'There's always a consolation prize.'

Ryan's brow furrowed. 'Will you do one last thing for me?'

'Anything, darling. Absolutely anything for you.'

Ryan breathed in the cold cell air.

'Why did you give up so easily? No solicitor, no defence. You didn't even struggle when we came to arrest you on the construction site. Why not?'

Webb laughed so loudly Ryan feared he'd blow open the door.

'It would have to end, sometime. I had no guarantee Morticia would continue to work for me, and my desires were growing more urgent more regularly. I'd miss it so much.'

'That's my point. Why get yourself locked away for thirty years?'

The Graveyard Shift

Ryan's blood curdled in his veins at the hauntingly dark sparkle in the depths of Webb's eyes.

'My dear, isn't it obvious? Just think of the infinite supply of gorgeous young men and their blood, available 24/7, three hundred and sixty-five days a year.'

Jackson Webb stared at Ryan, the sneer of a smile on his face once more.

Softly, tenderly, he began to serenade Ryan.

'Heaven, I'm in heaven
And my heart beats so that I can hardly speak
And I seem to find the happiness I seek
When we're out together, dancing cheek to cheek.'

****

Colin Youngman

COMING NEXT FROM

COLIN YOUNGMAN:

SAND DANCER

A Ryan Jarrod Novel

'Semilla Rachman is young, talented, and famous.
She's also missing.
The question faced by Ryan Jarrod is, did she go of her own accord - or has her mystery stalker finally achieved what he's desired for so long?'

Acknowledgement:

To you - for taking the time to read The Graveyard Shift. Your interest and support mean the world to me.

If you enjoyed this, the ninth Ryan Jarrod novel, please tell your family, friends, and colleagues. Word of mouth is an author's best friend so the more people who know, the greater my appreciation.

I welcome reviews of your experience, either on Amazon or Goodreads. Alternatively, you can 'Rate' the book after you finish reading on most Kindle devices, if you'd prefer.

If you'd like to be among the first to hear news about the next book in the series, or to discover release dates in advance, you can follow me by:

Clicking the 'Follow' button on my Amazon Author page
https://www.amazon.co.uk/Colin-Youngman/e/B01H9CNHQK

Liking/ following me on:
Facebook: @colin.youngman.author

Check my website:
https://colinyoungman-author.webador.co.uk/

Best of all:
Shout 'Free Beer' in the street.

Thanks again for your interest in my work.

About the author:

Colin had his first written work published at the age of 9 when a contribution to children's comic *Sparky* brought him the rich rewards of a 10/- Postal Order and a transistor radio.

He was smitten by the writing bug and has gone on to have his work feature in publications for young adults, sports magazines, national newspapers, and travel guides before he moved to his first love: fiction.

Colin previously worked as a senior executive in the public sector. He lives in Northumberland, north-east England, and is an avid supporter of Newcastle United (don't laugh), a keen follower of Durham County Cricket Club, and has a family interest in British Gymnastics and the City of Newcastle Gymnastics Academy.

You can read his other work (e-book and paperback) exclusive to Amazon:

Bones of Callaley (Ryan Jarrod Book Eight
The Tower (Ryan Jarrod Book Seven)
Low Light (Ryan Jarrod Book Six)
Operation Sage (Ryan Jarrod Book Five)
High Level (Ryan Jarrod Book Four)
The Lighthouse Keeper (Ryan Jarrod Book Three)
The Girl On The Quay (Ryan Jarrod Book Two)
The Angel Falls (Ryan Jarrod Book One)

The Doom Brae Witch
Alley Rat
DEAD Heat
Twists (An anthology of novelettes)

****

Printed in Great Britain
by Amazon